carved IN SCARS

ELLE MITCHELL

Book Cover by Beautiful Book Covers by Ivy

Carved in Scars is a dark high school lovers-to-enemies-to-lovers bully romance meant for an adult audience, and its content may be triggering or inappropriate for some readers. Please read the following trigger warnings before proceeding.

This book contains on-page sexual content, including dubious consent, as well as graphic language and profanity in abundance. The main characters struggle with mental health and hopelessness and experience verbal, physical, and sexual abuse, including rape (off-page). Throughout the story, a main character struggles with their own mental health and depression while living in an unsafe environment, and there are graphic depictions of self-harm (including cutting), depression, reckless and criminal behavior, and suicidal ideation.

Graphic on-page depictions of violence in this book include bullying, gun violence, murder, manslaughter, domestic/familial violence, starvation, and neglect. Religion is used by adults in positions of authority to justify abuse and mistreatment of others.

Additional trigger warnings include death of a friend, false imprisonment, religious trauma, abandonment by a parent, underage drinking, grooming (not by MCs), and mentions of drug use/dealing.

The main characters are 17-18 years of age in this story, and are physically and verbally abusive to each other at times, but not while in a relationship.

National Sexual Assault Hotline: 1(800) 656-4673

National Mental Health Hotline: 1(866) 903-3787

Crisis Text Line: Text HOME to 741741

To the ones who really needed a light in a dark place but had to be their own.

This is for you.

1

I lean over the sink and splash cold water onto my face, attempting to catch my breath and dry my tears. I take a good, hard look at the girl in the mirror, studying her face and knowing that others will be studying it, too. How do the tears make me look? Do they make me look sad, or do they make me look guilty, remorseful? Because that's the last thing I need. I'm not either of those things. Not for her, anyway.

I hate this. I hate *her*. I don't know how to do this.

I feel a million eyes on me as I return to the gym. And no, I'm not paranoid, and it's not my imagination. Okay, maybe I'm exaggerating in number, but they are watching me. It happens everywhere I go. At least half of them think I'm a murderer. A lot of them think I'm an accomplice. A few of them think I'm a victim, too.

They all know I'm a liar. I'm none of the other things.

I exhale slowly, attempting to steady my heart rate as I return to the sidelines. I pick up the white candle from my seat and prepare to join my teammates, lined up along the net in the middle of the court, but a hand on my shoulder stops me.

"Sorry, Ally," Coach Davis says. "The family asked that you not be here for this."

I guess that shouldn't come as a surprise. It's not like I want to face them. But...

"Where am I supposed to go? What am I supposed to do?"

"Go home, Ally."

"What about the next match?"

"It's just one game. I'll see you at practice tomorrow," she says, giving me what is supposed to be a reassuring grin. She seems sincere enough, at least.

I nod, set the candle back on the folding chair, pick up my duffle bag, and head toward the exit leading to the hallway. Before reaching the door, I stop, ducking under the bleachers instead—retreating to that old spot where I used to go when I felt lonely and needed to be alone. I set the duffle bag down on the ground as they lower the lights in the gym and lie down on my back, using the bag as a pillow. I look up at the letters carved into the wood, knowing they will hurt me and wanting them to.

"I don't know where to start. Um..." Principal Coleman pauses, and I hear her suck in a breath, attempting to stifle a sob. "It's been over four months since Darci Connelly was taken from her family and this community. Today, on what would have been Darci's eighteenth birthday, we remember her as she lived. Darci was an amazing student and an exceptional friend."

Was she, though?

"Darci had this force about her that was irresistible. She was the kind of person you were drawn to; she was a leader, a pillar of her community, her church, and her team. Those lucky enough to know her will always remember her for her energy, bright smile, passion, and drive to succeed. She was a force to be reckoned with, the kind of daughter who would have made any parent proud. Her death rocked our tiny island community to its very core, and she will be forever missed. Those who loved her are forever changed."

What the hell happened to you, Darci?

More tears begin to leak from the corners of my eyes. I guess she was—at least for a while and at least as far as I knew—a friend. *My* friend.

I'm sorry, Darci. I don't know what I could have done, but I'm sorry I didn't do it. I'm sorry for whatever part I played in it.

"But today, we don't want to focus on her tragic end. We want to celebrate her life. In honor of Darci's memory and birthday, we will add her jersey to the gym wall and officially retire #11. It will be hers forever. No other Black Rock Eagle will wear the number. We ask for a few moments of silence while the jersey is placed in memoriam."

The band plays something slow and sad while—I can only assume from my location—they hang Darci's jersey on the wall. Tears run from my eyes and into my eras while I reach up and trace the *A + D* etched into the bleacher above me hard with the tip of my finger until a splinter burrows into the skin. Sucking a breath through my teeth, I bring my hand back toward my body, examining the shard of wood. It's large enough that I can grasp it between my pointer finger and thumb and remove it with my other hand and deep enough that blood runs from my fingertip to my palm when I do.

I'm squeezing the tip of my finger, watching dark red blood flow from the wound, when a voice makes my heart stop.

"You've got to be fucking kidding me," he says.

All air leaves my lungs. I look up at the face of the person who couldn't possibly be standing there and feel that familiar ache in my chest that never quite goes away intensify until it becomes a crushing weight. I can't move *or* breathe. Until I remember...

"You're not real," I tell him.

And I can't do this right now. I can't get lost in this—not here.

I push off the ground, throw my bag over my shoulder, and attempt to walk past the guy who isn't real before a hand reaches out and grabs me by my throat.

"Are you sure about that?" he asks.

I can't speak, so I don't. I open my mouth, but no sound comes out, and stare ahead and the cold, steely blue eyes, once so full of life and now seemingly void, staring back into my own.

I want to touch him. Could I touch him, or would he fade to nothing like the ghost I know he must be? That'd be worse than this—worse than suffocating.

"I've never killed anyone before—but hey—you know that better than anyone, don't you, Ally?"

Yes.

"But seeing you here now, like *this*...really makes me want to."

He pushes me backward as he releases me, and I stumble, breath heaving as I grasp at my throat.

"Devon?" It comes out as a question. Those icy blue eyes look through me with nothing short of disgust. Repulsion—that's a better word. I want to throw myself at his feet and fucking beg for his forgiveness, even if I don't deserve it. "Devon, I'm sor—"

"Don't you dare finish that fucking sentence, or I really might kill you. Go home, Ally. Get the fuck out of here; I'll deal with you later."

I rush past Devon and exit the gym, then run down the hallway and out the door into the rain. Tears run down my cheeks as I cross the parking lot toward the transit stop just in time to board my bus.

I feel eyes on my back the entire time. He's there when I sink into my seat and peer through the window—in the doorway, watching me. My heart thuds against my ribcage strongly enough that I can hear it—the blood pumping, a distinct thudding in my ears.

But how?

I shift uncomfortably as we pull away from the school, noticing something wedged in the small space between the cushion and the side of the bus. Reaching down, I remove the small handbag, then look around to ensure no one is watching before opening it and rifling through its contents. I take out the cell phone, power it down and remove the sim card, then find an additional sixty-seven dollars in the wallet. I put both in my duffle bag before returning the small purse to the space where I found it.

I don't really need to do it anymore, but it's hard to resist when it's this easy.

It isn't a long ride to my stop—not long enough for me to think about it and not even long enough for the dread to truly settle in. Still shaking and questioning whether what happened was real or if I've just finally lost it, I walk the remaining two blocks from the bus stop to my aunt's home. It's your typical cool, misty Pacific Northwest October night. I welcome the barely-rain as it settles silently on my skin, waking me up and reminding me that there are worse things waiting for me at the place I call home—worse than anything Devon West could ever do to me—and I have to be alert.

But could Devon really hurt me? Would he? I know he hates me; I deserve that. But it wasn't long ago that it was something else, even if the last few months have felt like a torturous eternity.

I pause only for a moment before entering the home. Walking through the front door always sets my nerves on fire. It's hard to be in this house. After my mom was arrested, they told me my aunt and her husband had offered to take me in, then brought me to this house on Black Rock Island, and I thought...maybe it won't be so bad. The neighborhood was like the ones you'd see in movies: peaceful, upper-middle-class suburbia complete with a picturesque island backdrop—rocky shores, a small downtown with a beach boardwalk as its focal point, a place that runs on tourism in the summer and lives for Friday night football in the fall.

But I should know better than anyone by now that looks can be deceiving. Everyone everywhere is dirty. Places like this just make it easier for them to hide, to get away with it. The sickest parts of humanity go undetected in places like this. People look the other way, and they *want* to. They don't really care about the dirt as long as it doesn't get on them—as long as they don't have to look at it, to be aware of it. What gets us in trouble is when they can see it on our skin, seeping from the walls of a rundown house in a bad neighborhood, or in the eyes of the woman who's been working all day and selling drugs at night so that she and her daughter don't have to go back to living in a car.

Sometimes, the worst thing a person can be is desperate. That's something I know better than anyone now, too.

It's dark and quiet aside from the TV in the front room. My aunt sits alone with a glass of wine in hand. At least there's that. At least he's gone and will be for a while.

"Your mess just won't go away," she says as I close the door. I hear Devon's name, and my eyes dart to the television. My bag slides down from my shoulder and hits the floor with a distinct thud before I drag myself over to the armchair and let my suddenly heavy body collapse into it.

"The case against West was dropped shortly after police received this video from the backyard camera of a neighboring home. The original investigation missed the camera due to its location and the house being used as a vacation rental, with its residents only present for small periods of time throughout the year. We want to warn our viewers—what you're about to see may be disturbing."

The video shows a dark—but clear enough—view of a man emerging from the wooded area behind Devon and Darci's house, carrying a girl over his shoulder. Long, light-colored hair hangs down his back toward the ground, swaying along with her lifeless arms with each of the man's purposeful strides. Both wrists are lined with bracelets. It's Darci; I knew it when I saw her, but that alone is enough to confirm it—you could always hear her coming before you'd see her with those. And the man...well, he's not Devon. Not even close.

But of course, I always knew that, too.

He walks out of the camera's frame for a few minutes before we see him heading back toward the woods from which he came, now empty-handed.

"The video was enough to get the case against West dismissed, and sources say he was released from custody last night. Experts put the man in the video at around 5'10" and 200 pounds. West is 6'1.5" and weighed 175 pounds when he was taken into custody. Though wearing a hat, you can see that the man in the video also has his hair cut quite short compared to West's hair in the mugshot photo days later. This video has also given police a more accurate timeline of when the crime was committed, which they hope will help them zero in on potential suspects who may have been in the area at that time..."

"You better hope this isn't a problem for us," my aunt says. "They're going to start bringing this up again in the debates. It better not cost Mark the election."

I don't respond. I know better.

The good Christian republican congressman taking in his poor, orphaned-by-circumstances niece did look good on paper. It was great for his image. For those first couple of months, they paraded me around at events, dressed me up for newspaper photos, and graciously accepted praise from others at church for their good deed.

Then, everything changed.

"West became the primary suspect in the death of his stepsister after witnesses reported he had threatened her with a knife at a party the night of her death. Connelly was badly beaten and left for dead in the family's pool, where she was found the following morning. Police were unable to corroborate West's alibi at the time, and there was reason to believe the two had a sexual relationship."

That last part hurts. I cringe, biting down on the insides of my cheeks in an attempt to force down the feelings it brings up. It's hard to believe, but it's almost impossible to deny, too.

Grace snatches the remote from the table, and the television screen darkens. I know I should move, but I don't. I can't.

The remote flies across the room, slams against the back wall, then falls to the ground. I stay there, still, afraid to move, listening to the batteries roll across the hardwood floors in the dark, eerily quiet room. Then, she's in my face.

"You have *ruined* my life," she says. "You and your whore mother."

Still, I don't reply. My mom was a victim. We were victims. She got pregnant when she was sixteen, and her Baptist family threw her out of the house. They never spoke to her again—her older sister, Grace, included. Growing up, I never even heard the name.

We lived with my dad until I was four, and then he left, too. He never even said goodbye. That's when things really got complicated.

She reaches down and grabs a fistful of hair from the top of my head, using it to force me to my feet. "And you've ruined my marriage, too. God, if no one were watching, I'd throw you out on your ass so fast. I can't wait to be done with you. Just a few more months."

'Much less than that,' I think. The days had been crawling since Darci died, but we were still barreling toward my eighteenth birthday.

"Get out of my sight," she snarls, releasing me. "And you stay away from him. Don't talk to anyone about him *or* what happened."

I take a few steps backward, pick my bag up from the ground, and glance toward the kitchen.

"Grace, I—" I start weakly.

"Upstairs," she says, interrupting me. "Not the kitchen. There's nothing in there for you. I'd better not see anything missing from the fridge or the pantry in the morning, either."

I head toward the staircase and then down to my room at the end of the hall where I pull open the door, close it behind me, then change into pajama pants and a t-shirt. I crawl into bed, pulling the covers up to my shoulders, and sob quietly into my pillow, knowing I'll be in trouble if I make a sound. An hour must go by like this before I move, the tears bringing at least some relief to the weight crushing my chest and distracting me from my aching, empty stomach.

This is the only downside to when he's gone. I hate the sham family dinners; I hate the fear. But I hate being hungry, too.

I wait until long after I hear her bedroom door close before I get up. Then, I lie flat on my stomach and slide under the bed, slowly and quietly removing the loose board from the floor. I open the shoebox lid, take the phone and the money I found on the bus, and add it to my stash.

Slowly, quietly, I shuffle through the box's contents until I find another cell phone and remove it for the first time in months. Then, I reach further into the hole, feeling around until, finally, my fingers brush against plastic. Breathing a sigh of relief, I grasp the bag and extract it from my hiding place as well before replacing the board and sliding out from under the bed. I remove the black skull hoodie from the bag and pull it over my head before crawling back under the covers. It still smells like him. I can still make out his fabric softener and the cedar and sandalwood of his cologne. I power on the phone—surprised to find it still works—and stare at the one contact in my list.

No new messages.

Of course not. He probably has a different phone number, and even if he didn't, he wouldn't want to talk to me.

I lie awake for hours, thinking of everything I wish I could say to him, just like I have every night for over four months. The only difference is that before tonight, I thought I'd never get to see him again.

And when it happens in my head, he doesn't grab me by my throat and tell me he wants to kill me. But I don't know why I'd expect any better after what I did.

I pull the collar of the hoodie over my nose and breathe it in, my eyes watering as my mind takes me back to Devon's car on a cool spring night with the windows down, the music turned up, and a secret. *Our* secret.

I swallow a lump in my throat.

I'd sell my soul to try again if I thought I still had one. I'd give anything to go back and spend five more minutes in that car, to hit repeat on that last song and drive around the block one more time. But this is reality, and we don't get do-overs.

Only one life per customer. Try not to fuck it up.

But that's what I did.

I let the tears soak into the fabric until, eventually, sleep comes for me.

2

"Go back upstairs, Devon. No one wants you here," my stepsister Darci snaps as I pass through the living room to the kitchen.

"I need sustenance. If I die upstairs, our parents probably won't be happy."

"They'll be the only ones," she sneers. "Make it quick."

I walk through the group of jocks and cheerleaders who I wouldn't want to be around anyway and head for the refrigerator.

"So fucking weird, guys. I'm sorry," she says as I pass. I roll my eyes hard enough that I'm surprised they don't get stuck in the back of my head. "I literally paid him twenty bucks not to come down here and get *fucking loser* all over us."

"Stop, Darci!" Audrey's nails-on-a-fucking-chalkboard voice exclaims. "He's going to put a spell on us or something."

"I already did," I tell them. "It's called the Zero Fucking Personality spell."

"Just get your fucking...whatever you said and go back upstairs. Or I want a refund."

"Sustenance," I say. "Look it up."

I walk into the kitchen and find another one of Darci's...friends? Are any of them actually her friends? Anyway, it's Ally. She's leaning over the kitchen island, scarfing down pizza, and looks embarrassed that I caught her. I'm pretty sure she's the only one of those girls that fucking eats, even though she doesn't look like it. It's hard to tell, though, under her baggy jeans and oversized sweatshirt.

I'm not sure how she ended up tethered to Darci. Her aunt and uncle are public figures who are big into church, and her aunt is close to Darci's mom. I think they kind of threw them together, but she isn't really Darci's type. She always dresses like this and doesn't wear any makeup. I've heard she isn't allowed to have a phone or a driver's license, and it seems like our house is the only place she's allowed to go.

And then there's that stuff about her mom.

I'm not judging her. It's just that...it seems like Darci would. She's brought other girls to tears for far less more times than I can count. On the contrary, she's not someone I judge—she's someone I watch...closely. I can't stop myself. Whether here, in class, or in the halls where our lockers are across from each other, I'm aware of Ally Hargrove.

"Hi, Devon," she says, looking the other way.

"Hey, Ally," I reply. "I like your...shirt."

What.

"Oh," she says, looking down at her sweatshirt, confused. "Um, thanks. It's really old. It was my mom's."

She smiles—just a little—and her eyes meet mine. She doesn't need any of that other stuff to be beautiful. She just *is*. Her dark eyes are framed with thick dark lashes that I've spent more than enough time studying in art class, but this is the first time I've held them like this. Ally is always polite, but we never talk. Not that I haven't tried—I *have*. She's sat in front of me all semester. I'll try to come up with anything to start a conversation, and she'll answer without meeting my eyes. She won't look at me when she's over here, either. I assume it has something to do with the whole *Satan-worshipping* bullshit.

Equally dark hair sits piled in a bun on top of her head, and she nervously tucks a stray piece behind her ear before looking away. I watch, jealous of her own fingers brushing against her ear and trailing down her neck.

That's what I should have done. I hate myself for not being a riveting conversationalist right now.

I reach into the pantry and pull out a bag of Doritos. "You want some?"

She nods. I set it down on the island, and she walks hesitantly toward me.

"You have to answer a question for me first."

"Okay..." she replies nervously.

"Who are those people you're always drawing?" I ask.

"What do you mean?"

"The ones with no faces. Sometimes, they're kids. Who are they?"

I realize by asking that I've let her know I've been watching her, but I *want* her to know. Surely, she's caught on by now anyway.

"Oh...they aren't really anyone," she says, looking just over my shoulder. I want to grab her by the chin and make her look at me again. "Just a feeling. Sometimes, it feels better to get them out like that, you know?"

"Yeah, I do."

"Is that a good enough answer?"

"It is. Go for it."

She grabs a handful of chips from the bag.

"For what it's worth, you're really talented," I tell her. "I want you to know that...I've noticed. I always look for your work. It stands out."

"Thanks," she says. "Um, I'd better go back."

She looks down at her hands and then turns on the faucet. I reach across her and turn it back off.

"What are you doing?" she asks.

"Lick it," I tell her.

"...What?"

"The Dorito dust. You know you want to. Everybody does it."

"You're watching me," she says, shaking her head.

"Lick it or I will. Don't waste it."

A little bold, Devon.

She holds my eyes again when she brings her fingers to her mouth and sucks. Fuck me, am I really going to get hard over this?

Jealous. I'm so fucking jealous of those fingers. I'd love to see her take those wet fingers and—

"Hey, shithead," Darci interrupts. "I'll take that refund now."

I grab the bag from the counter and head for the door. "See you later, Ally."

"You don't have to be nice to him," I hear Darci tell Ally as I leave the room. "You don't have to talk to him if he tries to talk to you. Just ignore him—that's what I do."

Yeah, I wish. I wish she fucking ignored me.

When I get to the landing, I glance back over my shoulder in time to see Trevor pull Ally onto the couch beside him and drape his arm around her shoulders. Maybe he doesn't notice how she shrinks uncomfortably under his touch, but I do. I watch for only a few seconds, but it's long enough to see her make up some excuse to move and sit next to Morgan instead.

I shake my head and start back up the stairs, but catch Trevor's attention before I do.

"Hey, Devon," he says. "Your earrings look pretty."

His friends have done a terrible disservice to society by convincing this guy he's funny.

"Thanks," I say over my shoulder as I head to my room. "I bought them to go with my new purse."

A few of them laugh as I continue down the hallway, open the door, and step inside.

"Shit," I say to myself as I close the door.

I forgot my fucking purse.

I mean, my backpack. With my books. Since I have no desire to walk through that again, I resign to watching television. It's not that I'm afraid of them—I'm not small by any means, and I doubt any of them have actually been in a real fight before, and well...I have. And contrarily, most of them *are* afraid of me on account of the whole Satan worshipper thing.

I could probably walk back out onto the landing and start spewing some Latin, and they'd shit their pants.

I just don't have the mental space for any of that bullshit.

After a couple of episodes, it's quiet enough that I do risk that trip back downstairs. The living room is dark and empty when I pass through.

But Ally is there—again—sitting on the floor by the back sliding glass door. And she looks like she's been crying.

"Hey," I say, sliding down the wall and onto the floor beside her. I reach over and lay my hand on her shoulder. She winces and sucks in a breath through her teeth.

"Oh, shit. Sorry. Did I hurt you?"

"Yeah, I just...hurt my shoulder a few days ago. I...fell off my bike."

I noticed the scratches on her neck in the kitchen earlier, too. I bet those are from the same accident.

"Are you okay?"

"Yeah," she says.

"Where's Darci? Where's your friend?"

She shakes her head. "I don't care," she says. "I *don't.* I don't even like Trevor. But he said that he liked me. And...that's not why I'm crying. I can't really explain why I'm crying."

Oh.

"Fuck Trevor." Admittedly, it was a poor choice of words by me. "That dude is an idiot. I mean, Look at him—he's got like seven hairs on his fucking face, and he pretends it's a beard. It's ridiculous. And Darci's just as bad. I'm pretty sure if someone were to dissect her, they wouldn't even find a brain in there. There would just be like...a shoe, *maybe*. Or a selfie. Or a library of TikTok dance moves."

She laughs and—

"Did you just snort?"

"No," she says, still laughing.

"You *did*. That's adorable," I tell her. "I'm serious, Ally. Darci's as shallow as a fucking shower. And far less useful."

"That's what every guy seems to like, though."

"Not every guy. Not me."

"Because she's your sister."

"Don't call her—I have a sister, okay? And she's cool. Darci is not my sister. And no, not me. Because I don't do shallow."

"You don't?"

"No way," I tell her. "I wanna go swimming."

Her lips part like she wants to say something, but she doesn't. She stays quiet, and even though the room is dark, I can feel her eyes studying me.

"Do you want to go swimming, Ally?"

"What?" she asks. She turns toward the sliding door leading out to the backyard. "It's too cold to get in the pool."

"You know what I mean."

Before she can answer, we hear footsteps coming down the stairs.

"Do you think she knows?" Trevor asks.

"Yeah, obviously she knows," Darci says, the last part coming out with a laugh. "She has eyes."

"Well, maybe we can just tell her that—"

"Listen, you know I love Ally to death, but you realize you're wasting your time with her, right? She's not even allowed to have a phone. She's barely allowed to leave the house, and I know for a fact that she is not allowed to date. I don't even think she's ever been with a guy. I mean...she says she has, but I think she's lying. Her aunt and uncle won't even let her ride in other people's cars."

"Shit," he says. "I didn't know it was that bad."

"Yeah, it's really sad, honestly."

I hear Ally suck in a breath next to me. Unfortunately, I think a lot of that—if not all of it—is true.

"Anyway, I'll see you later," Darci adds. "I should try to find her. Make sure my brother didn't sacrifice her to the Dark Lord or some shit."

"See ya," he says, then closes the door behind him.

"The Dark Lord, really?" I whisper when I hear her footsteps on the stairs. *"Voldemort?"*

"Do you really worship Satan?" she asks.

"Does that scare you?"

"Not really. I don't believe in that stuff."

"Me either."

"Then why does everyone say that? And what's with the books?"

Right...the books. The entire reason I came down here.

"Um, well...it may not surprise you to learn that Darci never liked me. She made that pretty clear whenever I was around, but when I moved in with my dad full-time and started going to Black Rock, she raged against it in a really weird way. Because—well, I'm a loser, and that was her turf. And she looked at the way I dressed and decided she was going to tell everyone that I worshipped the devil. A lot of people believed her. I think her mom even believed her. Anyway, I went ahead and let her run with it—encouraged it, even—because it scares people."

"And you like that?"

"Sure. It gives me a wide berth, makes them think I'm crazy. People leave you alone when they think you're crazy; it's incredibly effective. And the books..."

I grab my backpack from the bench, open it, and pull out some books from inside. "This is just a dust jacket I made. For fun," I tell her, holding out a book I'd titled *666 Ways to Serve Satan*. "See for yourself."

She opens the book and pulls the cover back, revealing the third book in the Wheel of Time series.

"See?" I tell her. "Not a servant of Lucifer, just a nerd. Check this one out. I just made it last week, and I'm pretty proud of it."

I drop what's actually *The Great Gatsby* in her lap, and she reads the title aloud. "*Sacrificing Small and Medium-Sized Animals: The Complete Guide*. Oh, my god," she says, before laughing.

"I did get sent to the office for reading that one in English."

"Did you get in trouble?"

"No."

"No?"

"Believe it or not, Ms. Coleman actually finds my bullshit amusing."

"I do believe it."

"You think my bullshit's amusing, too?"

She shrugs. "I guess I do."

"You never answered my question earlier," I tell her.

"Which one?"

"About swimming."

"Ally?" Darci calls out, heading back down the stairs.

I didn't expect her to ever actively look for her or give a fuck. Her timing is shit.

"I better go," she says, pushing off the ground. She takes a couple of steps forward before she looks over and says, "But Devon? Yes."

"Morning," I say when I come downstairs much earlier than usual.

"Well, look who it is," my dad says. "What are you doing up?"

"I smelled food. I'm hungry," I lie. I grab a plate and sit beside him and across from Ally. She half-smiles when my eyes meet hers, then looks down at her plate. Darci glares at me before returning to her phone, and I shovel a couple of pancakes in my mouth while my stepmom drones on and on about church bullshit.

I take the opportunity to pull out *The Great Gatsby/Sacrificing Small and Medium-Sized Animals: The Complete Guide* and prop it on the table, turning to the bookmarked page.

"Mom! Do you see what he's doing?"

"Are you going to just let him do that?" Lydia asks my dad.

"He's not hurting anyone," he replies.

"Do you see what he's reading?"

"Devon, put the book away," my dad resigns. "We're going to leave in a few minutes, then you can do whatever you want."

"Maybe I want to go to church, too."

"Yeah, right," Darci says. "Why would you want to do that?"

I shrug. "Opposition research."

"Okay, girls. We need to get going," Lydia says. "Jeff?"

"If you're going, you better go change quickly," Dad says.

"Nah," I tell him. "Maybe next time, though. See you later, Ally."

I snatch my book from the table and head toward the staircase.

"Oh, my god. Stop talking to her. You're going to scare her, and then she won't want to come over anymore," Darci says to my back.

Really? I think she likes me.

But the last thing I'd do is say something like that to Darci. So instead, I look back and smile, giving her a wink before disappearing into my room.

Fucking Darci. She's used to getting whatever she wants, and it isn't fair that she gets Ally, too. I remember the first time she brought her over here—it was right before the school year started, and I thought it was some kind of mistake. She was quiet and introspective like she is now, but something else about her drew me in. Something fierce, unbreakable. It was the kind of vibe that would scare many people away, but not me. It sucked me into her orbit, and I got into the habit of making myself present but somewhere in the background whenever she was around, watching her and waiting for either of them to realize their mistake, but they never did.

But Ally looks tired now. I suppose almost a year of being Darci's sidekick would do that to a person. Or maybe it's just that she's realized what a shit hole Black Rock High School is and always has been, and it's left her disenchanted with both humanity and life in general.

I think that's what happened to me.

I spend the rest of the day alone in my room, mentally preparing for another week of being no one.

3

I feel my cheeks burn red when Devon walks into art class first period. I spent the rest of the weekend dreading this. I think maybe I told him too much; I let him get a peek at what's behind the wall, which isn't something I normally do. My other friends don't ask about my art. They never ask me anything about my life, and if they ever decided they cared, I don't know what I'd tell them.

I regret it, but he probably does, too. What Darci said about me is true—at least the important part of it. I am a waste of time.

I keep my eyes trained on my sketchbook when he walks past and slides into a seat at the table behind me.

"Hey Ally," he says from behind me. "You look really pretty today."

I almost turn around to say something—I don't know what, but something—stopping myself when Trevor walks over and leans against my table.

I wasn't lying when I told Devon that Trevor wasn't the reason I was crying. It wasn't because of him, and it *was* complicated. I cried because I'm afraid I'll always be alone, and it won't be because I chose it. It will be because I don't know how to be with anyone else anymore.

"Um, hey. What are you doing here?" I ask.

"I didn't get to say goodbye to you the other night," he says. "I just wanted to see your face."

So, this is what he's going with?

"Is this guy fucking serious?" Devon says aloud, laughing. "Yo, Ms. Gates. Trevor doesn't go here. Can you get him out of here?"

"Mind your own business, West. Or I'll rip that thing out of your nose."

"Holt, leave my classroom and go do whatever it is you're supposed to be doing," Ms. Gates replies, bored.

"See you at lunch," he says before he leaves the room.

"Whhaaaaat a fucking tool," Devon says. I laugh a little, then quieter he adds, "Ally, can I see you later?"

This time, I do turn around. "I'm really not allowed to go anywhere...not anywhere but school. What Darci said about me was true: you *are* wasting your time."

"I don't think so."

"Okay," Ms. Gates says. "You should be working. It should be quiet for the next fifty minutes. If you need guidance, you can come to me. Otherwise, you know what to do."

I turn back to my sketchbook and continue working on the people without faces. I can't look at or think about their faces.

Still, it does feel good to get them out, like I said. The problem is that it doesn't last, and they never go away completely. They come back, and I have to do it again and again. And I'm tired of it—this compulsion.

My existence has slowly become a collection of compulsions just barely keeping me from falling to pieces. They're the only things I have control over anymore, and even then, like I said, it's just barely.

Devon slides his chair to my table and sets his things down next to mine. I look over at him, confused.

"What?" he asks. "We're allowed to do this."

"I don't remember inviting you into my space."

He shoots me a crooked smile and runs his hand through his hair. "Can I be in your space, Ally?"

I shrug. "Why?"

"Because I like being in your orbit. And I want to know where you go."

"Where I go? What do you mean?"

"You always look like you're somewhere else in your head, and I want to know where that is."

"I think you'd live to regret that," I tell him.

"Hargrove, I hear too much talking coming from over there. If you're going to work together, you need to work quietly," Ms. Gates says.

I narrow my eyes at Devon, who shrugs innocently. "I can work quietly," he says.

Shaggy dark hair falls in front of his face when he leans over his paper and goes back to work without another word. I watch him for a few minutes, studying the strokes of his pencil, the way he furrows his brow and chews on his lip while he works. I think he must feel it because he smiles just a little. Embarrassed, I turn back to my own page but only stare at it.

I'm not sure how much time goes by like this before he speaks.

"Are you stuck?" he whispers.

"No. I'm just tired of drawing them," I tell them. "I'm not...enjoying it."

He takes the book from me and starts flipping through the pages. I feel like I'm choking—like he's seeing me naked—but I don't stop him.

"Which ones *do* you enjoy drawing?" he asks.

That's a difficult question to answer. Like the faceless people, much of my art comes from feelings or things I need to get out, and while I enjoy the process, the finished product doesn't necessarily bring me joy.

When I don't answer, he stops on a page and sets it down in front of me. "What about this one?"

It's a drawing of me standing in front of the door of our old apartment, trying to decide if I should open it for the police. It was right after my mom was arrested, but I didn't know that. I didn't know why they were there, but I had a bad feeling, and I was afraid. When they told me what happened through the door, I thought they were lying—my mom wasn't a drug dealer; she cleaned hotel rooms.

But it turned out I was wrong. My mom cleaned hotel rooms, but when everything got more expensive, and she thought we would lose the apartment, a coworker let her in on her side hustle.

"No. That one doesn't bring me joy, either." I nervously tap the desk with my pencil. I don't even notice I'm doing it until he does. He takes my hand in his and steadies it.

"I'm making it my mission to find out what does," he says.

"How do you plan on doing that?" I ask.

"I can read palms," he says.

I narrow my eyes at him, then feel his thumb tracing a line inside my palm and realize that his own has been resting on mine this entire time. Holding my breath, I slowly bring my hand back toward my body.

"I'm kidding," he says, smiling. "I just thought it would go with the whole satanic/warlock persona. But I *wasn't* kidding about the other part."

"Other part?"

I think I already forgot what we were talking about.

"I'll find out what brings you joy."

I stay there, locked in eye contact with him, for a minute before the bell rings. Then, wordlessly, I pack my bag and walk toward the door. He's still in his seat, slouched in the chair, smiling like he knows he got to me when I make a break for it. I don't reply when he tells me he'll see me later as I walk out the door.

I think I may have made a mistake. I need to find a way to get rid of him. Maybe he'll recognize his own before I need to worry about how to take mine back.

I race to my locker after fourth period, quickly dumping my things inside before heading to the cafeteria. Maybe part of it is to avoid Devon in the hall, but mostly, it's just my routine. If I'm quick, I can be one of the first ones into the lunch room, pick up a few extras, and then toss them in my backpack when my friends aren't looking.

As luck would have it, I am about the tenth person in line. I take my tray, pick up a couple of muffins and an extra milk, stuff them into my bag after paying, then sit down at the usual table alone and begin eating. Darci and Audrey walk in and sit beside me with their diet sodas. Only Morgan and the guys ever go through the line and get food.

"How does your skin look like that when you eat like this?" Audrey says, her lip turning upward as she watches me scarf down the sad excuse for a cheeseburger.

I only shrug and keep chewing.

"You look like a porcelain doll," Trevor says, sitting down next to me, flanked by Luke and Justin.

I scoff. "Well, I'm no doll," I reply, my tone overtly harsh.

I'm not a toy—certainly not his—and if I were fragile, I would have broken a long time ago.

He sighs and shakes his head, visibly frustrated. "I was just being nice, Ally."

I'm about to tell him that I don't need his brand of nice, but quickly reel it back in and turn my attention back to the sad cheeseburger. After a few seconds of silence, Luke changes the subject, and everyone moves on. I finish my food quickly, then return my tray to the kitchen and head back to my seat.

"He's texting me again," Darci says when I sit back down.

"Who?"

"The older guy I was with—the one I hadn't heard from for a while."

"The college guy?" I ask.

"Yeah," she says. "He says he misses me. He wants to see me soon."

"Are you going to go?" Audrey asks. "I mean, he blew you off for weeks, right?"

"Yeah, but he had a good reason," she says. "And this is different. I told you guys. This is like...real."

They're still talking, but I can't hear them, because now, Trevor drapes his arm around my shoulders while absent-mindedly scrolling on his phone. I know it's normal, but I fucking hate it. I *hate* being touched, and no amount of conditioning or holding my breath to get through it seems to help. Even when Darci or Morgan touch or hug me, I clench my jaw until it's over. Not wanting to make a scene, I let it sit there, even though my skin crawls. Resigning to make an excuse to get up and leave in a couple of minutes, I go back to listening to my friends' conversation, feigning interest while ignoring the weight on my shoulders.

But then, he starts whistling. And he keeps whistling.

My breath comes short. I dig my nails into my thighs, but through my leggings, it isn't enough to take the edge off. I grit my teeth, and when my eyes begin watering, push away from the table, grab my bag, and leave without saying a word.

"Hey, where are you going?" Trevor says to my back. I don't answer, determined to make my exit through the impossibly loud cafeteria.

I need to find a quiet place. *Alone.* And I need to get there before everyone witnesses one of my full-blown meltdowns.

I turn into the bathroom but quickly double back out when I spot a group of girls in front of the mirror, talking and waiting for their friend to finish her makeup. I continue down the hallway and then into the empty gym, where I duck under the bleachers.

I fumble with shaky hands through my bag for my sketchbook and charcoal pencils.

It's okay. You're fine. He's not here.

I manage to find both, open the book, and just barely touch the pencil to the paper when I feel a hand on my shoulder. I react before I think.

"Ow! Shit! You stabbed me," Devon says, cradling his bloody forearm close to his body.

"I'm sorry!" I say, mortified. "I'm so sorry. You...you can't sneak up on me!"

"Yeah, I'll remember that for next time. Fuck," he says, shaking his head. "I didn't mean to scare you."

"You didn't scare me—you surprised me. Believe me, I've seen far scarier things than you."

"I *do* believe you," he says. "I saw you run out of the cafeteria; I just wanted to make sure you're okay."

"Yeah, I bet you regret that now."

"Not at all," he says with a half smile. "I think you just got a whole hell of a lot more interesting."

"Yeah, right," I scoff.

"I'm serious. What the hell happened back there?"

"I don't want to talk about it."

"Okay, but—"

"I'm not weak. Or helpless."

"I can see that."

He sits there, watching me, waiting for whatever I'll say next. He is attractive—more so even than the guys who sit at our table. I'm not really sure how he got lumped into the freak pile, and I didn't. If anyone is worthy of that pile, it's me. He's tall and fit with a defined jaw and shaggy hair as dark as mine that I want to run my fingers through. Enough that I could really get a hold of it if I wanted to—not that I do...or would.

Piercing blue eyes, though. That's all I see now—so pale in contrast to his other features.

I don't even mind the gauged ears or the septum ring the rest of them always make fun of. I think I like it.

If I could, I think I'd get one through my eyebrow. Maybe my lip, too. I wonder what it would feel like. I wonder how it would feel if he rolled his tongue over it—or sucked it into his mouth.

I realize that I'm biting my own lip and stop.

I think a lot about how I would decorate my body, my face, if I had the chance. Other people's bodies, too. I used to love clothes and makeup when I was allowed to wear it. It's just another form of art, our bodies just another outlet, a canvas, even.

But what's happened to mine, it's—if I got the chance, I'd wipe it clean and start over.

We all come into the world as blank canvases. And we leave it carved in scars—some we show the world and others that remain invisible unless someone knows exactly where to look—but they make us who we are, whether we want them to or not. I'd like to make my own canvas into something pretty or at least something I'm not ashamed of. Someday, I will.

"I'm gonna go," I tell him. I toss my things in my bag, stand, and throw it over my shoulder.

"You have a track meet tomorrow, right? In Mount Vernon?"

Yeah, I do.

"Don't sneak up on me anymore," I say. "And...no whistling."

"Whistling?"

"I don't like it."

"Okay, no whistling. No problem."

I leave just as the lunch bell sounds without saying anything else. It's not like I want to be alone. It's not my choice, it's my circumstances. It's not that I'm entirely uninterested, but that I don't have the mental space or energy to think or feel things like that anymore.

But that has taken a toll on me and made me wonder if I'm now incapable. I wonder if I'll ever want to be touched and what it would take. I want to think the answer is yes, but I'm not sure.

I think maybe I'd like it if Devon touched me.

I spend the rest of the day zoning out—not that my grades are important to me. Track practice is an easy one since we have the meet tomorrow. I take the city bus home, the familiar sense of foreboding settling in the closer I get.

I wonder what I'm going to walk into this time. I think that makes it worse—the not knowing, the trepidation. At least this time, I know I have food in my bag.

When I walk inside, Grace is in the kitchen cooking. It smells like chicken and green beans.

"You can go fold the laundry and clean the bathrooms," she tells me. "Then we'll eat together."

Thank god.

Fuck the together part, but I didn't have dinner the day before or breakfast this morning. I'll take the win.

I fold and put away the laundry, then scrub the house's two and a half bathrooms, at least enjoying the silence. Once finished, I head down to the kitchen, wash my hands, and sit across from Grace at the table.

"We need to pray," she says.

I follow her lead—the routine—bowing my head while she thanks someone for all the blessings surrounding us, but I don't think it's any type of god who brought me here.

"And I know, Lord, that you will bless this family with a child when the time is right. A *real* child," she adds.

I fight the urge to scoff and roll my eyes.

"Amen."

She finishes before I do but stays at the table—manners or whatever. Maybe it's just to watch me. I feel her eyes boring holes through me. She wants to say something, and I know better than to ask what it is.

Eventually, I hear it anyway.

"You look ugly when you eat," she says. "Like a rat. You know that?"

"I'm sorry," I say after I finish chewing. "What do you suggest I do instead?"

"I don't think there's much hope for you, I just wanted you to know that. You look ugly right now."

Six more months.

"Your mother was at least taught better. Prettier than you, too. You got your dad's nose. Have you ever even seen him? Do you remember what he looks like? I'm sure he's in jail, too, wherever he is."

I grit my teeth and push back my chair. "Do you want me to take your plate?" I ask.

"Clean it all up," Grace says before standing. She hits the corner of the table with her hip hard, rattling the plates and utensils and knocking over her glass of wine. It topples onto the floor and shatters, its contents splattering across the white tile. "That better not leave a stain, either, or you'll be sorry."

She waits, again, for a reaction I'm not willing to give her.

"I have a track meet tomorrow," I say calmly as I grab a towel. "It's in Mount Vernon. I'll be home late."

"I'll be waiting. If you miss the last bus, you're walking. And you'll be punished when you get home."

I clear the table, load the dishwasher, and head straight to the shower. I wash the day from my skin and try to pretend I'm somewhere else, anywhere else.

Maybe on a beach somewhere, washing the sand from my feet after a long day. Somewhere quiet, somewhere I can rest. Maybe somewhere I can put my art on the walls, in a world where someone tells me they love me before I fall asleep.

But reality pulls me back.

A waste of time.

Ugly.

Have you ever even seen your dad?

The whistling.

I crack the side of my disposable razor and remove the blade. The last one had grown dull, and it's worse when they're dull. I'm getting better at this; I barely cut my fingertips when I remove it from its plastic casing.

Then, I sit at the bottom of the shower and run it across the inside of my thigh in three identical strokes, like I always do.

3...2...1

I watch the blood run down my thigh, becoming one instead of three separate streams before trickling onto the white porcelain and spiraling down the drain. I lean my head against the cold tile wall and let the relief wash over me as it pours out of me. I breathe a little easier afterward, just as I always do.

We come into the world as blank canvases—all of us. Innocent, eager for love. Then the world gets ahold of us and leaves us with scars we don't deserve, that we never asked for. But like I said before, it feels better to let it out, even if it's only temporary.

4

It's raining, but just a little—not enough to cancel the track meet—when the bus pulls to a stop in Mount Vernon. I make my way over to the high jump mat and take a few practice jumps, trying to get a feel for their setup and the surroundings before the real thing.

Not that it really matters how I do. I'm the third-best jumper on the team; I almost never place.

Grace and Mark won't be here. Sometimes, when he's in town, they do show up, especially at home meets—to show what a part of the community they are and to remind people what great Christians they are for fostering their niece.

God, if they only knew.

Once the meet starts, I tell the coach I need to go inside and use the restroom. It will be a while before they call high jumpers to check in. As soon as I can, I slip away, sneaking into the school, searching for the gym and then the locker rooms.

I look around, checking for anyone who may be watching me, then slowly slip into the one labeled 'men,' ensuring there's no one still inside. There are a couple of reasons why I do this. The first is that guys are always lazier when it comes to protecting their things due, I'm sure, to a sense of security that's innately male. They don't know what it's like to be afraid walking on dark streets at night, sleeping in a first-floor bedroom, or moving through parking garages alone with keys between their fingers. They run at night with headphones on and take for granted that they're safe, so they leave their bags out on the floor. Another reason I choose the men's locker room is because maybe if they start trying to figure me out, they'll assume it's another guy who did it.

As expected, there are several lockers unlocked and bags left out in the open. I end up with $280 in cash and three cell phones.

I make it back to the track just before they start calling high jumpers, spotting a familiar...book...in the stands behind me when I do.

666 Ways to Serve Satan.

Devon peaks out at me from over the top. I bite back a smile and turn back toward the opposing team's coach, waiting for my turn. We don't speak, but I know he's watching me. Every cell in my body is aware of it. I try harder than usual once it's my turn and only end up really fucking up on the third jump.

Afterward, I join the rest of my team in the grass alongside the track. I feel it when he sits on the bleachers behind me.

"I'm announcing my presence," he says. "Please don't hurt me."

"I know you're there," I tell him.

"Is this what you do now?" he asks. "You just sit here?"

"Yep," I say without looking over my shoulder. "Until all of the events are done."

"Sounds boring," he says. "Isn't it boring?"

"I enjoy the fresh air," I tell him.

"Okay," he says. "So, you're outdoorsy. I wouldn't have guessed that."

"Sure," I reply with a shrug. "Let's go with that. I'm outdoorsy."

"I'll add that to the very short list of things I know about you."

"Is this a physical list, or are you writing it down somewhere?"

"I'm writing it down," he says.

"What do you have so far?"

"Well, you're beautiful...obviously. You're a talented artist. You like Doritos. And...Darci, which is weird. And I shouldn't sneak up on you if I don't want to get stabbed. I'm still trying to work out what brings you joy since, apparently, it isn't your art."

Yeah, so am I.

"That's pretty much all there is."

"I don't believe that for a second," he says. "Do you want to go...somewhere else?"

"I can't," I tell him. "I have to be on the bus when we go back. And I'm not allowed to go anywhere...ever. Add that to your list."

"That's not true. You're allowed to go to my house."

"Yeah, I guess."

"Why is that?" he asks.

"I don't know. Darci and your mom go to the church—"

"Whoa," he says. "I'm going to stop you right there. Not my mom. Not my sister. *Step*."

"Okay, well. My aunt and uncle love your stepmom. And Darci does all that youth group and camp stuff, and they think she's like...a model citizen or some shit."

Devon laughs. "Oh god. That's fucking ridiculous. So they like...set you guys up?"

"Yeah, basically. She's supposed to teach me how to...not be a shitty human, I guess."

"What have you learned so far? And—Jesus—how bad were you before? I guess that should be my next question."

Now, I laugh. Hard. "Not a lot. But you know what? She has been my friend. She's been good to me. She could have easily ditched me, and then I wouldn't have any, so I don't really wanna—I mean, I can't—say anything bad about Darci."

"Okay," he says. "I'll do my best to hold it in."

It's true. I know she's not always good to others, but she has been good to me. At first, I could feel the pity coming off of her, and I felt like the charity case that I was, but it eroded into something that does feel like a genuine friendship.

I don't like all of them all the time. Audrey is mean because she likes it, and it gives her power. We tolerate each other at best. Morgan is just as pretty as the other two but more laid-back and the athletic type. She isn't concerned with high school social politics the way the others are, but she effortlessly falls into her place. She plays volleyball with Darci and me in the fall, but basketball is where she stands out. There are already colleges paying attention.

And then, there's Darci. She's smart but also selfish. I've seen her scheming first-hand; it's not always easy to watch, and she's not the kind of person whose bad side you want to be on. Still, there's only one reason people at this school don't say shit about me being a foster kid or my mom being in jail—one tall, blonde reason.

I've also seen another side of her that I don't think the others have—someone who is maybe hurting a little more than we know, but people like that always are, aren't they? I wonder where I'd have to look to find Darci's scars.

"Hargrove!" Coach P yells, waving me over.

"He doesn't like the whole fraternizing with our peers at meets thing," I tell him. "Unprofessional."

I push off the ground and walk away from the bleachers to where Coach Parks stands, glaring at me over his clipboard.

Devon scoffs. "He fucks students, but okay."

What? My head whips back in his direction. *"Really?"*

"Oh, yeah. Absolutely. How long have you been here?"

Not quite a year now, but I think he knows that. I have *so* many questions. Since I can't ask them, I shake my head and keep walking in Coach's direction.

I sit in the grass next to him and a few other field event girls, trying to reconcile this new information. I guess it isn't that surprising—the part where he'd do shit like that. Short, beefy dude with a complex. How original.

But who would sleep with him? He wears white Oakleys with one of those strings attached to both ends, for fuck's sake.

"Hargrove, are you okay?" he asks, likely noticing I'm staring. I get a look at my reflection in the yellow lenses of the aforementioned sunglasses and realize I'm grimacing.

"Yeah," I tell him. "I'm good."

After we lose, we board the bus home. No one is surprised; we expected it. The only thing I didn't expect was that their school would hand out ribbons through sixth place; they usually only do this at larger events. I run the fourth-place ribbon through my fingers, laughing when I think about adding it to the box under my bed with my other three. Still, it feels good to win something, even if it's only this and even if I don't have anyone to give a shit, and I'm weirdly proud of it. Maybe I could mail it to my mom; I wonder if they'd let her keep it. I make a mental note to look that up.

The bus makes it back to the school around 8:00 PM. I'm one of the last ones off, purposely taking my time watching my teammates disperse to their own or their parent's vehicles. It's always awkward when one of them offers me a ride, and I have to refuse it.

"Hey, do you want a ride?"

Exactly like this.

"Did you come all the way back to the school just to wait here to ask me if I wanted a ride?"

"Yeah," Devon says, shrugging.

"I can't. I have to take the bus."

He takes a couple of slow steps toward me, closing the space between us. I take a step backward and run into a parked car. "My car's right there," he says, nodding over my shoulder.

"Why are you doing all of this?" I ask. "You shouldn't do this. I mean, didn't you hear Darci? I'm a waste of time."

"Hmm...I don't think so."

"What do you want, Devon?"

"I told you what I want—swimming, remember? You said you did, too."

"I shouldn't have said that," I tell him.

"Yeah? Why's that?" He takes another step forward, effectively eliminating the remaining space between us. One hand settles on my hip while he leans on the other against the car.

All of the air leaves my lungs.

"Well?" he presses.

"I don't even...I don't know if I like to be touched anymore," I say.

"Do you want to find out?"

My eyes dart around the empty parking lot.

"No one is watching," he says. "We're alone."

I manage a slight nod.

"Close your eyes."

"What?"

"Close them," he says again.

I close my eyes and wait for what feels like minutes before I feel lips softly kiss each of my eyelids—the right first, then the left—before cautiously trailing down my jawline and over to my earlobe. I lock my arms tightly at my sides as he sucks it into his mouth and runs it through his teeth. I feel something I haven't felt in a long time low in my gut, something I wasn't sure if I could feel anymore, and it's almost a relief. When his mouth moves to my neck, I gasp, embarrassed when I hear the sound, but that feeling—that ache between my legs—doesn't really give a shit.

Eager to have him closer, my hands reach out, each grabbing a fistful of his shirt and pulling him into me. His lips move to my mouth when I do, finally kissing me, tasting me. His tongue thrusts into my mouth, circling and teasing my own. The hand on my waist runs over the curve of my ass, then continues to dip lower. His fingers graze my pussy through my thin running shorts when his hand moves to grip my inner thigh, using it to hitch the leg up around his waist.

I feel the ridge of his hard cock press between my legs and moan against his mouth. He rolls his hips into me, eliciting a low rumble from his throat, and I just want more—more of this feeling I forgot, more of that sound, more of him. With my back firmly against the car, I push up onto the tip toes of the one foot remaining on the ground and hook my fingers in his belt loops, bringing him closer, spurring him on as he grinds his dick into me.

I hear the bus pass the stop, and I don't give a fuck.

His hand moves under my shirt, then inside my bra, his thumb circling my nipple while the other still holds me firmly in place as he rubs his cock into my clit. He pulls his mouth away from me and stills, still pushing into me, and I want to fucking scream.

"Seems like you still like being touched to me," he says, leaning in and kissing me again. "Actually, it sounds like you're about to come on my dick through those tiny ass shorts. Are you?"

Yes.

I stare at him with lips parted, breathless, but don't reply. Surely, he knows the answer to that question, anyway. If he were to touch me right now, he'd probably be able to feel how wet I am right through these *tiny ass shorts*.

"You can, if you want. Or you can get in the car, and I can take them off of you."

I still don't move or say a word.

He releases the thigh hitched around his waist and backs away. At first, I think he will leave me here like this. Then he opens the back door to the car and looks at me, waiting.

I steady myself on shaky legs and climb inside.

He follows, closes the door behind him, then moves in and starts kissing me again. He grabs my hips and pulls me down flat on my back on the seat and then slips his fingers under the waistband of my shorts on each side.

"Wait..."

"What?"

I don't say anything. I lie there for a few seconds, heart pounding, staring at the dome light until it goes off. "Okay, go."

There are things about my body that I don't want him or anyone else to see. In this dark car, in a dark parking lot, I should be able to keep hiding.

I slip my shoes from my feet while he pulls my shorts off my body, leaving me bare and exposed. I suck in a breath as he runs his fingers over my slick center before pushing two of them inside me.

"God, you're soaked," he says, moving them in and out of me. I grip the side of the bench seat hard in my hands and grit my teeth to try to keep myself from crying out while he fingers me, slowly at first then faster. I lose the battle and drop my head back as he pulls the moan from my lips.

"You really were about to come, weren't you?" he asks. He removes his wet fingers and circles my clit.

"Would you just...fuck me?" I groan.

He furrows his brow. "Is that what you want?"

"Yes."

He pulls his hand back, and I hear him fumbling with his belt. I sit up and help him pull them down over his hips, freeing his hard cock. I'm admittedly shocked when I see how big he is, and he must see it on my face, too.

"It will feel good," he says. He pushes me back down onto my back, stroking it in his hands before pulling a condom from his wallet and rolling it down the length of him.

He reaches down under my ass, bringing my hips toward him and positioning himself between my legs. Then, I feel him push past my entrance in one smooth, slow motion. His size stretches me; I feel it burn at first, but I'm so wet that there's no resistance.

"Oh, my god," I say, digging my nails into his forearms.

"Fuck," he says back, almost sounding pained as he starts thrusting in and out of me. "You feel so damn good, Ally."

I arch my back and whimper at his words. I'm so close already; I want so much more. I take one of my legs and prop it on the center console in the front of the car, spreading wider, and feel that tension at my core about to unravel.

"Devon...harder."

He looks absolutely feral when he pushes my shirt and bra up, revealing my breasts before he gives me what I asked for—again and again—until my legs are shaking and my toes are curling. My eyes actually roll back into my head when I come in the backseat of the car, and I'm such a mess I think I even yelled his name. My body is still spasming when his own stiffens, and I feel his dick pulsing inside me.

We lie in the back like that for a minute—sweaty, winded, and half-naked.

I start to panic a little, losing myself in my head. Not wanting to go down that hole, I reach for him, looking for anything that will anchor me in reality right now. I push my hands through his hair, then down over his gauged ears, running my fingers over the plugs, and for whatever reason, it actually works. I'm out of my head. I'm back in my body, in this car.

I'm...fine.

But...what the fuck did I just do?

Devon props himself on his elbows, then leans down and kisses me on my mouth. "Well, this is not at all how I thought tonight was going to go. In the best way."

"Yeah, me either."

"Do you have any idea how many times I've thought about this?" he asks, brushing my hair away from my face. "That's kind of a weird thing to say, isn't it? I don't mean it in a creepy way, but also...kind of in a creepy way. You know what? I think we should—"

"Devon, can you take me home now?" I interrupt.

"Yeah, but—"

"I just—I missed the last bus, and if Grace didn't hit the bottle hard tonight, she's going to be waiting for me, so..."

"Did I do something wrong?"

"No, I just...I'm going to get in trouble. I shouldn't have done this." My tone is harsher than I mean for it to be, and I'm sure he hears it, too.

He sighs, his own tone changed when he speaks again. "Yeah, okay. We can go."

"Okay, thanks."

Shit, I'm terrible.

Devon sits up, and I push my bra and shirt back into place while he fixes his pants, then feel around for my own shorts on the floor and pull them on.

He holds out my shoes, and I take them from him. I can tell he wants me to say something, but even though I feel the need to fill the silence, I can't.

I'm sorry. That's what I would say if I could.

I set the shoes on the floorboard, then lean forward, place a hand on the back of his neck, and kiss him, sliding my tongue past his lips, letting it linger for a few seconds before I pull away. He leans forward and rests his forehead against mine, looking into my eyes. There's something about the way he looks at me that just...it hits me right in the gut. And he just *feels* different from other people. I don't know how to describe it other than that it's something that feels familiar.

I guess that's why it was him.

I wait only a second before I break away from his gaze and slip into my shoes. Then, I go for the door handle, step out of the car, and retrieve my bag from where I'd dropped it in the parking lot. I hear the car start behind me, then a Slayer song blaring from the speakers before I get into the passenger seat.

"Can you drop me off at the bus stop?" I ask. "Do you know where it is? I'm not supposed to be in cars with people, and there's a doorbell camera."

"Yeah, Ally. I know where it is."

He's so fucking beautiful. I hope it doesn't hurt him when he realizes this can't ever happen again—that I really can't even talk to him again. But...he's a guy. He'll be fine, right?

The thought of it makes me feel like there's a vice around my chest. I want to touch him again, but I don't. Instead, I rest my head on the center console, and fingers run through my hair for the rest of the short drive. I close my eyes and wonder how long it's been since someone touched me like this—out of kindness. I hope he doesn't see me cry.

I get my shit together when I see the car turn into my neighborhood, stopping just a few seconds later.

I sit up and look at him. Again, I feel like I should say something, but all that comes out is, "Don't tell anyone."

"I won't," he says.

Then, I practically throw myself from the car.

Somehow, despite the vice crushing my chest, I manage the walk back to the house. I step inside the unlocked front door, pleased to see that Grace did have too much to drink tonight and passed out on the couch, as she tends to do when Mark isn't here. I tiptoe past her to the staircase, set my bag on the floor in my bedroom, and head straight for the shower.

I turn on the water, letting it warm as I strip down. I pull the shower curtain closed and let it wash over me, rinsing his scent and any other evidence from my skin. Then, I sit down at the bottom of the tub and remove the small razor blade I hid in the soap bar a day before. I turn it over in my fingers and look down at the marks lining the inside of my thighs, trying to pick a side.

It takes me a little longer than usual. I realize that—for the first time in a long time—I just don't want to.

5

I wake to my alarm the next morning feeling hungover. What happened instead was I probably got around two hours of interrupted sleep on an empty stomach. I roll out of bed, and my heart stops when I look down and realize I slept in Devon's hoodie. What was I thinking? What if she'd seen it? I pull it over my head, taking a moment to let it linger near my nostrils before stashing it between my mattress and the box spring. I hear Grace moving around downstairs, so I won't risk getting into my treasure box right about now. I pull on a pair of straight-legged jeans that are at least one size too big for me and pair them with a long-sleeved black t-shirt. All of my clothes are plain like this. I remember a time when that bothered me, but it doesn't bother me at all now.

I comb out my thick, straight hair, brush my teeth, grab my bag, and head for the side door, slowing down but not stopping in the kitchen.

Grace hands me a bagel and says, "They probably won't send him to school. He may not even be living on the island now."

"I wouldn't know."

"Either way, you stay away from him. If I find out otherwise..."

"I will," I say as I head out the door.

On the bus, I begin to wonder the same thing—will they send him to school? He missed the end of junior year, and his dad and Darci's mom divorced. I don't even know if his dad still lives on the island. I know I'd want to get the hell out of here if I were him. It's also possible he moved in with his mom.

When I get to school, I go to my locker and apply just a tiny bit of the lipstick I was gifted months ago, just as I do every day, and head to first period art class. I get an answer to my question fairly quickly.

This classroom is always loud, especially with the new art teacher being super laid back, but all the sound dissipates once Devon enters the room. You can feel the shift in energy, the shift of attention to the front of the classroom. He hands Mr. Ames a slip of paper.

"Okay, everyone. Looks like we have a new student. Devon...West. If you'd like to introduce yourself to the class, be my guest. Otherwise...go ahead and take your seat."

"Oh, I'm not new. *You're* new," Devon says to the teacher before turning to the class. "I think you all know who I am. I'm Devon. And I missed a bunch of school because I was arrested for a crime I didn't commit...all because that girl right there didn't want people to know she was fucking me."

A handful of people laugh, but most of them are afraid to react at all. I'm in the latter group. I think Mr. Ames realizes now exactly who is standing next to him because he's also too shocked to react. Devon grins before strutting down the aisle, stopping at the desk behind me.

"Get the fuck out of my seat," he says to Sofia. I hear her scramble to gather her things and find a new spot before he slides into his old seat.

We're starting a new section today, so Ames turns down the lights and puts the slides up on the smart board. I don't think anyone is paying attention to what's going on in the front of the room—they're watching him, whispering. I can hear my heart beating in my ears.

I feel Devon's breath hot on my neck before he speaks.

"I gotta ask—how do you sleep at night, Ally? How do you live with yourself?"

"I don't sleep," I tell him over my shoulder. It's not a lie. He knows me, so surely he can see it. "Devon—"

"No."

When the lights are back on, he gives us the theme for the Fall Art Fair: Identity/Secret Self.

Secret is the only self I have, but most of them aren't really things I can put on display. Not that it matters—the art fair isn't until the very end of the month. I'll be gone by then.

I do have something I've been working on, though, that I could finish and submit. I wonder if they'd display it after I leave, and it could serve as a farewell of sorts. There aren't many people I'd want to say goodbye to, but there are a few who have made the days a little easier in small ways that maybe they didn't even think mattered—that maybe they didn't even notice—but I did, and it mattered to me.

I wait in my seat after the bell rings. I half-expect him to wait for me or try to speak to me, even if it's just to yell at me or grab me by my throat again, but he doesn't. He breezes past me like I'm nothing, but I'm glad to get another look at him, at least. I can still feel it—everything that ever was there, heavy in my gut.

He's thinner now—I can tell. I recognize the shirt he's wearing and remember the way it clung to his shoulders and chest before. His dark hair is buzzed close to his head. He wore a hat last night, and I'd been so shocked I didn't even notice. He's paler, too, and there are no more piercings on his face or ears.

I don't see him again for the rest of the morning, but he's all anyone talks about in the classroom or in the hallway.

At least he's out. That's a good thing, right? I should be happy about that—I *am* happy about that. And with the video they found, no one should think I had anything to do with it anymore.

So, why do I feel worse? It's not like I'd rather have him in jail than not holding me; he doesn't belong there.

And he cheated on me, so I shouldn't want him, anyway. But that still doesn't feel like it's right, either.

As usual, I get to lunch early and slide into my seat at our table. Morgan goes through the line shortly after, and Audrey walks in a few minutes later with nothing but her phone in hand. Trevor sits next to me, and a few of the other basketball guys follow suit.

"Hey, beautiful," he says, taking his seat.

I've entertained the idea of it for a while now—I've let him think that maybe we could be a couple, but only because I'm leaving soon, and no one likes to be alone. And it's not like Trevor is a bad person. Maybe he isn't exactly a good one, but he's far more innocent than he'd like the rest of us to know, I'm sure, and that's more than I can say about myself. He isn't dangerous.

But now *he's* here. And I can't.

I don't see him in the lunchroom, so maybe he isn't on this schedule.

"How are you?" Morgan asks. "Are you doing okay?"

"Yeah, I'm fine."

"Devon was in my English class," she adds. "It was the quietest that class has ever been. Everyone acted like they'd seen a ghost."

"It was the same in art," I tell her.

"You had a class with him? Did you talk to him?"

"No."

"If he tries to fuck with you, you better tell me," Trevor says. "It was sick what he did—trying to use you as an alibi or whatever."

"He didn't kill her, though. You saw the video. It wasn't him."

"Yeah, well...I'm still not so sure," Trevor says.

"We all saw him threaten her that same night, Ally," Morgan adds. "You need to be careful. And what Coach did at the game last night...that was fucked up, too, by the way."

"It's fine. I get why she did it. Her family didn't want me there."

"Yeah, well, too fucking bad. You guys were friends. *Best friends.* It's unfair what they've done to you and your reputation..."

"My reputation?" I scoff. "Is shit. And honestly, they had very little to do with that. Anyway, I can't be mad at Darci's mom. How could I?"

"Maybe they'll finally find that guy she was dating now," Morgan says.

"How is it you guys don't know more about this mother fucker?" Trevor asks.

"I think she made him up," Audrey says. "I always thought so—ever since the first time she brought him up sophomore year."

"Why would she do that?" Morgan asks.

"Because she was jealous," she says. "She was the last one to lose her virginity, and so she—"

"Would you stop?" I interject. "That's ridiculous."

"And she's dead, Audrey," Morgan adds. "You can't talk about her like that."

The bell rings, and we gather our things and head back to the lockers. Trevor follows me to mine and waits to walk to the math wing with me.

"You're quiet today."

"Yep."

"Are you sure you're okay? With him being here? Are you scared?"

"No, I'm not scared. I don't want to talk about Devon, okay? Ever."

"Okay, fine. But if you do want to talk..."

"Then I'll get a fucking therapist," I snap.

"Relax. I'm just trying to help."

"I don't need any help, Trevor."

He shakes his head in resignation and says nothing.

We're some of the last people to leave the hall, and when we turn the corner, Trevor reaches for my hand and laces our fingers together. It feels...unnatural, like cockroaches crawling up my arms. I casually remove my hand from his grip, pretending to need to adjust the bag on my shoulder.

"I can carry that for you if you want," he says.

"No," I tell him. "I've got it."

He grabs my free hand again, and I let him, inwardly cringing, thankful that his classroom is the next one.

"See you later, Ally."

The bell rings as he leaves me there in the hall, indicating I'm late again. It's hard to care when it's a class I'm failing, especially when I won't be here to see it through.

I'm lost somewhere in those thoughts when a hand grabs me by my forearm and jerks me into an empty classroom.

"Devon? Devon, stop! You're *hurting* me. What are you doing?" I protest, trying to break free of his grip. He says nothing, dragging me through the dark room to an industrial-sized paper cutter. He lifts the handle and holds my hand flat against the cutting mat, the blade aligned at my wrist.

"Trevor!?" he shouts at me through clenched teeth. "Trevor!? Are you fucking kidding me, Allyson?"

"No," I tell him. "No, there's nothing going on, I promise. I never touched him or anyone else. I—"

"You're lying! God, do you ever stop fucking lying?"

"Devon," I start. I lay my free hand on the side of his cheek. "Devon, I'm so sorry. You can hurt me if you want to—if it will make you feel better. I've been hurting, anyway. It won't make a difference to me."

He jerks his head away from my hand. "I can't believe I ever fell for this shit," he laughs. "You're pathetic, you know that?"

"I'm just glad you're okay."

"You think I'm okay?!" he replies, his tone drenched in rage. "Does it look like I'm fucking okay?"

He releases both the paper cutter and my wrist simultaneously, and I yank it out of the blade's path just in time. I clutch the hand to my chest, pulse racing and breath heaving.

"Devon—" I start again. I scream when he reaches around me, grabs me by my hair, and jerks my head down toward the cutting mat. I hear the distinct sound of the blade rising again and squeeze my eyes closed when it comes down, slicing through my hair.

"What did you do?!" I exclaim, looking at the ten inches of hair still gripped in his fist. I run my hands through my hair and watch it fall to the ground in chunks. What's left seems to settle just past my chin. "I'm going to get in trouble for this!"

"Do you think I give a *shit* what happens to you now? This is just the beginning, Ally."

"This isn't you," I tell him, my eyes filling with tears. "At all."

He closes the space between us, grabbing me by my chin and tilting my head up so that we're face-to-face, despite me standing at only 5'7" to his 6'1". "Take a good look. Because I promise you, it's me."

"You can't hurt me," I tell him. "There's nothing you could do that would make me feel worse than I already do."

"If that's what you think, then you really are as stupid as everyone says."

I jerk away from his grip and turn toward the door, letting the tears I've held onto fall when I do. A sob escapes my throat, and he laughs.

Laughs. Him.

I pick up my pace, and instead of walking in late to math class, I head to my locker and dig through it until I find a pair of scissors.

"What...happened?"

I close the locker, scissors in hand, and turn to face Laurel, a junior I ran track with last year, and sigh. She's one of those people who once showed me a moment of kindness—a small one that mattered.

"Devon...he...can you help me?" I sob, holding out the scissors.

"Come on," she says. She links her arm through mine and leads me down the hallway to the locker room. I sit on a bench, and without asking for the details, Laurel evens out my hair while I cry.

"It's not that bad," she tells me. "It looks chic—highlights your cheekbones."

"Yeah, right."

"What are you going to do now?"

"I don't know. Just hide in here until volleyball practice, I guess. I don't want to...deal with people right now."

"I bet he still loves you," she says.

"No," I tell her. "He *hates* me. And he should hate me. *I* hate me."

Not as much as I hate Darci. I wish she were still here. Not just because I wouldn't be in this fucking nightmare, but because I never got to scream at her; I never got to shake her, break her nose, or punish her for what she did.

"Fuck!" I scream before standing up and punching the metal locker in front of me.

"That's a good way to end up benched with an injury," Laurel says.

She's right. I'm lucky the lockers are low quality, like just about everything else at our small town, underfunded school. But I also don't really care. I participate in school sports so I don't have to go home. It's nice that I'm actually decent at volleyball, and I do enjoy it.

The bell rings, signaling the end of fifth period. I should find a stall to hide in.

"Do you want me to stay with you?" she asks. "I can. We can go sit in my car. We can talk if you want."

"No," I tell her. "I'll be fine. Thanks for helping me...again."

"I'm here if you need me," she says. "It's just hair, Ally. It'll grow back."

"Yeah, I know."

After she leaves, I run my hands through my DIY bobbed hair, eventually working up the courage to get up and stand in front of a mirror.

I do look ugly. I *am* ugly...and it's more obvious now.

But I can do this. I just have to get through this week. Then I'll be gone, and Devon will still be free, and he can move on and be happy and pretend that none of this happened. And I'll be safe somewhere, remembering it did, with that vice-grip feeling crushing my insides whenever I allow my mind to wander.

And it will be what I deserve.

6

Ally is late to art the next morning. It's almost like it was a strategic move—like she knew if she was late, she could slide into her seat without looking at me or talking to me, and it would be normal because, well...class started already, and unfortunately, today is a quiet work day. So, that's how it went. I sat behind her, and she didn't turn around. I watched her work on her charcoal drawing—the people with the blurry faces, the ones who aren't anyone, just a feeling.

When the bell rings, she bolts for the door without bothering to put any of her things away—she just tucks it all under her arm and makes a run for it.

"Hey!" I call after her, speed-walking to catch up. "Would you stop?"

"Stop what?"

"Moving. I want to talk to you."

"I can't talk to you here, Devon."

"Well, where *can* you talk to me?" I ask, standing behind her as she digs through her locker.

"Nowhere," she says. "We cannot do this."

"Ally, what—"

"Ew," Darci says, leaning against the locker next to Ally. "What are you doing? Why are you bothering one of my friends?"

"He's not bothering me," Ally says. "We have art together. He was just asking me about our assignment."

"Oh...well, did you answer him?"

"Yes," she says, closing her locker.

"Okay, then...bye, Devon."

Darci puts her arm around Ally's shoulders and leads her away from the lockers, and I'm left standing here like a fucking tool.

What the fuck?

I guess I'm not that surprised after the way she jumped out of the car last night. Still, I expected a little more than this. Ally likes me. Ally is *like* me, not Darci, Trevor, or the rest of them.

I spend the next couple of classes convincing myself that if I could get her alone—if I could just get her to look at me—she'd tell me that I'm not crazy and she wants me again, too. Making that happen with my evil stepsister always at her side will be the complicated part.

I sit at the lunch table with Seth and Isaac but can't focus on anything they say. I'm staring at Ally—sitting with Darci and the rest of her friends, laughing and not looking at me at all. Completely unfazed.

"Devon!" Isaac says, snapping his fingers in front of my face. "What are you doing? Are you glaring at your sister or staring at Ally Hargrove again?"

"Darci is not my fucking sister."

"Whatever, man. What the hell is up with you?"

"What does she want with her?" I ask them. "It just doesn't make any fucking sense."

"What are you talking about?" Seth asks.

"*Ally*. What the hell does Darci want with Ally?"

"What do you mean what does she want?"

"She wants something. Darci isn't nice, and Ally's..."

"Ally's what? Not cool?"

"That's not what I mean," I reply, shaking my head. I'm not quite sure what I mean.

But of course, he doesn't get it. Everyone fucking likes Isaac. Whatever rules apply to Seth and me don't apply to him because he plays basketball with them a few months out of the year.

"You mean, why would Darci want to be friends with someone who lives with weird, religious nutjobs, has all these crazy rules, doesn't wear makeup or any clothes that fit, and whose mom is in jail for dealing drugs when she could be making them hate themselves?" Seth asks.

"YES." I point at Seth and turn back to Isaac. "What he said. That's exactly what I mean."

Except she does wear *some* clothes that fit. Her track shorts fit. I feel my dick grow hard when I think of how wet they were when I pulled them off her last night.

"Glad I could help," Seth says. "I'll see you guys later."

He grabs his tray and leaves the table, his girlfriend following behind him, leaving just Isaac and myself in the emptying cafeteria.

"Maybe she's just trying to be nice," Isaac offers.

"Not possible."

"Maybe they have...other stuff in common."

"No."

"Well, what do you want, Devon? What are you looking for here? Do you want me to go ask her?"

"No, I don't—"

"Oh, hey, Darci. Just curious—what is it you want from Ally? Oh...why am I asking? Because your stepbrother is weirdly obsessed with her and sees you as a barrier to whatever imaginary relationship he thinks he has with her."

"It's not imaginary."

"Sitting behind her in art for a semester does not make a relationship."

"We had sex."

"You're lying," he says.

I glare at him. “Don’t...repeat that.”

“You’re *not* lying?”

“No, I’m not lying. But now she won’t talk to me.”

“Maybe it was bad for her.”

What.

“That’s not it.”

“How can you be so sure?”

“Because I was there—that’s how. You know what? You—”

“What?” he asks.

But I don’t answer. He distracted me, and I almost missed Ally leaving the cafeteria. I leave the table and follow her down the hallway and into the women’s restroom.

Good thing it’s empty.

I hear the toilet flush, and then the door opens. Ally gasps when she sees me standing in front of it.

“Hey, Ally. How’s it going?”

“What are you doing in here?”

I step into the stall and lock the door behind us.

“Are you trying to ghost me?”

“Maybe.”

“Seriously?”

“What? Guys do it all the time.”

“Well, it’s severely damaging to my ego, for one. Don’t you care about my ego, Ally?”

She bites back a smile, but I see it. “Not really. Now move.”

Ally reaches for the lock, and I grab her hand before she can, then shift to the left, blocking it.

“Why’d you fuck me then?”

"Devon...please."

"That sounds familiar."

She crosses her arms in front of her body and rolls her eyes. A group of girls enters the restroom before she can reply, speaking loudly, and I lower my voice. "You *like* me. Don't be like this. It doesn't have to be like this."

"I just..." she whispers.

"What?"

"I just wanted to do something for no reason other than because I felt like it," she says. "That's why I did it. And I wanted to know if I could."

I shake my head. That's the truth; I can tell. But it isn't the entire truth.

"Devon, I'm sorry. I just can't do this. Please don't hate me."

The bell rings for the next class period, and the rest of the girls leave the bathroom.

"Great, now I'm going to be late," she says.

"Yeah, for study hall with Parks—like he gives a shit."

Yeah, I know her entire schedule. She doesn't even look surprised.

Ally reaches around me and unlocks the stall door. This time, I step to the side and let her pass.

I stare at her reflection in the mirror while she washes her hands, but of course, she refuses to look up.

I walk up behind her, brush some hair away from her neck, then lean down and kiss her exposed collarbone. She closes her eyes and leans into it for only a second before she turns to face me, placing both hands on my cheeks.

"Devon, I *do* like you. This is hard for me. And you're making it worse. Please...just stop."

She looks pained this time, not snarky and unbothered like she did when we were talking about ghosts and egos and shit. For that reason, I don't follow her when she leaves the bathroom. I don't stay and watch her at track practice, even though I want to and even though I have a small argument with myself about whether or not I could get her naked in the back of my car again if I did.

That doesn't mean I'm going to give up, though.

What I do instead over the next few days is what I've been doing for months—I watch her. It isn't easy. I trace the freckles on the back of her neck in my mind and barely resist the urge to reach out and run my fingers through the curtain of dark hair running down her back.

I watch her cringe when even Darci puts her hands on her, and I remember how she melted so easily into mine.

And sometimes, she does meet my eyes, and there's a flash of hurt and regret in them. I want to know which part she regrets.

I still want to know where she goes when she's in her head.

And if she won't tell me, I need to figure out a way to get her the fuck out of mine.

7

An entire week goes by just like this. I watch her while she works on her portfolio. I watch her draw a blindfolded girl with a fist full of roses and blood dripping from her hands, then crumple it up and throw it in the trash. I watch her draw more kids with no faces.

I watch her go to her other classes and wonder if I misjudged her. Maybe Ally isn't like me, and I made it all up like Isaac said. Maybe she's shallow, just like Darci, and there could never be any swimming.

I've just been distracted by her talent and those goddamn freckles and read too much into her quiet, mysterious persona, and when it looks like she goes somewhere in her head, she's really nowhere because there's nothing in there, either. Growing angrier by the second, I slam my locker shut. She looks at me from the corner of her eye but continues walking toward the cafeteria.

And then, I watch her not go to lunch.

Ally goes through the line, stuffs a few things into her backpack, then doubles out the doors. She makes her way down the hallway and then slips into the men's locker room. Rage boils up in my chest as I settle on the most obvious conclusion: she's meeting up with some other guy. Probably someone popular—someone Darci and the rest of her shithead friends would approve of her sneaking around with, like Trevor.

I clench my fists at my sides and prepare to confront her for being a fucking liar—for disappointing me by being typical and predictable when I thought she was different.

But I should have known better. It's official...nothing about Ally is predictable.

I watch as she looks for open lockers, pulling wallets from pants pockets, cell phones from bags, and removing the sim cards with a pin on her backpack before tossing them inside. From one, she pulls out an orange pill bottle. She reads the label, then shakes it once to see if it's full before tossing it in the bag, too.

What...the fuck.

I take another step closer, attempting to get a better look, but she hears it. Ally freezes, glancing around the locker room for a few seconds before letting out a breath, throwing her bag over her shoulder, and bolting back into the hallway.

And then out the back door to the parking lot. What the hell is going on?

She walks to the bus stop just a block from the school, and I get in my car and wait to follow.

The bus I know stops at her neighborhood passes, and she doesn't get on it.

Interesting.

About ten minutes later, a bus bound for downtown pulls up, and she does get on this one. I follow it for about fifteen minutes, including stopping time, before I see Ally hop off and disappear down an alley.

No.

I park in a handicapped spot and run to the alley where I last spotted her, but it's empty. I race to the other side just in time to see her disappear inside a pawn shop.

Shortly after she does, the guy comes out from behind the counter. He crosses the store to the front door, flips off the 'open' sign, and turns the bolt lock. I watch Ally put what must be at least ten cell phones up on the counter and hand the man the bottle of pills.

The guy doesn't look like he gives a shit at all where they came from. No, wait, let me try that again—he looks like he knows *exactly* where they came from. Not only that, but it looks like he knows Ally, too. And he knew when he saw her that she was bringing him some stolen shit.

Damn. What happened to ethical business practices?

I watch him count out the bills from the register and hand them to her. She wads up the cash, puts it in her backpack, and leaves—even taking the time to flip the 'open' sign back on for her buddy in there. She walks to yet another bus stop, and this time, she does get on the bus that takes her to her neighborhood. That will make it a bit easier because I can at least predict where she's going.

I hope.

I get in my car and drive toward Ally's neighborhood, then park near the bus stop on Cypress and hope that I've anticipated her next move correctly and this is where she's going.

For once, I'm actually fucking right.

She gets off the bus and cuts through the yards toward her house. I follow behind her slowly, staying close to the buildings and hoping she doesn't look back and see me. Naturally, I expect her to go through the front door when she arrives, but she doesn't. She walks around the back of the house, then up the furthest side, peeking around the corner into the garage window before backtracking and opening another window on the side of the house.

Ally tosses her bag through before using the air conditioning unit to help her crawl inside.

Again...what the fuck?

I wait for about five minutes before following through the open window. The house is pristine and expansive, with rich wood floors and white furniture. It's big but a typical size for this neighborhood. It's weird, though—it barely even looks like anyone lives here. But I guess the congressman travels a lot, and when he's here, he works at a law firm downtown, and the aunt runs the daycare at the church. The house spends a lot of time empty, which is something I'm entirely unfamiliar with. A single portrait of Ally's aunt and uncle hung over the fireplace—a large canvas print. Other than that, nothing personal.

Certainly no sign of Ally.

I creep up the stairs, peering into each room and coming up empty until I get to the very last one—a closed door with no fucking doorknob.

I push it open with one finger and see her on the floor between her bed and the wall. I walk around to that side, then see what she's hunched over is a box filled with cash.

"Who *the fuck* are you?"

My voice in the eerily quiet space startles even me, so I'm not surprised when she screams and jumps back, knocking over her secret cash stash and sending the contents in all directions across the floor.

"Are you a drug dealer? *Why* are you a drug dealer?"

"You didn't go in the front door, did you?" she asks, panicked.

"No, I climbed in through the bathroom window right after you did."

"You can't be here."

"I'm not leaving until you tell me what the fuck is going on. You're stealing from students? How much money is in there? Why don't you go in through the front door, and why don't you have a fucking doorknob?"

"I'm not allowed to have a doorknob. Or...to be here without permission."

"What?!"

"I'm not a drug dealer. It was just some kid's Adderall. And I don't want to hurt anyone, but I *need* money."

I watch her quickly stuff what must be thousands of dollars back into the box, then slide under the bed. I get down on all fours, lift the bed skirt, and watch as she removes one of the floorboards and stashes the box inside before replacing it and sliding back out.

"*Why* do you need money?"

"So that I can get the fuck out of this never-ending nightmare, Devon. You need to go—now. Back out the window." She stands and begins pushing me toward the bedroom door.

Then, we hear the door slam. I watch Ally freeze; all the color drains from her face. She slowly lowers her body down to the floor and starts to slide back under the bed, gesturing for me to do the same.

Fuck. Am I really going to fucking hide? I look at her face, at her pleading eyes, and decide I have no choice. I'd refuse if she didn't look absolutely terrified.

I get back on the ground and slide under the bed next to her, listening to Ally's uncle whistling downstairs as he rifles through the kitchen. A microwave door opens and closes. Sounds like he's in town and decided to come home for lunch.

I glance over at Ally, who has her hand covering her mouth and silent tears rolling down her cheeks.

No whistling. I don't like it.

What the fuck did these people do to her? Why the hell is she so terrified of them? I reach for her other hand and lace her fingers with mine, squeezing her palm, trying to tell her with my eyes that it'll be okay, but hers don't look convinced.

We stay like that for at least half an hour before we hear the door slam, and Ally starts to sob.

"Hey, come on. Let's get out of here."

I roll out from under the bed and wait for her to do the same, then pull her into my lap. She wraps her arms around my neck and sobs into my shoulder.

"You're okay," I tell her. "I'm not going to let anyone hurt you. I promise."

For whatever reason, what was supposed to be comforting only makes her cry harder.

"I didn't think he was back yet," she says. "Otherwise, I wouldn't have done this."

"It's okay." I let her cry for a few more minutes, stroking her hair, before asking, "Ally...what's going on?"

"They hurt me," she says.

"What?" I heard what she said; I just wasn't expecting that. "What do you mean?"

"They starve me sometimes, too. I can't stay here."

"You should tell someone," I say. "Call the police. I'll go with you."

"Devon, come on. Look at them. Look who they are and look at me. How do you think that's going to go? Do you really think they'll take me out of the house?"

No. I know better than that. I don't say it, but she must see it in my eyes.

"There has to be something else we can do."

"We? No. I am doing something—I'm saving the money so I can leave when I turn eighteen in October. That's it for me—that's my *only* out. I already snuck a withdrawal form from the office and filled it out with the date. I'll get a bus ticket, hand it in, tell people goodbye so they all know I left on purpose, and then I won't come back. I'd go now, but I wouldn't even be able to check into a hotel, let alone find a place to rent if I'm underage. And if I'm eighteen and leave by choice, the police won't come for me. They can't make me go back."

"It sounds like you've thought about this a lot," I reply, shaking my head. "What about graduation? Or college?"

She laughs. "Devon, I'm stupid. You didn't know that? Seems like you know just about everything else about me."

"You are not stupid."

"Maybe not, but I'm not going to graduate, and I'm certainly not getting into any colleges. I didn't always go to school when I was younger. My grades are horrible, and I can't pass math or science. But...that's okay, because I have a plan."

"Stealing isn't the best long-term plan, Ally. Not unless you want to end up in jail—"

"Stealing *isn't* a long-term plan. It's a means to an end. I'm going to find a cheap place to live, a job, and a tattoo apprenticeship."

"You want to do tattoos?"

She nods.

"That's actually...smart."

"Thank you."

"Where are you going to go? Not far, right?"

"I don't know," she says. "I was thinking maybe Florida."

"Florida? Why Florida?"

"Because it's far. And because if they did look for me, they'd never look there."

"I don't want you to go."

She shakes her head. "This is why we can't get to know each other, Devon. I don't want to have anything in my life that will make leaving hard. I don't know how much more I can take."

"We already know each other."

"Devon..."

"My sister's dad used to beat me and my mom," I tell her. "He's in jail now, but it took a long time. He had to almost kill her first."

"I'm so sorry."

"One time, it got really bad, and he beat me until I lost consciousness...and two of my teeth. My dad stepped in, though, and said I was never going back there again—not until that guy was in jail."

"Well, you're lucky, then."

"Don't you have a dad, Ally?"

"Technically, yes, I have a dad."

"Where is he? Why can't he help you?"

"Can I see your phone?" she asks.

I take it from my pocket, unlock it, and hand it to her. She opens the Facebook app and types 'Adam Hargrove' into the search bar. I watch her scroll until she gets to a photo of a man with the dark hair and eyes almost identical her own and clicks the picture.

"This is him," she says, handing it to me. "He left us when I was four, but I know it's him. When I realized...how it was going to be here...I looked him up on the school computer. I made an account and sent him a DM. He blocked me after he read it. See the shirt?"

Yeah, I do. *MY FAVORITE PEOPLE CALL ME DAD.*

His wall is private, but the profile pics are visible. There are pictures of him with a blonde woman and two blonde babies who can't be much older than four and six in the most recent photos. There are pictures of them camping, celebrating birthdays, playing soccer, riding bikes, lined up on a staircase, and...

They all look fucking familiar.

"This is them, isn't it?" I ask. "These are the people with no faces. It's your dad and..."

"The kids he wanted," she finishes. "I tried. He doesn't care what happens to me. He cares about them, though. And I can't get them out of my head."

"Ally, I'm—"

"We should go," she says. "I'm already going to be much later than I planned."

She leaves the room, and I push up from the floor, follow her down the staircase, and then to the small bathroom window. She stands on the toilet and starts climbing through, grimacing when she pushes up onto her arms, using them to support her lower body. I reach for her legs and help her through, then follow the same way. She waits in the grass, her left hand holding her right shoulder.

I think of when I'd touched it and the scratches she had on her neck that weekend.

"Hey, Ally...you know, you live pretty close to the school. Why don't you ever ride your bike? It would probably be faster."

"What? I don't have a bike."

I sigh, déjà vu rolling through me. My mom used to make up excuses like that, too. "I parked over on Cypress. I'll drive us back."

"...Okay."

We walk back through the grass to where my car sits parked, about a block down the road from the bus stop. I unlock the doors, and we both get in.

Ally's eyes dart to the back seat and back up front again.

"What are you doing?" I ask. "Looking for your cum stain?"

"What? No, Devon. Jesus."

I shrug. "I'm just saying that's what it looked like."

She covers her face and turns toward the window. "Would you just drive?"

"Fine," I tell her.

We drive in silence for a few minutes—up until I pass the school parking lot.

"What are you doing?" she asks. "Where are we going?"

"McDonald's or Taco Time?" I ask.

"What? You don't need to get me food."

"I missed lunch because I had to stalk you, and I'm hungry."

"You didn't have to stalk me; you *chose* to."

"Whatever. And I can hear your stomach. So, which one? Hurry up, we're getting close. Don't be that person who can't pick a place to eat when—"

"McDonald's," she says, and I swing into the parking lot.

There's no one in line; we both order Big Macs, fries, and giant sodas, and I watch Ally practically inhale hers as we drive back to school.

"Now you know more things about me—things Darci doesn't know. You have more to add to that list you made," she says.

"Yeah, I do."

"So, on a scale of one to ten, how disappointed are you now?"

"I thought you were hooking up with Trevor."

"What?"

"When I started following you, I thought I was about to catch you fucking around with Trevor. That would have been far more disappointing than finding out you're a thief and a drug dealer."

"Would it really?"

"One hundred percent, yes."

She laughs and shakes her head.

"So...tattoos, huh?"

"Yep," she says, finishing off her sandwich.

"What would you do to me?"

She smiles. "You mean like...if I could tattoo you?"

"Yeah."

"I don't know. I'll have to think about that and get back to you."

"You do that."

We pull into the school parking lot a few minutes later. I put the car in park, and Ally goes for her door handle.

"Wait," I say. "You can't steal from people anymore, Ally."

She shakes her head. "I told you—I need money."

"We'll figure something else out. You said you don't want to hurt people. That hurts people, Ally. And you could get caught. I mean, I caught you. Someone else is going to, too, and then what?"

"No one watches me like you do."

"They don't have to; it wasn't that hard. Do you have a backup plan for when they figure out that a bunch of kids are getting robbed at school?"

"I usually just do it at other schools. Or I look through cars, but yeah. I have a backup plan."

"Well, what is it?"

"Sell nudes to old pervs on the internet," she smiles.

"Okay, no. Fuck that. You're definitely not doing that."

"What makes you think you have a say in it?" she asks before she jumps out of the car.

I take a second to roll my fucking eyes and mutter a few choice profanities under my breath before I do the same and jog to catch up with her.

"Well, how much money do you have? How much do you need?"

"I have just over two thousand dollars," she says.

"Jesus."

“And I figure I can live on two thousand a month—and if I have enough money for three months, then I’ll be okay.”

“Okay. Okay, so...maybe we just need to steal a lot of money from...someone who deserves it. You know, like the TV show *Dexter*, but with stealing. What about your aunt and uncle?”

“No,” Ally says. “If I steal from them and run, they’ll send the cops after me. They’ll know.”

“Okay, someone else, then.”

“You find me someone I can steal that much money from and get away with it, and I’ll stop doing this. But I have to go. I’ve missed two classes already, and I have no idea what I’ll say to get out of this.”

“Well, you’re a girl. Can’t you just like...blame period stuff or something?”

“That’s offensive.”

“Sorry.”

“But also...not a bad idea. Maybe I’ll tell Martinez I bled through my pants. I bet he’ll be terrified.”

“See?” I tell her. “I’m useful. I’m a problem solver; you should keep me around.”

“You’re good for more than that,” she says.

“Oh, yeah? Like what? Be specific.”

“Bye, Devon,” she says.

“Wait!”

I grab her hand and pull her back into me, then lean down and kiss her. Her lips part for me, and I slide my tongue past them, tasting her mouth for only a second before she pulls back.

"You know, you're really beautiful," Ally says.

"I feel like I'm the one who is supposed to say that," I tell her, tracing her jawline with my fingertips, lost in those sad, dark eyes again.

"I mean it," she says. She starts to walk away, and I follow before she shoves me. "Go the other way, Devon. Don't walk next to me, seriously."

I shake my head but hang back anyway as she turns the corner down the hallway. "Bye, Ally."

I can play this game if she wants...for a while. I lean against the wall and watch as she walks to her locker, passing Mr. Parks on the way.

"Hargrove, I didn't see you in study hall. You going to be at practice this afternoon?" he asks.

"Yeah, I'm feeling better now," she says.

I watch his eyes run up and down her body. "Yeah, you look like it. See you then," he says.

He continues in the other direction, stopping to turn and check out her ass before disappearing into his classroom, and my blood boils.

Then, it hits me.

Someone who deserves it.

8

I sit on my bed with my sketchbook in my lap, drawing *them* again—the people without faces, as Devon calls them. I call them the kids that he actually wanted or the family he chose. Sometimes, I call them brother and sister or by their names. I hate that I know them. I hate that I can't seem to draw anything else right now. My mom and I never asked for anything, and they got *everything*. I would have settled for scraps. I'd take phone calls and lunch dates and call it good enough because it would be better than being thrown in the trash.

Since learning about them, I often think about what it would be like to be a big sister. Kids have a lot of love to give, and I bet they'd be happy to have one. Sometimes, I picture ringing the doorbell at their home and little footsteps running to greet me and then throwing their arms around my neck. Then, I'd go upstairs and read them books, play with dinosaurs, and have tea parties. Maybe my stepmom wouldn't like me, but she'd realize that I could be helpful. She'd let me take them for ice cream and eat dinner with them.

Fuck, I need to get out of my head. Usually, when Grace and Mark go out of town and leave me with Darci, I'm able to do that. I can relax at her house. I can sleep.

I think I made a mess of that.

I hear the doorbell ring and race down the staircase, hoping to get there before Grace and Mark have the opportunity to invite her in.

Of course, I'm not so lucky.

"Darci, come on in," my uncle says, leaning in to hug my friend.

The sight makes the hair on the back of my neck stand on end. If she knew what kind of people they were, she'd know better than to let him touch her. I hold my breath until he stops.

"Darci, you look beautiful as always, sweetheart," Grace says. "So grown up."

"Thank you," she says. "And Grace, I signed up to volunteer at the daycare after choir every week this month."

"Oh, that's wonderful!" she says.

"Ally, you should do it, too," Darci says.

"Oh, I think Ally needs the sermons more," Grace says. "You know she grew up without church in her life. And it takes a certain personality to work with children. You need to be...warm, caring, and, well, more like you, Darci."

"Yeah, you know me," I say, "cold and negligent. I'm ready to go if you are, Darci."

Grace shoots me a look that tells me I'll pay for that one later, but I know I'll be paying regardless, so I don't really care.

"Did you pack a bathing suit?" Darci asks. Her eyes run down my body, taking in my black joggers, high tops, and an oversized band tee.

"No," I tell her. "I thought I'd just hang out. I...don't know how to swim."

"Oh...okay. Cool."

"So, you guys have the pool open already, Darci?" Mark asks.

"Yep," she says. "We've got it up to eighty-five degrees. It's warmer in the water than it is outside."

"Well, maybe I'll have to come over for a swim, too," he says.

"I'll tell my mom," she smiles.

"You ready?" I press.

"Yeah, let's go."

"We'll be back tomorrow afternoon by four or so; just make sure you have her back in time for dinner," Grace says. "We're going to eat at six thirty. You're welcome to join us."

"Oh, that'd be great," she says. "Maybe I will."

"And you girls behave yourselves," Mark adds with a wink.

"We always do," Darci says.

After a prolonged goodbye, I follow Darci out the front door and over to her Honda. I want to ask her if Devon will be there, but I know that will look suspicious. My stomach flips just thinking of seeing him and maybe ending up alone with him again.

"You should be nicer to them, Ally," she says as we back out of the driveway. "I know you know how to be nice to people. They're trying really hard."

"I'm trying, too," I say.

"Right," she says, shaking her head. "Anyway, Morgan and Audrey are going to meet us at the house. Do you really not know how to swim? How did I not know that?"

"I don't know. It's embarrassing."

And it's not true. I know how to swim; I just don't want to be seen in a bathing suit.

"I could have sworn you got into the pool last year."

I was different then.

I shrug. "Nope. I don't think so."

"Well, I could teach you. You could stay in the shallow end. You could wear one of my suits. I mean...they'd be big in the top, but—"

"It's okay, Darci. Really."

"Well, if I knew, I would have asked you to do something else. I don't want you to be uncomfortable."

"I won't be. I'm happy to just...hang out there. I'll be fine. Any excuse to get out of the house on the weekend. It would be nice if you could come to dinner tomorrow, though."

As annoying as it is, the show they put on for Darci does tend to work in my favor. She's an excellent buffer.

"Well, I was supposed to meet up with that guy later that night, but..."

"What guy? The old guy?"

"He's not an old guy," she says. "He's in college. But I could probably do both."

"Okay...thanks."

When we pull up to the house, Morgan's car is in the driveway, and she and Audrey are already waiting for us by the pool. I follow Darci through the living room and out to the back patio, pretending I'm not scanning the first floor for Devon as we go.

I did see his car. That doesn't mean he didn't leave with someone else, though. What if he comes back with another girl? He probably wants to after everything I told him.

I think I'm going to be sick.

I put on my sunglasses, lie back on a lounge chair next to my friends, and listen to them talk about prom dates and dresses and wonder if Devon will go to prom. Maybe he's even asked someone already. It seems like almost everyone has a date by now.

Yeah, I definitely fucked up. *Fuck.*

I hear the sliding door close, and Darci yells, "Go back inside, Devon. We're using the pool right now."

"Too bad it's not just your house," he says. He pulls his shirt over his head and sits down on the edge of the pool.

"Are you going swimming, Ally?" he asks.

"What? No," I reply.

"Ally doesn't know how to swim," Darci says.

"Really? I thought Ally liked swimming."

"Why would you think that?" she asks, annoyed.

"I feel like she mentioned it."

"No," I say. "I definitely didn't."

"My mistake," he says, smiling.

"Honestly, Devon," Darci says. "Would you go inside? I know you probably get off on seeing my friends in bikinis, but..."

"That's definitely not what I get off on," he says. "But yeah, I'll go in in just a minute. Just wanted to cool off. You can pretend I'm not here."

"That's all I ever do," she says.

I zone out, ignoring whatever they're talking about, instead watching him in the water through my sunglasses, until Morgan passes me a phone.

"What?" I ask, staring at her outstretched hand in confusion.

"Have you been listening?" she asks. "Tell me which one you like best."

It's hard to pick; they're both so beautiful. Not for the first time, I'm aware of what I'm missing out on. That I'm different, and I didn't ask for it.

That I'm a waste of time.

"Um...the green, I guess."

"No, the purple!" Audrey bemoans.

But Morgan smiles as I hand it back. "Thank you. That's what I thought."

Devon gets out of the pool, walks over to the chair next to mine, and grabs a towel. He dries his face and chest, then runs his fingers through his hair and, when they aren't looking, flicks the water in my face before going inside.

"Darci, Devon is—" Audrey starts.

"Don't say it," Darci says. "Don't you dare fucking say it."

"I mean, he's kind of hot."

"Don't. He's *awful*."

"Yeah, but looks good with his shirt off," she says. "He's got that 'v' that dips down..."

"Stop," she says. "If you fuck him, you can't come over anymore."

"Have you ever thought about it?" Morgan asks.

"You mean for the kink?" Darci asks. "I'd have to keep looking at him and living with him afterward, so it's a hard no."

"It may be worth it for me not to come over anymore," Audrey says.

Yeah, I'm going to be sick. My eyes sting with fresh tears.

"I'm going to go to the bathroom," I announce, heading inside the house.

Blinking back tears, I walk through the living room to the half bathroom near the front of the house and close the door behind me. I take a good look at the girl in the mirror—her sunken cheeks that were once full, the bags under her eyes. I forget what I look like with makeup. I may not have been thrown into the freak pile, but I'll always be the ugly friend. Maybe that's why they keep me around.

I resign not to cry—I need to suck it up. I wipe my eyes again and then take one more deep breath before opening the bathroom door and finding myself face-to-face with Devon.

"Hey, Ally," Devon says. "So, you don't know how to swim?"

"I do know how to swim. I lied," I tell him. "I just don't want to."

"And why's that?"

"No reason in particular," I say, walking around him.

"Don't do that," he says, grabbing my arm. "There's a reason, right? Tell me what it is."

"Audrey thinks you're hot," I tell him. "Maybe you should go for her instead."

He steps inside the bathroom and closes the door behind him. "That sounds boring," he says. "And I'm realizing that I've been perpetually bored with everyone and everything for a very long time, but I'm not bored with you."

"Well, I'm sure you will be. Or you'll find out that's not a good thing," I scoff.

"Are you really going to be shitty to me because of something Audrey said? Hmm? Come on, Ally."

I shake my head. "I don't know. I don't know what to do with you. I didn't think about any of this."

"What's 'this'? What are you talking about?"

"I don't know," I say softly, averting my gaze.

What I would do when someone else wants you and can give you things I can't. What it would feel like to be here with you and not be able to touch you. How this *might affect one of the only friendships and safe spaces I have.*

He runs his hand through my hair, then down to the nape of my neck, and leans down and kisses me.

"Devon, I can't..."

"We're not doing anything wrong."

"Yeah, but..."

"I missed you," he says before diving into my neck, licking and sucking in that way that makes me completely crazy, causing wet heat to pool between my legs even before I feel his erection against me.

I wrap my arms around his back and kiss him back, feeling his tongue caress mine while he nips and bites at my lips.

"You're going to get me in trouble."

His thumbs slide into the waistband of my joggers, and I break away.

"What's wrong?" he says. "If you can be quiet, they won't even know. I promise."

"I just...I don't want you to see me."

"What do you mean?"

"I have scars," I tell him. "A lot of really ugly scars. I can't wear a bathing suit. That's why I'm not getting in the pool—I don't want people to see them."

"Where?" he asks. "I've seen you naked. I didn't see any scars."

"It was dark," I say. "Um, they're down the sides of both of my hips. And on my upper thighs...across the front and inside."

"Okay," he says. "Where did they come from?"

"Um, I did it...to myself."

"Let me see."

I laugh so that I don't cry. "Haven't you seen enough?"

He places his hands on my cheeks and uses his thumbs to wipe the tears pooling in my eyes. "Never. Okay?"

I nod my head, and his fingers go back to my waistband. My cheeks burn, and my heart hammers in my chest while I wait.

Devon works my joggers and underwear down my legs before dropping to his knees, and I forget how to breathe. I feel his eyes on me—on my skin, my scars, my pussy. I close my own eyes, afraid to look—afraid to see disappointment on his face...or worse. He runs his fingers over the marks on the outside of my hips—the deepest of my scars—then the newer marks I started making inside my thighs. A few of them are still scabbed over, red, and irritated, painful to the touch. I wince and suck in a breath. His eyes search my face, but still, I don't look back.

Then, I feel his tongue on the same wounds, kissing and licking the insides of each of my shredded thighs before he spreads me and runs his tongue down my wet slit.

"Devon..." I gasp as he slowly licks up and down my center. "They're gonna..."

I give up my protest when he slides his fingers inside of me, slowly pumping them in and out of me, two at first and then adding a third, and I have to slap my own hand over my mouth to keep from crying out.

"Shit, you're tight," he says. "Does that feel good, or is it too much?"

"It...feels good," I force out.

His other hand pushes my legs further apart then his tongue goes back to work on my clit, circling it, running back and forth, up and down, while he fucks me with his fingers. I arch my back against the wall to give him better access, and he rewards me with quick, deep strokes that make my knees go weak. I'm teetering on the edge of my orgasm when I reach down and thread my fingers through his hair, rolling my hips against him like I'm trying to ride his damn tongue.

"Ally?" Darci calls from the hallway before knocking on the door. "Are you still in there?"

I freeze, and my eyes go wide.

"Um, yeah," I say, hoping I don't sound as breathless as I feel. "Sorry. I just need a minute."

I go for my waistband, but Devon pulls it back down. His fingers start moving again, and he looks up at me before his mouth closes around my clit and sucks.

I gasp and squeeze my thighs together. *Fuck.*

"It's fine," she says. "I just wanted to make sure you're okay. You've been in there for a while."

His fingers curl inward as he flicks my clit with his tongue. My head drops back, and I silently beg my body not to come before I answer. "Yeah, I'm okay. I just..." *Oh god, I'm going to come.* "I just need a minute."

"Oh...okay. I'll just use the one upstairs."

Once I hear her footsteps fade away, I grab a fist full of his hair again, lean back into his tongue, and let go of the orgasm I've been holding in.

The intensity of it takes me by surprise. I do my best to bury a scream in the back of my throat as it rolls through my body, threatening to take my legs out from underneath me. I'm still shaking when he removes his fingers and licks the cum dripping out of me.

He gets back on his feet and kisses me on the mouth.

"That was fun. Can you taste yourself on me?" he whispers.

I nod my head. That was close. Terrifying, even.

"You're so fucking sexy," he says. "And you know what else?"

"What?"

"I think I may have come up with a solution for your money problem."

"Well, what is it?"

"I'll tell you when I get the details hammered out, but...you don't have to steal anymore, okay?"

"What are we going to do?"

"Don't worry about it," he says. "You're mine now. And I take care of what's mine. All right?"

"I don't know, Devon..."

"What do you mean you don't know?" he asks. "You sure come on my dick and my mouth like you're mine."

"You are going to be a really big problem for me," I say, shaking my head. "I need to go. She'll be back."

He shoots me one of those half-smiles, then leans in, burying his face in my neck, and traces my throat with his tongue. "Say you're mine, and I'll let you leave."

I attempt to step around him toward the door, and he moves into my path.

"Seriously, Devon?"

He shrugs.

"I'm yours," I tell him.

He grins at me, then side steps away from the doorframe. I crack the door and look out.

"No one's there—get out, hurry," I whisper to him. "Go...the other way...away from me."

"So *rude*," he says as he steps out.

I wait until he makes his way down the hall and before exiting the bathroom.

"You taste so good," he says from the base of the stairs as I walk through the room.

"Stop!" I say, continuing toward the back door. I glance back toward him, my eyes meeting his first, then moving down his body to where I can see him hard against his shorts.

"Keep looking, and you're not going to make it out of the room without me bending you over the couch."

My cheeks turn red, and I look around to make sure no one else is in the house to hear him, too shocked to reply.

"And Ally?"

His serious tone stops me. "Hmm?"

"There's nothing wrong with you. Not a damn thing."

Not wanting to argue but also not willing to agree, I only offer him a smile before turning and heading back to the patio with my friends. *My friends,* who don't know half as much about me as I've told Devon in the past week.

My mind tries to argue that I didn't want to tell him any of that—he made me tell him. But that isn't necessarily true. I think I did want to tell him. Again, I can't explain why it's him, but...it is.

Audrey and Morgan both stayed for dinner, and Devon stayed clear of us all the rest of the evening—I assume playing video games in his room like he usually did before all of this—and I was grateful for it.

"I can't stay for dinner tomorrow," Darci says out of nowhere while we're lying in her bed later that night. It's dark except for the light from the TV. Darci has *Teen Mom* on again—it's her comfort show.

"I texted my boyfriend, and he said the timing just wouldn't work out for him," she adds.

She sounds genuinely upset. Surely, she didn't really want to have dinner at my house that badly.

"That's okay," I tell her. "Maybe some other time."

She stares at the ceiling, and I wait for her to say something else. When she doesn't, I tell her, "I'm going to go to bed. I haven't been sleeping much."

"Ally, there's so much I want to tell you *so badly*," she says. "I feel like things have been different between us lately, and I don't want it to be like that. You're my best friend. Honestly, I feel like we're closer than I am with Audrey because I can tell you things that I can't tell her...that's why I really hate that I can't tell you this."

"Okay..." I say. And it isn't a lie. I know she tells me things that she doesn't tell the other girls—things that she thinks they'll make fun of her for or judge her for or whatever. She feels like she needs to maintain a certain image with them that she doesn't with me; that's the real reason she keeps me around.

"I wanted to tell you that because I know you probably feel it, too, and I wanted you to know that it has nothing to do with you personally. I just...can't tell you what's going on yet. But I will...soon."

"Yeah, I have noticed something was weird," I lie. I haven't noticed much of anything lately. My mind has been too preoccupied with Devon.

"Okay, well, it's not you," she says. "It's me, so don't worry about it."

"I'm here...whenever you do want to talk," I offer.

"I know you are," she says. "That's why you're my favorite. You're always there, and you never push. I know I can trust you."

"Yeah," I tell her. "Yeah, thanks. I feel the same way."

I only feel a little bit guilty as I drift off to sleep.

9

I wake up to someone rustling through my desk and shoot straight up in bed. I almost jump the guy before I realize...it's not a guy. I see a curtain of dark hair running down her back and pale, toned legs I'd know anywhere in the moonlight.

"Ally? What are you doing?" I whisper-rasp.

"Do you have a Sharpie in here somewhere?"

"Yeah," I tell her. "Um, there's a cup on the left corner. There should be a couple of Sharpies in there. Why?"

"Shit!" she says as she knocks it over, sending the contents flying. I start to get up to help her, but she stops me.

"No, stay there," she says. "I've got it."

She uncaps the lid and walks toward the bed. "Lie down on your stomach. I need your back."

I turn over, and she sits on top of me, her legs on either side of my waist.

"Pretty sure you need my front," I tell her.

"Shhh."

I feel the felt tip of the pen on my back, running up and down the length of it.

"That feels good," I say. "What are you doing?"

"You asked me what I would do to you..." she says.

"You want to know what I'd do to you?"

"Shhh," she says again. "I haven't been able to draw anything but those fucking faceless people for weeks now, and now I finally want to draw something else. So, I need you to be still, and I need to do it now, you know? Like if I don't get it out now, then maybe I won't, and I'll be stuck again."

"You do what you have to do," I tell her.

I lie down, close my eyes, and try to enjoy the sensations—the strokes of the pen, her hands and fingertips on my back, her weight on top of me, her long legs on either side of me. My dick swells in my boxers, begging me to flip her over and bury myself inside her. I just barely resist.

I think this goes on for an hour before she caps the pen, sets it on the nightstand, and tells me she's finished.

"What is it?" I ask.

"You'll have to see for yourself," she says. "But it's you."

"Me?"

"Goodnight, Devon," she says.

"Hey...no," I say. And now, I do flip her over. "You came into my room. I have you in my bed. I'm not just going to let you leave."

"We can't. She's going to hear us through the wall."

I pull the straps down on her tank top, exposing her chest, then flatten my tongue and run it over her nipple while I roll my hips into her.

"Devon..." she moans.

"I'll go slow, and you'll be quiet like in the bathroom, and she won't hear anything," I tell her, sliding her shorts down over her hips, then position myself between her legs. "Can you be quiet, Ally?"

She nods.

I slide my cock into her warm, wet pussy in one long, torturously slow motion, feeding it to her inch by inch until it's buried to the hilt, and hold it there for a couple of seconds before pulling it all the way out just as slow, and repeating the motion.

"I don't have a condom," I tell her.

"It's okay," she whispers breathlessly. "Don't stop. It feels so good."

I continue moving in and out of her slowly, enjoying the tortured look on her face and the way she lifts her hips and digs her nails into my skin, trying to set the pace a little faster, but I don't let her.

"Devon," she whimpers. "Devon, please. Faster...I can't take it."

I thrust all the way into her again, and she moans.

"I don't know, Ally," I groan, continuing to fuck her slowly. "You're going to have to be quieter than that if you want me to give it to you faster."

"You're...torturing me," she forces out.

I smile. It doesn't get much better than a girl you've fantasized about for months underneath you, telling you you're torturing her with your big dick and a slow fuck.

"Quiet," I repeat.

I give her what she asks for—just a little faster, rolling my hips a little harder as Ally meets me with every thrust, silently begging for more. The headboard starts to tap but doesn't slam against the wall.

I put one of her legs over my shoulder, then reach my hand between us and circle her clit with my fingers.

She turns her head to the side and bites into my pillow when she comes, burying the scream I would have pulled from her inside of it, and the sight of that is enough to drive me right to the edge.

"Fuck," I groan. "Can I come in you?"

"Yes..."

Her legs are still shaking when I reach both hands under her knees and spread them wide. Maybe I lose control a little bit because she feels so good like this, and I slam into her and let the headboard pound against the wall.

"Devon..."

"Fuck...yes." I grit my teeth, pin her legs next to her head, and come hard inside her.

I lie down next to her, and she sits up and starts digging through the blankets for her shorts.

"No way," I say, pulling her back down onto the bed. "You have to stay with me for at least two whole minutes before you run away this time."

She doesn't even bother fighting me on this one. She lies down with her head on my shoulder, wraps one arm around my chest, and pulls on my earplug with the other hand.

"Can I ask you something?"

She nods.

"Why do you do it? The cuts?"

She sighs. "Um, it's like an outlet, I guess. Kind of like art, but for letting out the pain. It gives it a physical exit point, and I don't know...gives me a false sense of control, I guess. Does that make sense?"

"No."

I run my fingers through my hair and try not to picture it in my head—Ally in so much pain, suffering enough that she wants to hurt herself. I can't take it.

"I don't want to, but it's become kind of a compulsion or a routine, even. I feel bad, I do it, I feel a little better. I started with just one...and then I decided that three at a time was better. Then, I decided if there needed to be three, I couldn't do it more than two days in a row, and just added more rules from there. I want to stop, though; I'm trying."

"Can I help you?" I ask.

"You do help me," she says. "More than you know."

"How?"

"I don't know. You talk to me."

"Your friends don't talk to you?"

"No, not like this. I can't tell them, and they don't ask."

I'm not sure how to reply to that without saying something shitty, so I don't.

"Are you...disgusted?" she asks.

"Is there anything about what just happened that would make you think I'm disgusted by you?" I ask. "No, Ally. I'm not disgusted. I'm just worried about you. I *care* about you. I want to *take care* of you."

She doesn't reply, continuing to run my earlobe through her fingers. I grab the pen from the nightstand, uncap it, and pull the blankets away from her body. Then, I move down the bed, lean in, and kiss her hip bone.

"Devon..."

I touch the marker to her hip and start working, etching three small black roses onto her skin.

"You're beautiful," I tell her. "Perfect, even. I can't think of a damn thing that would change that."

"Your two minutes are up," she informs me, sliding out of bed and back into her shorts. "See you tomorrow."

"Ally, are you on birth control?"

"Um, yeah. I got an implant...before I moved in with them," she says.

"Okay, because...I want to keep fucking you like that."

"Who says I'm going to let you fuck me again?"

I shake my head. "You're a jerk."

A few minutes after she leaves the room, I remember why she came in there in the first place. I grab my phone from the nightstand, then head down the hall to the bathroom to try to get a look at this picture she drew of me on my back.

Except that it isn't really me at all.

It's more like a dark forest. The entirety of my back is covered in tall, menacing leafless trees, with dark filling the spaces between them. I tilt the camera to see down to the very bottom of the drawing—there's a stump with a single candle burning on it.

I'm not really sure how that's me, but I'll take her word for it. Maybe she meant that it felt like me—because it's dark. The forest gives off kind of a Sleepy Hollow vibe, and maybe the candle is part of all those animal sacrifices I don't really do.

Whatever it means, I like it—both because she's a talented artist and because it's her, and I'd let her carve anything she wanted into my skin.

The following morning, I surprise my family by rewarding them with my presence at breakfast again.

I walk past the four of them at the table, grab a plate from the kitchen, and then backtrack and sit next to my dad.

"Where are you going this morning?" he asks, likely noting that I'm dressed.

"To church," I tell him. "This is next time. I'm ready to worship the lord."

"You can't let him mock it like that and then take him with us," Darci says.

"Everyone is welcome at church, Darci," Lydia says. "Devon, I think it's great that you want to go with us."

She passes me the pancakes, and I take four, then a couple of pieces of bacon from the middle of the table.

"Are there doughnuts?" I ask. "From what I remember, they usually have doughnuts at these things."

"God, like you don't have enough food already," Darci sneers.

I shrug. "No, not really."

I look over at Ally, who is staring hard at her plate, trying not to look at me.

"Do you like doughnuts, Ally?" I ask.

She looks up and laughs.

"Well...do you or not?"

"I guess," she says.

"He's not funny, Ally. Don't laugh at him," Darci says.

She shakes her head, then goes back to eating and not bothering to look up.

Darci's mom changes the subject to prom court and limos and whether or not Mark and Grace would let Ally come if she just went with her friends. Ally nods and pretends to be interested in the conversation, but I'm pretty sure there's not a chance in hell they'll let her go. She either doesn't care about going, or she knows it too—it's written clearly on her face.

After breakfast, we all pile into my dad's Nissan. I make sure to get in on Ally's side of the car so she ends up in the middle. Darci looks at me with revulsion, like I've committed some unspeakable atrocity just by getting into the vehicle. It's obvious that she wants to say something...anything that will get me out of the car, but she comes up empty-handed.

My stepmom puts on some Christian rock channel, and something cringy plays through the speakers about some dude who wants to get it on with Jesus or something while Darci buries herself in her phone, her fingers flying furiously over the keyboard. I take advantage of how distracted everyone else is and move Ally's bag so that it's covering her hand, then hook her pinky in mine.

"You look really pretty," I whisper in her ear.

She smiles but doesn't look at me or say anything.

I glance over at Darci one more time, then lean down and kiss her quickly on the shoulder. But when I look up, I meet my dad's eyes in the rearview mirror.

Shit.

I lean back in my seat and resume my usual bored, slumped against the window position for the rest of the drive.

When we get there, there aren't any doughnuts.

My dad and Lydia shake hands with people and make small talk while I follow behind them. People I don't really know tell me how nice it is to see me there and that I should come more often, and I pretend to care before we all file into the pews and Darci and Lydia leave to join the choir.

"What the hell do you think you're doing?" my dad whispers to me once they're gone.

"Praising the lord?"

"You're going to get all of us in trouble."

I look at Ally, sitting just a foot away from me. She's chewing on her lip and staring straight forward.

"Are you going to tell them?"

"No. But you need to knock it off."

"Okay," I say.

He shakes his head, and we both sit back in our seats, fully aware that I'm not going to knock it off.

10

People are fucked up. And incredibly disappointing.

I spent four years at this school a loser. Unknown at best, detested at worst until they all decided I was a murderer. Then, they all knew exactly who I was. Everyone suddenly claimed they'd been paying attention to me for years and that none of them were surprised.

Those days between when we found her body and when we knew my arrest was inevitable—they feared me. They gave me a wide berth in the hallway and averted their eyes.

And it felt...good.

Now that I've been to jail, but it turns out I'm not a murderer, something changed again. Some of them are definitely still terrified, but a lot of them are intrigued. They all seemed to want a piece of me today.

I can't decide how I feel about that. I mean...I'd be stupid not to take advantage of the girls breathing down my neck, but I think I liked the fear better. It was genuine and warranted, at least as far as they knew, and I felt powerful.

This new thing where I'm suddenly interesting after all these years because I went to jail for something I didn't do? It's a weird reminder of how I'd been nothing before and how I'm actually still the same, and I think maybe I'd like to give them something to be afraid of again—maybe when I'm done with Ally.

I park at my mom's house and walk inside. I've always spent Thursday nights here, so I figure I might as well fall back into that routine—try to feel normal, even though I don't feel normal at all.

"Hey, Mom," I say when I walk inside.

"Hi, honey. How was school?"

"Fine," I tell her.

"Fine?" she asks. "That's it?"

"I'm interesting now, apparently," I tell her, shrugging.

"I wish you wouldn't have gone back there," she says. "I wish you'd just finish the year out at home or enroll here again. You still could, you know."

"I need to get out. I need to leave the house." I can't just lock myself in another prison. "And everyone here knows, too."

"Yeah, but people here are different, Devon. It's not like at Black Rock. It's not where Darci died, and...it's not where Ally is. Did you see her?"

"No," I lie. "I didn't see her. I don't care if I do. And I don't want to hear that name again."

"You know, when you love someone, you can tell when they're lying," she says.

Not always.

"Where's Ivy?" I ask. "Shouldn't she be off the bus by now? Is she still afraid of me?"

"I don't think so, but it may take her some time to adjust. Also, something happened while you were gone, Devon. I didn't want to upset you, but...he got out."

"What? How the fuck did he—"

"Good behavior. Overcrowding. It doesn't matter, but he did. They've been letting him have supervised visitation with Ivy once a week. It's just for a couple of hours during the day."

"Well, can't you do something?! How the fuck is he allowed around kids?"

"I tried," she says. "This is just how they do things. Please don't be like this. It's hard enough for me without..."

I shake my head. "Without me here making it worse? God, the world is so fucked."

"That's not what I was going to say."

"Does that mean he's coming over here?"

"No," she says. "I'm going to go pick her up in about an hour. The social worker will be there and—"

But I'm already done listening. For the second time in the last twenty-four hours, I think I could become a murderer.

I leave her in the kitchen, storm down the hallway, and slam my bedroom door. Sighing, I pull open my desk drawer, then reach into my pocket, take out the handful of long, dark brown hair, and throw it into the drawer. I don't know why I brought it home; I guess it's just because I hate her. I fucking hate her, and I can't stand to look at her stupid, fake-innocent face. I sat behind her in art and stared at that curtain of dark hair running down her back, and then she brushed it over her shoulder, and I could smell it—lavender, just like before. I remembered what it looked like against her bare back or draped across my pillow while she slept. And I just wanted it to go away.

And now, I have it in my desk drawer like some fucked up serial killer trophy. I shake my head, run my hands over my face, and my fingers through the fuzz that is what's left of my own hair. I'm still not used to that feeling.

I can't believe I fell for it. I still can't quite figure out how she did it—how she manipulated me so completely and faked it so well the whole time.

I didn't just fall in love with Ally Hargrove. I got lost in her.

I wonder how much of it was a lie. I did a lot of that while I was locked up—once I realized Ally really was gone. I've wondered if she made all that stuff up about Mark and Grace abusing her. I've never seen any concrete evidence of anyone hurting Ally except for Ally, and I've known them since my dad and Lydia got married years ago. From what I can tell, they're ordinary people, aside from the strict religious values they try to use as an excuse to control Ally. And everyone else in Washington state—in Mark's case, anyway.

I've also wondered if Darci was involved the whole time—if they both played me and the picture was part of it, if they were involved in some shit that ended up getting Darci killed. Darci knew about my mom's ex, and she'd know that something like that would be an easy way to get to me. It's the only thing that really makes sense.

No one ever found any evidence of this college boyfriend Ally claimed Darci had, even though Audrey and Morgan attested they'd heard the same story. There were no pictures, no text messages. No digital evidence at all, which is next to impossible.

No, Ally and Darci needed money for something. And Darci decided to take it a step further and blackmail me. Ally knows more about whatever happened, and she lied and left me there to rot.

And it should have been her. I'll make sure that it *is* her.

I'm not quite sure how I'll do it. It's not that I didn't have plenty of time to think while I was in there, I just never thought I'd actually get out without going to trial. *That* I was prepared for—to put her on the stand, to make her look me in the eye while she tried to lie through it all as it came out. It would have gotten messy. We were relying on *messy* to set me free after the knife incident. It was the only card left to play.

I spend the next few hours googling myself—something I haven't been able to stop doing since I got out, even though I promised my parents I wouldn't. For the most part, Ally has seemed to elicit sympathy from our peers, but the internet has come up with several conspiracy theories that, as usual, are far from the truth. Many of them believe Ally and I killed Darci together, but she turned on me afterward, hoping to save herself. Some think it was just Ally, which—although it would work in my favor—isn't true, either.

There's a lot of stuff about her childhood on here. They go on about how she spent a lot of time homeless while her mom had an addiction and worked as a dealer to feed it, although Ally always said she was only ever a dealer, not a user, and it was because she had no other choice. They talk about the family, their religious beliefs, and how Ally's mom was thrown out when she became pregnant at sixteen. They even found her dad, and the same pictures Ally showed me on Facebook wound up in the threads. There appears to be a universal consensus that a background like this would inevitably breed a sociopath or a killer, but she's only the first one.

They mention my mom, too, and our experience with Ivy's dad and draw the same conclusion about me.

The internet sleuths have been all over it, though. My favorite is the 'What happened to Darci Connelly' subreddit. One of its active users was the one who found the camera on the side of our neighbor's shed, which ultimately led to my release. He drove all the way from Boise to investigate the area for his podcast. The dude had a theory that Ally and I killed Darci in the woods behind the neighborhood, and that was why there was no physical evidence found inside the house. Still, there were holes in this logic—our security system shows that only one door was opened and closed one time after everyone left that night. It was at 2:12 AM, and now we know Darci's body was left in the pool an hour later.

We can also be pretty sure that her cell phone didn't leave the area, even though they never found it. Anyway, the internet's focus seems to have shifted away from both of us and back to a secret boyfriend.

I scroll past threads I've read and reread and pictures I've seen a thousand times over. There are a couple of images of Ally walking into school and a few of her playing volleyball. I heard they had to start banning the general public from attending the matches for that reason; only students and their immediate families can attend now. Our small island runs on tourism in the summer, but apparently, murder tourism is frowned upon.

I spend hours diving deep into this trash bag, and when I come up for air, it's after midnight, and I haven't found anything useful.

What a fucking waste.

Luckily, after living in a concrete shithole waiting to be tried for murder, sleep comes easy for me now. I close my eyes and instantly fall into a deep sleep. I dream of Ally's hands on me, of felt-tipped markers running down my spine and the weight of her body on mine.

And when I wake up the next morning, I hate myself a little more.

11

"Ally, are you okay?" I ask.

She jumps at the sound of my voice. She must have fallen asleep again; this will be the fourth day in a row.

"Yeah, I just...I haven't slept," she says. "I need to sleep."

Her portfolio has been open to the same practically empty page for days now. It's not like her.

"You're stressed," I tell her. "Maybe you should skip the meet. Go find somewhere to sleep."

"Like with you?" she asks.

"Yeah, if you want."

I reach forward and start to rub her shoulders. She lets me, but only for a few seconds before she snaps.

"Stop," she hisses. "You can't touch me here. You probably shouldn't talk to me so much, either."

"I'm sorry," I tell her. "I miss you. I'm just trying to help."

"Yeah, well—you're not."

I spend the rest of class trying to figure out what the fuck I'm going to do with this girl. Five months doesn't feel like much time, but it's a lot to let whatever is happening to her in that house keep happening.

The bell rings; I gather my things and head for the door, looking back at Ally, still in her seat, before I do.

She mouths the words, *'I'm sorry.'*

"I know," I say back.

It doesn't make me feel much better. I hate that I can't talk to her or touch her at school. I hate that I can't see her on the weekend and that everything has to be hard for reasons that don't make any fucking sense. I don't mean to be mad at her for it, but I am. I mean, fucking in my car after her away meets over the last few weeks has been great and all, but it's just making the space between even worse.

I take my seat in Mr. Parks' health class and pull out my notebook. He's on my list, too. I've just been waiting for my chance with this dumb mother fucker, and I get it at the end of class.

"A lot of you have asked about how you can get your grade up before the end of the year," he says. "I have an opportunity for you—an essay. I will post a few topics for you to choose from on the class site, and if you choose to participate, you'll turn it in on Monday, and it will be worth twenty points."

I approach his desk after the bell rings and the room empties.

"Hey, can you tell me what I have in this class?" I ask. "I want to know if the extra credit will be worth my time or not."

"Sure," he says. "But I'm pretty sure you're fine."

"Yeah, well," I say as he turns to his computer. "I'm ranked third in our class. There's a difference between an 'A' and an 'A-' for me."

I lean in as much as I can without making it obvious and focus as he types his password. It's easier than expected because he doesn't set down the Monster energy drink in his left hand and just kind of pokes at the keys with his right.

Bigdick79!

Are you fucking kidding me?

I run my hands over my face and cover my mouth to help hold in a laugh.

"Let's see...West..." he says. "You have a 98.2."

"Thanks," I tell him with the most ridiculous and seemingly unwarranted smile on my face before turning and going for the door.

Doesn't he know the administrators can probably see his password? Fucking embarrassing regardless. Still, I hope he's stupid enough to use the same password for everything.

Later, I walk into the cafeteria, grab my tray, sit at the usual table, and scan the room for Ally like I always do.

"Looking for your secret girlfriend?" Isaac asks.

I swear this mother fucker still thinks I'm making it up.

"Yes," I reply curtly.

"I saw her duck into the gym on my way here," he says.

I eat the rest of my pizza in three bites and leave the table.

"Hey, you're welcome, you fucking dick!" he yells at my back.

"Thanks," I tell him, flipping him off over my shoulder as I go.

I toss my tray through the window and head down the hallway toward the gym, walking through the doors and then back behind the bleachers.

She's there, sleeping with her head against her track bag.

She found a place to sleep.

I want to lie down next to her, wrap my arms around her, and hold her like I'm never able to, but I stop myself a couple of feet away.

"Allyson?"

Her eyes flutter open, and she turns and looks up at me.

"I didn't want to wake you up, but I know I'm supposed to announce my presence first, so I'm doing that now."

"I'm sorry I yelled at you," she says.

"Well, technically, you whispered at me. But it *was* a harsh tone."

Now, I do lie next to her; I wrap my arms around her and pull her back against my chest.

"Are you mad at me?"

I sigh. "I'm frustrated with you as a general rule, but no, I'm not mad."

"I won't be able to go with you after the meet," she says. "I won't be able to talk to you. Mark is in town, so he'll either be there to pick me up when it's over, or he'll send Grace."

"It's okay," I tell her.

"It's not okay with me. It shouldn't be okay with you, either. You get nothing from this. I don't know what I'm going to do when you figure that out."

"It's okay because it's you, Ally. That's what I get from this."

"But we never get to see each other. We can't go to the movies or talk on the phone. I can't go to prom. Are you going to go to prom?"

"No. I don't want to go to prom." That's the first lie I've ever told her. I *do* want to go to prom, but I want to go with her. I'd love to take her and see her dressed up and smiling; I'd love to show everyone that she's mine. "I want you. I want swimming, remember?"

"I wish we could go together," she says.

"I know it seems like a big deal, but it'll probably be lame, anyway. And ten years from now—actually fuck it, probably far less—prom is going to look and feel like nothing. We aren't missing *anything*, Ally."

"I don't deserve you," she says, closing her eyes.

"Just go to sleep. I'll wake you up, okay?"

It isn't long before her breathing slows, and she slips back into a deep sleep, even snoring lightly.

It's cute.

And when she's like this, I can't be mad at her anymore. I know it's not her fault, and she's suffering, too, but something needs to give soon. I don't know how much longer either of us can keep doing this when sometimes it feels like we're just barely not tearing each other apart, and Ally is hanging on by a thread.

It keeps me up at night, too.

12

Our meet tonight is at home—the first one in weeks. That means it'll get out a lot earlier. It won't be dark, the parking lot won't be empty, and Grace or Mark will be there to pick me up.

I won't get to be with Devon.

Still, he's there in the stands with a book in his hands. He's onto the fifth book in the Wheel of Time series now, but as far as anyone else is concerned, he's reading *Summoning Demons and Other Ways to Do Lucifer's Bidding on Earth.*

I watch someone's grandparents almost sit down next to him before getting a glimpse at the cover and moving to the entire opposite side of the bleachers.

I meet his eyes and laugh. I'm still so fucking tired. It's always hard to sleep in that house, but it's impossible when Mark is there. Sleeping with Devon's warmth against my back was a comfort I can't describe. I got to smell like him the rest of the day.

Unfortunately, I'm not as lucky when a pretty girl from our class with blonde and blue hair sits next to him. She has bright red lips and fake lashes, a tattoo near her collarbone. She looks like she'd be his type. He sets his book to the side to talk to her, laughing at whatever she says, and I feel like I'm choking.

I can't compete with that.

She playfully shoves his arm, and he pretends to fall over from the force of it.

I think about how she could leave here with him right now if she wanted to. They could go to the movies, she could take him back to her house, and he could take her to prom. I bet her life is simple, and she doesn't steal money and prescription pills.

It makes me want to rip her hair out.

I feel my cheeks burn red, and my eyes fill with tears, and I fucking hate it. I feel so stupid. I try to talk myself out of this unwarranted panic attack, but I can't seem to do it.

"Hey, Ally...are you okay?" one of my teammates asks.

Instead of answering, I turn and break for the building, not stopping until I'm in the empty locker room. I sit on the bench with my elbows on my knees and my head in my hands and just try to get a fucking grip.

"Ally?" the same voice calls.

Shit. She followed me.

"Are you okay?" Laurel asks.

"Yeah, I'm fine," I tell her, drying my eyes. "I just...I have allergies."

"You like him, don't you?" she asks. "Devon?"

"How did you..." I pause.

"He's been at all of our meets lately," she says. "I've known Devon since I was in seventh grade. He doesn't do stuff like that. And he sits there with a book, not paying attention to anything. He watches you, though."

"I *love* him," I tell her. It's the first time I've said it aloud, but it's in my head all the time. Letting it out—giving life to the words—is a relief in itself. Maybe I won't want to cut it out later. "But I can't compete with anyone. I'm ugly."

"That is crazy," she says, digging through her locker. "You are not ugly. And Riley...she just has a lot of makeup on."

She pulls a bag from her locker and sits on the opposite bench, facing me.

"It's not obvious—if you're worried about that. I notice things about people," she says. "Those of us in the field events have a lot of time to do that, you know?"

I nod. She lifts my chin with her thumb and pulls an eye-shadow pallet from the bag. "Close."

I close my eyes and feel the brush on my lids.

"And the way he looks at you...that's something to envy. It's the kind of look that makes someone not on the receiving end want to clear the room. Open," she says, snapping the pallet closed and pulling mascara from the same bag, "but just a little."

She brushes the mascara over my top lashes. "Look up."

I do what she says, and she runs it across my lower lashes.

"You know about me, right?" I ask.

"It's a small island," Laurel says. "If you're asking if I know about your mom and how your aunt and uncle keep you locked up, then yeah. I know about that."

"He's going to get tired of it," I almost whisper.

She gives me a sympathetic look and pulls a couple of lipsticks from her bag. She examines the two shades before deciding on one and facing me again.

"Part your lips."

I do what she asks, and she runs the bright red color over my lower lip.

"I don't know, Ally," she says. "I wouldn't."

She finishes with my lips and lifts my chin again. "I wouldn't even put anything on your skin," she says. "Your complexion is flawless."

"I'm not allowed to wear makeup."

"So? Wash it off before you get home."

"I can see why everyone likes you so much."

"I can see why Devon likes you so much," she tells me. "Some people are just...worth it."

She stands and puts the bag back in her locker. I notice she's left the makeup she used on me out on the bench.

"You should keep those," she says. "You don't need it, but everyone deserves to feel pretty."

Once the sound of her footsteps fades, I stand and walk over to the sinks to get a look at myself in the mirror. I almost cry again when I see the girl looking back at me. It's been so long since I've seen my face with makeup on—nearly a year now.

And I *do* look pretty.

But I also feel like an imposter, like I'm not allowed to look like this.

Still, I pull out my hair tie and shake out my long, dark hair. I put the makeup Laurel left for me in a compartment in my duffle bag and then shove it back into my locker. I mentally prepare myself to make space for it in my box of secrets under the bed.

The school itself is pretty empty since nothing is going on inside at this time aside from a few clubs, but still, I feel like the few people I do encounter are staring at me...and not necessarily in a nice way. It's more of a questioning way.

"Hey," Devon says when I turn the corner. "I was looking for you. Where'd you....what's going on? What's up with the makeup?"

"Um...Laurel Lindley did it," I tell him.

"Why?"

My heart drops into my stomach.

"I don't know. I just wanted to look pretty, but I guess I got that wrong, too."

"You do," he says. "You do look pretty. But you always look pretty, Ally."

I shake my head. "Not like Riley."

He pinches the bridge of his nose. "Oh, my god, Ally. You're kidding, right? On top of all the other shit, now you're going to do this, too? I didn't do anything. I don't like Riley."

I scoff. "All of the other shit, huh? That's telling."

I walk past him toward the door that will lead me to the parking lot and then back out to the field.

"I didn't mean it like that," he says. "I just mean—"

"What?"

"I just hate that I can't talk to you at school; I *hate* that I can't see you over the weekend, and I spend those days waiting for Monday to come so I can sit behind you in art and not talk to you there, either. Maybe we should tell people, Ally. I *want* to. Maybe if people like Riley knew I had a girlfriend, they'd back off."

"I knew you'd get sick of me," I tell him. "That's exactly why I didn't want to do this."

"If Darci really is your friend, she won't care."

"You know she will. And you know this isn't just about her."

"Allyson—"

"Leave me alone," I tell him. "Or go do...whatever you want. I don't care."

I rush out the doors and down to the track with that feeling in my chest again—the one where it feels like there's a vice grip around my ribcage, crushing my insides.

I think I'm starting to realize that feeling is regret.

After the meet, I head back to the school and into the locker room to get my stuff. Devon's car is gone.

I wash my face before I meet Grace in the parking lot and head home for another family dinner. Mark compliments how strong my thighs look when I walk into the house, causing bile to rise in my throat. I say nothing in response and head straight to my room to change into sweatpants.

Just as I pull them up over my hips, Grace pushes the knob-less door to my room open.

She storms across the room and backhands me hard enough to knock me off balance. I fall onto the hardwood floor, curling into the fetal position to protect my stomach from what I know will come next. The kicks to the gut hurt. Sometimes, I end up vomiting, and that's the last thing I need. I get in trouble for that, too.

I hold my breath, waiting, and when she can't get to my stomach, Grace kicks me in the back twice instead and then lowers her body onto the ground next to me. She grabs my hair and pulls my head back so we're face to face, close enough for me to feel her breath hot against my cheek. I smell the wine on her before she speaks.

"Don't come into this house looking like a whore again," she says. "Or you're done with track—DONE. Do you understand?"

I nod as much as I can with her fist still holding my hair.

"What are you going to do?" she asks.

"Change," I tell her. "I'll change my clothes before I come home."

"You better."

She stands up and kicks me once more before heading for the door.

"She should have aborted you," Grace says. "God, I bet she spent so many nights wishing she did over the last eighteen years. We'd all be a lot happier."

I don't reply. I stay on the floor, still curled in a ball. I don't want her to see me cry; I know she likes it too much.

"You know, she tried to ditch you once. She brought you to my parents' house after your dad left her—asked them to take you. They said they weren't responsible for cleaning up her mistakes. I wish we would have done the same."

She pauses for a moment, waiting to see if she'll get a reaction from me like she wants. I can feel the disappointment coming off of her when I lie there, not saying a word and not letting her hear my stifled sobs.

"You can join us for dinner now," she says as she leaves the room.

I pause momentarily at the door to gather myself before pushing it open and heading down the staircase, my hands still shaking.

Mark sits on the living room sofa, watching the evening news, while Grace sets the dining room table like nothing happened.

"There you are. Finally," Grace says as if she wasn't just upstairs kicking me, and she'd been down here waiting on me all this time. "Go wash your hands; I'm sure they're disgusting like the rest of you. Mark, dinner is ready!"

I wash my disgusting hands, and then we sit there like we do every night when Mark is home and eat like we're an actual family. Mark asks me about school, how the meet went, and my grades. Grace mentions that I spend too much time in my room with my sketchbook and should be using that time to study, and Mark reiterates the importance of time management skills in every profession.

It's eerie, really—the way we all sit here together, engaging in mundane small talk about our days as if everything that happens between these walls is completely normal, like we don't all know exactly what the fuck is going on here. Like I'm not counting the times they refill their glasses, and I don't fall asleep afraid I'll wake up with a hand covering my mouth.

Just as long as we keep up appearances, right? As long as it doesn't get on them, as long as they don't have to look at it, nothing will ever change. No one will care.

That night in the shower, I dig my razor from the soap bar. I look at the ugly scars on my hips and thighs—the ones Devon licked before he told me there was nothing wrong with me.

And there it is again, crushing my insides. *Regret.* I wish I hadn't gotten involved with or dragged him into any of this. I don't know what I was thinking.

And I'm running out of canvas I can carve into and still hide under my track shorts.

I lift my left arm instead and drag the razor across the soft flesh on the underside of my bicep. There's a lot less muscle here—a lot less of anything here—and it hurts more than it does on my leg. Or maybe I dig in a little deeper—the razor is starting to get dull from being in the soap bar for so long, and it's probably time for a new one. It bleeds...a lot. I add a second and then a third before leaning back and watching it run toward the drain, swirling with the water and running down pink. It doesn't slow for quite some time.

Afterward, I replace the blade in the soap bar and towel off my body. I wrap my arm with tape and slip into my oversized hoodie and sweatpants.

I get into bed, and I don't sleep again.

The following day, I head downstairs for school and find the kitchen empty. A feeling of relief washes over me—he's gone again. He mentioned he was going to Olympia next week, but I didn't expect him to leave so soon. There's no breakfast on the table, so Grace must have slept in. After double checking the first floor for her, I grab a banana from the counter and slip out the door. I stand and wait for the school bus with a bunch of younger kids from the neighborhood, like I do every morning.

That vice-grip feeling returns when I step off the bus. I'm going to see Devon in art. I bet he won't even try to talk to me or look at me.

Just like I've been telling him I wanted...

At least the pain in my chest takes my mind off the pain in my arm. I'm trying hard not to scratch it or pick at the tape covering it, but it doesn't feel quite right.

I open my locker and find a greasy McDonald's bag sitting on top of my books. I pick it up and look inside. Biscuits and gravy—my favorite. Even though I have eaten regularly over the last couple of weeks, my stomach churns.

There's a small, folded piece of paper inside. I dig it out of the bag and open it.

Don't go to art. Meet me at our spot first.

Our spot? What's—

Oh.

I wait for the bell to ring before I head to the gym and find Devon under the bleachers scrolling through his phone.

I stop about two feet away from him.

"Hi," I say.

"Hey," he says. "Come here, sit down."

"Can I eat the food?" I ask when I sink onto the ground next to him.

"Yes."

I dig the Styrofoam container of biscuits and gravy from the bag and open the small plastic fork that came with it. Devon waits a few minutes while I eat before speaking.

"I didn't mean what I said yesterday," he says. "Not like that, anyway. I'm sorry."

"I'm sorry, too."

"I got you something. Close your eyes and hold out your hands."

I set the nearly-empty box on the ground next to me and do as he asks. He sets something rectangular in my hands.

"Open them," he says.

"You got me a phone?" I ask. "I can't take this."

"Yes, you can," he says. "It's on a month-to-month plan; it's a shitty carrier, but the signal is okay, and it was actually really cheap, so please take it. It will make everything better, I promise. You can put it under your bed with your drug money and only turn it on when you are somewhere you can talk or text."

"I don't know, Devon..."

"Here," he says, pulling his own phone out from his pocket. "I'll send you a text. Let me know if you get it."

The phone vibrates in my hand, and a little red '1' pops up next to my inbox. I click on the message and open it.

I love you, Allyson.

I read it at least three times before shooting him a puzzled look.

"That's what I should have said," he says. "I should have just told you that you looked pretty—because you did—and that I love you. I love you, and I miss you when you're not around and I can't talk to you, and it's hard for me. When something funny or terrible happens, you're the first person I want to tell, and I hate that I can't. That's all I meant by it. I'm not sick of you. I just love you, that's all."

"I love you, too," I tell him. "It's hard for me, too."

"This will make it better. It's cute that you get jealous, though," Devon says.

"No, it's not. It's ugly, and I hate it. I never used to be like this; it's just...the circumstances."

"I know," he says. "How are you? Are you okay? You look tired again."

"I *am* tired."

"All right, come here," he says. He pulls me into his chest, and we lie there on the ground.

"But I am better," I tell him. "Mark left today. I think he's going to be gone for at least a week. Grace will be back on the bottle, and it'll be quieter. Hey, what are you doing tonight?"

He pulls a knife from his pocket and opens it with a flip of his wrist, then starts to carve into the wooden bleachers over our heads.

"I have something that I have to do while you're at track practice, but that's it. Why?"

"Well, maybe...we could see each other."

"Really?"

"Yeah, maybe. If Grace drinks enough and goes to bed, then I could text you and..."

"Yes! Whatever you want to do. Let me take you somewhere—you want to go somewhere?"

"I just want to do something normal...somewhere no one knows who I am."

"We can do that," he says as he finishes carving the letter 'D' into the wood.

A + D

"Okay...maybe."

"Thank you."

He smiles, then leans in and kisses me. It's been days since I've felt his mouth on me, and I missed it.

I think he did, too.

He moves on top of me, sliding a hand under my ass before settling between my legs. He grinds against me, slowly and deliberately, torturously. I lift my hips into him, desperate for more friction. I try to decide if I'd fuck him right here. It's empty enough that every sound would carry, and I'm sure there will be a class in here next period. Still, I'm pretty sure I couldn't tell him no if that's what he wants. And I'm pretty sure it's what he wants.

He runs a hand up my shirt, slips it inside my bra, cupping my breast, and then he freezes.

He removes his hand from my shirt, and I see fresh blood on his palm.

"Ally, are you bleeding?" he asks.

"What? No."

But I sit up and lift my bandaged arm and see that both the sleeve and the side of my shirt are wet.

"Maybe," I say, panicked.

"Shit. Okay, come here," he says.

He takes my hand and pulls me into the hallway, then the nearest bathroom, after ensuring no one is inside.

"Let me see it," he says.

I sigh, pull the soaked shirt over my head, and wince when he removes the tape from the cuts on my underarm.

"Sorry. Does that hurt? I'm not trying to hurt you."

"It's not your fault," I tell him as he removes the last of the tape.

Devon exhales loudly, and I look at him instead of at my arm. He looks scared.

"Jesus, Ally," he says. "This is bad. This looks *really* bad. I think the cuts are infected. There's bruising all around them—and a couple on your back, too. Did you do this?"

I nod my head. "I'm sorry."

"No, don't be sor—" he sighs, running his hands through his hair and shaking his head. "I have a first aid kit in the car. I'll go get it."

"Um, I have a hoodie in my locker."

"I'll get that, too," he says. "You need to wash those, Ally."

He leaves the bathroom, and I turn on the water, lifting my arm so that I can see exactly what I did to the underside in the mirror.

The sight surprises even me.

It's much worse than I've ever done to my legs. The skin is greenish around each of the deep, angry red cuts. I pump some soap into my hand and maneuver my body so that I can get my upper arm under the water. It's tender to the touch when I try to clean it.

I pat it dry with a towel and hold it up to the mirror again, for some reason expecting it to look better just because it's clean now.

It doesn't.

Devon doesn't say anything when he returns with the first aid kit. He sets it down on the sink, then sprays my arm with some kind of antiseptic before wrapping it with gauze.

"I'm ashamed," I tell him quietly.

"Ally..."

"I'm really embarrassed that you had to see this and do this."

Devon shakes his head and finishes with the tape, then hands me my sweatshirt. I glance toward the door, then remove my soiled bra and throw it in the trash before pulling the sweatshirt over my head. After shaking out my hair, he places his hands on my cheeks.

"Is this my fault?" he asks.

"No," I emphasize. "No, it's not your fault. I just..."

"I don't want to tell you what to do," he says. "But...you can't steal and you can't sell nudes to old pervs and you can't do *this* to yourself. I mean...it looks really bad, Ally. Those cuts are deep. That scares me."

"I didn't mean to."

"You can't do this again. And I'll know; I'll check you."

"I don't want to do it again, Devon. I *want* to stop. I want there to be a time in my life when I can move on and forget about this part. I won't be able to forget if every time I look in the mirror, I see it staring back at me, carved in scars."

He wraps his arms around me and pulls me into his chest. I lock mine around his waist and breathe him in—cedar and sandalwood and a hint of fabric softener—and try to focus on the fact that I have someone who actually cares instead of the overwhelming shame.

"What happened to your back?" he asks. "Did Grace do that?"

I nod.

"This is going to get better, okay? We'll figure it out. I'm already figuring it out, so don't worry."

"The bell is going to ring soon," I tell him. "We should go."

"Yeah. Hey, I'll text you, okay?"

"Okay."

"And you text me tonight and tell me when I can come and get you, and I'll be there. I know where we can go—somewhere you can feel normal, and no one will know you."

"Really? Where?"

"A party. One of my friends who lives in my mom's neighborhood is having one. It's about a twenty-five-minute drive from here. No one from our school will be there."

I smile. "Okay."

"Allyson, I love you," he says before kissing me on the lips. "*Please* be good."

"I will. I promise."

He laces his fingers through mine, and we leave the bathroom, walking together only for a few seconds before we hear the bell. Then, I let go and turn the other way.

And go back to pretending for the rest of the day.

13

I've been watching this fucker for a week now, waiting for the right time.

Parks lives in an apartment in Downtown Black Rock. It's in a newer, trendy building with beach access and a pool. And a lot of younger residents.

I guess that last part shouldn't come as a surprise.

He doesn't leave much—not from what I've seen. He doesn't go to bars at night and doesn't seem to have any friends or family. There are no pictures in his classroom of anyone but himself.

I guess that part is kind of sad, but not enough to make me feel bad.

Anyway—the leaving. It doesn't really happen. I hoped I could do this under the cover of night, but now I'm banking on his neighbors not knowing each other well enough to realize that I'm out of place around here.

I lock my car and walk around the back side of the building, then up the staircase to the second floor. I pass another guy on my way down the hallway, and he gives me a nod before continuing on his way. I stop in front of #213 and remove the set of keys I took from his desk. I flip through them until I find the one that looks most like a house key and turn it in the lock.

The small apartment is trendy but bare, and while it appears to be clean, it smells like stale laundry or dirty towels. A plate with a half-eaten microwave dinner sits on the countertop, and I wonder how long it's been there before reminding myself that I'm on a tight schedule and need to do what I came here for.

I resign to breathing from my mouth for however long this takes.

I panic a little when I look around the apartment and don't see a computer anywhere. He has to have one—it's got to be here somewhere, but I don't even see a desk or anything resembling an office or workspace in the apartment.

But if I were an old perv, would I leave my computer out for other people to find? No, probably not.

I head to the bedroom—the apparent source of the worst of smells—and start turning out drawers, looking for hiding places. I wish I'd worn gloves for the sake of sanitation, not because I'm worried about fingerprints. I don't plan on remaining anonymous.

I notice a power cord plugged into the wall beside the bed, lying on the floor.

I lift the mattress and find the laptop wedged underneath. Then, I pull out the computer, sit cross-legged on the ground, and power it on. It feels like it takes an eternity for the computer to load and bring me to the sign-in screen. My heart pounds along with a figurative stop clock counting down in my head. Eventually, it does load, and I attempt to log in, typing the same password he'd used at school when prompted and hoping for the best.

Bigdick79!

The word *Welcome* flashes across the screen.

Idiot.

It isn't difficult from there to access his text messages and email history. Even though I expected to find something incriminating, I have to admit I'm shocked by the sheer volume of garbage he's saved on this computer.

His search history is wiped. Not surprising, and I'm sure I know why.

I take out my phone and start taking pictures of what I've found—the messages, the photos—and I feel like I'm a creep, too. It makes me feel like whatever is wrong with him is getting on me, as if it's in the air here, seeping into my skin. I mutter a silent apology to my classmates for looking before closing the computer and returning it to where I found it.

I open the door just a crack and peer into the empty hallway before stepping out and closing the door behind me. After locking up, I head back down the staircase to my car. I only have about ten minutes left before track practice is over—and that's just barely enough time to make it back to the school. Let's hope he's a lingerer.

The track is empty when I park my car and head inside the building. I proceed down the empty hallway to Parks' room and turn the knob.

It's locked.

Fuck.

The custodians probably close and lock all the doors after they go through the rooms in the evening. I didn't think of that.

"West!" a voice calls from behind me.

Shit.

I wince, then turn and find myself face-to-face with the douchebag himself.

"Do you need something?"

I hold out the keys in my hands. "Found these in the parking lot next to the red Chevy Silverado. It's yours, right?"

"Oh, shit. Yeah, I was looking for those. Thanks."

"No problem," I say and quickly walk in the other direction.

"Hey, what are you doing here anyway?" he asks.

"Nothing," I tell him. "I forgot some stuff I need for the weekend."

"Oh, right. I always forget you're one of the smart ones," he says. The urge to roll my fucking eyes is overwhelming. "I've seen you at a lot of the meets. Thought you had a girlfriend on the team you were waiting for or something."

"Nope, don't have a girlfriend on the team. What about you?" I ask.

That slack-jawed look on his face tells me he wasn't ready for that one and isn't sure how to react.

I smile and point at him, saying, "Gotcha! Just kidding, Mr. P. Have a great weekend," then turn to leave.

He forces a laugh. "Yeah, good one. You, too."

"Oh, I *absolutely* will!" I say as I turn the corner. "Talk to you soon!"

"Dude, don't go in there! You're going to get us both killed! NO, NO, NO, SHIT! FUCK!" I yell, taking off my headset and throwing it across the room.

"Would you shut the fuck up?" Darci yells, banging on my bedroom door. "God, don't you have a life? An animal to sacrifice or something? Can't you just leave for once...ever?"

"Fuck off," I say back to her.

"Darci, he's leaving you alone, so leave him alone," my dad shouts from downstairs.

"You don't have to have your room next to his!" she yells back. "I don't want to listen to his loser shit!"

"Darci, enough," her mom says.

My phone vibrates in my pocket, and I pull it out.

Ally: She's asleep…do you still want to come and get me?

Me: Yes. I'll be there in ten. I'll park near the bus stop.

"...If you guys would just make him shut up, it wouldn't be a problem," Darci shouts back, still arguing. "I can't ignore him when his video games and his music and his voice are *so loud* that..."

"Hey, Darci?" I say, pulling open the bedroom door. "It turns out I *do* have an animal sacrifice tonight that I almost forgot about, so no worries—I'll be leaving soon. Thanks for the reminder."

She stomps back to her room, and I go to my desk for my wallet and keys.

"Devon? Are you still there? Don't leave me hanging."

Ah, right.

I pick my gaming headphones back up from the ground. "Nah, man. I'm leaving, actually, but...we'll talk about that other stuff later this week. I'm going to get the money soon—I'll text you."

"Whatever, dude. Fine. Enjoy having a real life," he says before I sign off.

I walk through the house, out the door, and get in my car. After starting the engine, I put it in reverse, and...shit.

Darci parked me in again.

Fucking idiot thinks her Honda CRV is a massive truck that can't fit on one side of the driveway.

Not wanting to deal with her bullshit, I back the car up the entire two feet I've been gifted with, then put it in drive and go through the neighbor's yard to the street.

I'll probably catch shit for this, but how many times have we had this fight? Maybe now, they'll deal with it.

When I get to Ally's neighborhood, I park and send her a text. Ten minutes go by without a reply, and I start to worry that she's changed her mind or gotten caught. I'm contemplating whether or not I should get out and go to the house when I see her emerge from the tree line.

"Hey," she says when she gets in the car. She leans over and kisses me, then pulls down the visor and starts digging through her bag. I look her up and down, taking in the bare legs in her short denim shorts and her exposed stomach in a tight, black lace long-sleeved cropped top.

"Hey. You okay?"

She laughs. "Yeah. I can't imagine a scenario where I don't get caught, but...other than that, I'm okay."

She takes down her hair before opening a tube of mascara and applying it to her lashes. "Just tell me I look pretty this time, all right?"

"You look pretty," I tell her. "You always look pretty."

She looks happy, too.

She finishes with her eyes and applies lipstick, then runs her fingers through her hair.

"What?" she says when she catches me staring. "I *have* normal clothes. I just haven't worn them in a long time. Can I turn up the music? I'm not allowed to listen to music at home."

"Do whatever you want," I tell her.

And she does. She turns it all the way up, rolls the window down, and props her feet up on the dashboard.

She's lucky I love her.

I watch her sing along to my playlist with her hand out the window, moving it as if surfing through the cool night air as we drive.

"So I guess it's greasy food, loud music, and the windows rolled down," I say.

"What?!" she shouts over the music.

"The things that bring you joy. I told you I'd make it my mission to figure it out."

She shakes her head. "*You* bring me joy, Devon. That's it—that's the entire list."

We pull into a driveway about twenty minutes later and get out of the car. "Is this where the party is?" Ally asks, taking my hand.

"No," I tell her. "This is my mom's house. I left my laptop here on Wednesday, and I need it for something."

"Well...is she here?"

"Yeah, I think so."

She freezes at the front steps.

"What? You said you wanted to do normal stuff. Come on."

I usher her into the front door of the smaller ranch-style home and close the door behind us.

"Mom?" I call from the kitchen. Ally stands beside me with her arms folded over her chest, awkwardly shifting her weight on her feet.

"Come on in, sweetheart—we're in the living room!" she calls out.

I grab Ally's hand again and pull her through the dining room and into the front room, where my mom and Ivy sit together watching television.

"Just wanted to pick up that computer," I tell her. "This is my girlfriend, Ally, by the way. Ally, that's my mom, Stephanie, and my little sister, Ivy. She just turned six."

"Hi," Ally says, her pale cheeks blushing.

"Hi, Ally," my mom says. "It's so nice to meet you. It's been a long time since Devon brought a girl over here."

"Stop," I say, shaking my head.

"I like your shirt," my sister says to her.

"Thanks," Ally replies. "I heard you were the cool sister."

"I am cool," Ivy says. "Devon said your mom was in jail."

Shit.

"Um, yeah. She is."

"My dad is in jail, too. Do you miss her?"

Ally nods. "All the time."

"Okay, we're just going to go and get that now. Come on."

She follows me down to the small bedroom at the end of the hall.

"Are you mad at me for telling them about you?"

"No," she says. "It's kind of nice. Normal, like you said."

"I only told Ivy about your mom because I thought it might make her feel less lonely. Her dad wasn't a good person who did something bad like your mom, though. She knows he hurt us, and that's hard for her. But...my mom knew that the other kids' parents would know the truth, so she wanted to make sure that Ivy knew it, too."

"Yeah, that makes sense," she says. "Does your sister miss him?"

I think it over for a minute before replying. "That's difficult to answer. I don't think she remembers him, really, but I think she's aware that she's missing *something.* I think she misses the idea of him. My parents divorced when I was that same age, and I don't remember them ever being together, but I remember missing the idea of us all being together, if that makes sense."

"I remember my dad," Ally says. "There's a handful of really clear memories—distinct, ordinary moments that just stayed with me for whatever reason. I think maybe I miss the idea of him, too. So...it makes sense; that's what I mean. I miss my mom, too. I wish I could see her."

"You will, Ally. We can go see her—I'll figure something out."

She shakes her head. "You've got a solution for everything, don't you?"

"Smart ass, yes, I do," I tell her. "Do you still want to go to the party? If you don't feel like it, we can do something else—anything you want."

"No, I'm fine. I want to go."

"Okay, you ready?" I ask.

She nods, and I wrap the charger around the laptop and toss it into my bag.

"Bye, Mom," I say as we walk back through the living room.

"What? You're not staying?"

"Nope, going to Tyler's."

"Are you staying the night here then?"

"No, I have to take Ally home, so I'm just gonna go back to Dad's."

"Okay," she says. "Well, remember...you said you'd watch Ivy tomorrow."

Ugh. Right. I did. "What time was that again?"

"I have to be at work at two," she says.

"Why don't you bring her over to Dad's house, then? The pool is open; she can swim."

"Are you sure they won't mind?" she asks.

"Yeah, I'm sure. They like having Ivy over. And they always complain that we don't use the pool enough anyway."

"Okay, have fun," she says. "Ally, you come back over here again sometime, and I'll make you guys dinner."

"I will," Ally says.

We get back in the car and drive just two streets down to Tyler's house, then park and walk up to the front.

His house is an older two-story home with matted beige carpets and a kitchen that needs updating like my mom's. The place is loud and packed with people I used to go to school with when I lived here full-time. A cloud of smoke hovers over the living room.

"Devon!" Tyler calls from the kitchen. "No way. You actually showed up."

"Hey, man. How's it going?"

"Who's this?" he says, gesturing at Ally. "I know she's not here with you."

"That's Ally, and she's with me," I tell him.

"You're too hot for him," he says pointedly. "Do you guys want a beer?"

Does Ally drink? I don't even know. "Umm..."

"Yes," Ally answers before I can.

"Yeah, we do," I say.

As the designated driver, I nurse my beer while we mingle. I'm surprised that Ally seems at ease here and social—she fits. And not like how she fits with Darci—all uncomfortable and in a way that doesn't make sense.

She fits here because she fits *with me*. I'm a little nervous when my friends invite me to play beer pong, and she encourages me to go, opting to stay and socialize with some girls I know, but I do it anyway. I give her the space because I want to give her what *she* wants—a chance to feel normal.

When I inevitably lose, I return to the kitchen and find her sitting on the kitchen table with a Sharpie lid between her teeth, drawing on another girl's bicep. I take a couple of steps forward and get a better look at the drawing: a naked woman with comically big tits. We make eye contact, and I laugh, shaking my head.

"What?" she asks, flashing me a grin. "They wanted tattoos."

"Nothing," I tell her. I lean against the counter, watching as she finishes one and then another, taking swigs from a red solo cup, laughing and talking.

And for once, I feel normal, too. Or like *we're* normal.

A normal couple.

Ally caps the marker and sets it on the table next to her, and I move to stand between her legs. She wraps her arms around my neck, leans in, and kisses me. Her warm tongue glides along the space between my lips before dipping into my mouth, teasing me with slow, deliberate motions that have me rock hard, wondering what it would feel like to have that pretty pink tongue on my cock like that.

And she knows what she's doing.

I grab her hand when it starts to dip down into the waistband of my jeans.

"Well, you're in a good mood."

"Mmmhmm," she says, going for my dick again with the other hand. "I'm free. And I'm horny."

I grab both of her wrists and lean in close to her ear. "If you're going to try and grab my dick in a room full of people like a thirsty slut, then I'm going to take you upstairs and fuck you like one. Is that what you want?"

"Yes," she says.

"I was hoping you'd say that."

I toss her ass over my shoulder and carry her up the staircase to Tyler's parent's bedroom, locking the door behind us as Ally works on the button of my jeans.

"Get on your knees," I tell her. "I want your lips around my cock."

My dick springs free of my jeans, and she pumps it in her hand as she drops to her knees and gives me what I've wanted—licking, sucking, and teasing the head. I watch her tongue glide over the bead of precum at the end before she takes it all in her mouth.

"Oh fuck, Ally," I moan.

Her other hand moves to my balls while she bobs up and down on my cock. I watch her pretty mouth work while her cheeks hollow out around my dick, and I can't stop myself from thrusting into her. She responds with a moan, and my eyes roll right back in my head. It's all I can do to keep from coming right down her throat.

But I still want to fuck her pussy, so I don't.

"Take everything off and get on the bed on all fours."

I lie back on the bed and stroke my cock in my hand while I watch her take everything off. Once she does, she climbs onto the bed.

"Like this?" she asks, crawling toward me.

"Just like that, baby," I tell her.

I move to my knees and position myself behind her, nudging her legs further apart before sinking my dick into her wet cunt.

"Oh, my god!" she gasps as I thrust into her. "Oh god, that feels so good..."

She places her palms flat against the headboard and arches her back, pushing against me as I slam back into her, the sound of heavy breathing and skin against skin filling the room.

I slap her ass once before gripping it with my hands and spreading her wider, making my cock sink in a little deeper.

"Fuck, Devon..."

"Does that feel good, baby? Is this what you wanted from me?"

"Yes..."

"You look so good, Ally...taking all of my cock like this."

At some point, someone knocks on the door, but I ignore it. They'd have to be deaf not to realize the room is occupied. It occurs to me that I've never been able to fuck her like this—in a bed, not worried about if someone is going to hear us or find out what we're doing. I take full fucking advantage of it, spurred on by moans each time I drive into her.

Ally's cries turn to desperate whimpers just before she comes. I push her head down into the mattress when I feel her pulsing around my dick, thrusting hard and deep before I come inside her.

I lie on the bed next to her, and she reaches for me, running her fingers over my earplugs like she always does.

I lean in and brush her hair away from her face.

"I love you, Ally."

She gives me a small smile. "I love you, too."

"I should probably take you home," I tell her. "It's almost 2:00 AM."

Ally goes to the bathroom to clean up and get dressed while I wait on the bed, and then we head back downstairs. I find Tyler and the guys in the kitchen and tell them we're leaving, but we get lost in conversation again—this time about all I've missed and how I need to come around more. Somehow, in those ten minutes, I manage to lose my girlfriend. I find her in the kitchen with the same group of girls and three empty shot glasses in front of her.

"Do I need to throw you over my shoulder to get you to the car, too?" I ask. "We need to go."

"Fine," she says, rolling her eyes.

I take her by the hand, and we head out the front door and then down to where I parked my car.

"Turn on the heat," Ally says when she closes the door. "I'm freezing."

The temperature did drop a little, but it's not that cold. I reach into the backseat and grab one of my hoodies.

"Here," I say, handing it to her before I start the car.

She laughs before she pulls it over her head.

"What's funny?" I ask.

"Nothing," she says. "Just...regular couple stuff."

I turn away and shake my head, trying to hide my own smile.

"Those girls asked for my phone number, and I had to tell them I don't have a phone," she says, then laughs again. Hard. Way too hard.

Uh oh. I may be in trouble here.

"They were so confused," she adds. "Devon!"

"What?"

"Let's go swimming! *Real* swimming."

"Not tonight, baby. Maybe some other time."

"You're always mean," she pouts.

"Literally the opposite is true, but that's fine."

It's at this point I realize that maybe I should have watched her a little better. It seems like those last few shots really did her in.

"Devon, I want to drive. Can I drive?"

"Fuck no, you can't!" I tell her. "There's some water bottles on the floor in the back, Ally. You need to drink some water."

She unbuckles her seatbelt, turns around, and tumbles head-first into the back of the car.

I laugh for a few seconds before I realize...I'm in deep shit.

"Why did you do that!?" she asks when she pops back up.

"I didn't do anything! Ally, seriously. Get a water, then get back up here and buckle your seatbelt before I get pulled over."

"I can't!" she says.

Shit.

I turn down a quiet street and find a place to park the car, then I go to the back, open the door, and buckle my girlfriend back in the front.

"Drink the water and stay in your seat, Ally. I'm serious."

I close the door, shake my head, and silently degrade myself as I return to the driver's side and climb into the car.

"Devon?"

"Yeah?"

"I don't want to go home," she says. She chokes on the words just a little, and it's enough to tear me apart.

I sigh. "I know, baby. It won't be much longer, I promise. I've got it figured out."

"You keep saying that," she says. "I don't know what that means."

"I'll tell you soon, okay?"

She doesn't answer, and when I look over a minute later, she's asleep.

Once we're back in Ally's neighborhood, I park slightly closer to her house than she'd normally want me to, but far enough away that the camera won't see us. I walk around to the passenger side, open the door, and wake her up.

"Hey, Ally. We're back. You need to go inside and go to bed."

Ally groans and climbs out of the car. She takes a few wobbly steps away from the vehicle before I throw her arm over my shoulders and help her across the yards and to the side of the house—the one with the bathroom window I know she probably used to get out earlier.

"I'm going to go in first, and then I'm going to help you climb in, too, okay? And you need to be really, really quiet, Ally. Can you do that?"

She replies with something like a groan that I'm going to have to hope means *yes*, then I climb onto the AC unit and through the window.

I lower myself onto the floor carefully and peek out the bathroom door. The first floor is dark and quiet—no sign of anyone up and moving around.

I gesture for Ally to climb through and help her onto her feet, but her every move is loud. After shushing her several times, I give up and carry her up the staircase to her room.

I find the door without a knob and push it open, then set her down on the bed. Instinctively, she lies down on her pillow and pulls her covers over her.

"Ally, where should I put your bag?" I whisper, knowing it contains what's considered to be contraband in her house.

"In the hole," she slurs. "And turn the phone off, please."

I dig through the bag, power down the phone, and crawl under the bed. It takes me a minute to find the loose board, but I do, and then I drop the bag inside and replace it.

"I love you, Allyson," I tell her and kiss her on the lips. "Be good."

"I love you, too," she says, running her fingers over my gauged ears again.

"Why do you do that?" I ask.

"It makes me feel better."

"What do you mean?"

"Someone...hurt me."

"What does *that* mean?"

"You *know* what I mean," she says.

Oh...shit.

"And sometimes I get...confused. And it makes me feel better. Like I'm safe."

"You're always safe with me, Ally. I'll never hurt you."

"I know," she says, closing her eyes.

"I have to go, Ally. Text me tomorrow when you can, okay?"

"Mmmhmm," she says, pulling the covers up to her neck.

I glance out into the hallway to make sure it's clear before I leave the room, creeping back down the staircase and out the window I came from. A wave of relief washes over me when my shoes hit the wet grass.

I can't fucking believe we didn't get caught.

That sense of relief fades quickly as I walk to my car, remembering that Ally's still stuck there—that someone hurt her, and people are *still* hurting her.

When I get home, I crawl into bed, and despite how exhausted I am, I don't sleep.

14

When I do finally emerge from my room the next morning, I find the house quiet and empty—a rarity around here. I go to the kitchen, scarf a couple of pieces of cold pizza from the fridge, and drink some orange juice straight from the carton, then head back upstairs to my cave.

I almost have everything I'd taken from Parks' House of Horrors copied over onto my laptop when my phone vibrates on the table next to me. I snatch it up, prepared to ignore whoever is calling, before seeing Ally's name on the screen.

"Hey," I say when I answer. "How are you feeling?"

"Like shit," she says, then laughs. "I threw up all morning, and my head is killing me. I remember falling into the backseat of your car, and then...that's about it. I don't remember how I got inside the house."

Then I'm sure she doesn't remember what she told me before I left, either.

"I carried you," I tell her. "I was scared shitless. I'm sorry you're sick. I should have...done better."

"It's okay. It kind of worked out. Grace has some things she had to do at the church today, and she thinks I have the flu or something, so she left me here and has been keeping her distance so that she doesn't get sick, too. I plan on milking it the rest of the weekend."

I force a laugh. "I miss you. It's nice to hear your voice."

"I miss you, too," she says. "I had fun, though. So...thanks."

"Yeah, me too."

"Anyway, I think I'm going to go back to bed for a little while. I just wanted to talk to you...make sure you're not mad at me for becoming a problem."

"You're not a problem," I tell her. "I'm not mad at you at all."

"I love you, Devon."

"I love you, too. Text me when you can, okay?"

"Okay...bye."

"Bye."

After ending the call, I send not everything, but enough to prove my point, to the printer in my dad's office and then run downstairs to grab it all. I stand there for what feels like the longest time waiting for everything to print. My body must be on high alert due to what I'm trying to do because I actually jump when I hear her voice.

"What are you doing?" Darci asks.

"Fuck! Homework," I answer.

"Why are you so jumpy?"

"I thought I was the only person here, and I find your presence disturbing."

"Hey, have you read *Animal Farm*?"

I scoff. There it is.

"I'm not doing your homework for you," I tell her.

"I'll pay you."

"I have to watch Ivy; she'll be here any minute, actually. So, no. And the answer would be no, anyway. I don't have time."

I breeze past her and back up the stairs, ignoring whatever protests she yells at my back. After stashing the papers in my bag, I pull out *The Fires of Heaven*, and go back to reading until the doorbell rings.

When I get downstairs, my mom and Ivy are already standing in the living room with Darci.

"Devon said I could go swimming," Ivy says.

"You look adorable," Darci tells Ivy. "I love your unicorn towel. I wish I had one."

"You can borrow it if you want, but you have to give it back," she tells her.

"Hey, Devon," my mom says. "I have to run; I got a late start. I'll leave the booster seat on the front porch. I don't have any cash, so I sent some money to your Venmo."

I don't need her to pay me. I don't want to take her money, but I also know she won't take no for an answer.

"That's fine," I tell her. "I'll bring her home after we eat."

"Try to get her to bed. She has school tomorrow. I'll see you later."

"I'll try," I say as she closes the door, knowing it won't work out, just like it always doesn't. Ivy will still be up when my mom gets home around ten.

"Hey, Ivy," Darci says. "Wouldn't you rather play with me today? I can swim with you, and then we can do our hair and makeup. We can have a Girls' Day, and *Devon* can write a book report."

I shake my head. "No."

"Come on. I'll pay you, *and* you can keep the babysitting money."

"I want to have a Girls' Day!" Ivy says. "Maybe Devon's girlfriend can come, too."

Darci laughs. "Devon doesn't have a girlfriend."

Shit.

"Okay, come on, Ivy. I think we have ice cream. Do you want some ice cream before we get in the pool?"

"He does have a girlfriend. He brought her over to our house. Her name is Ally."

Darci's eyes dart toward me, and if they could shoot lasers, I'm pretty sure that's what they'd be doing right now.

"What does Ally look like?" she asks Ivy.

"She has long dark hair and dark eyes. Devon said her mom is in jail."

Darci shakes her head and feigns laughter. "Well, that's just...fucking great. I hope you enjoy never seeing her again."

"Darci...you can't tell them."

"That lying fucking...bitch. I'm going to kill her."

She storms off toward the staircase, and I run after her.

"Okay, what do you want? You want me to write your stupid fucking essay? I'll do it."

She ignores me, throws open the door to her bedroom, and grabs her phone from the charger.

"I should call Grace and tell her right now."

"What do you want?" I ask her from the doorway. "What do you want to just...let it go? At least for now."

"Why should I let it go, huh? That fucking bitch lied to me; she betrayed me with *you*."

"If you do this, I'll make sure you regret it."

She scoffs at my threat.

"Where do *you* go at night, Darci? Does your mom know?"

She paces back and forth across the room.

"If I keep your secret, then you're going to stay out of my way and out of my business."

"No problem. I don't like you anyway."

"And you *are* going to do my essay and *every other* assignment I have for the rest of the year."

"Fine," I tell her.

"My chores, too. And if I want my car washed or anything like that, you'll do it."

"Great."

If everything goes according to plan, I won't have to do it for long anyway. Surely, I can manage extra homework for a couple of weeks.

"The essay is due tomorrow. I have a math assignment, too. I'll email it to you. Have fun babysitting."

She starts to close the door in my face.

"Wait," I say. "Are you going to tell Ally that you know?"

She freezes, and I watch her think it over for a minute. "No, not yet—not until I thoroughly torture her. So...you aren't going to tell her that I know, either. That's part of the arrangement."

"What do you mean, *torture*?"

She laughs. "Aw, look at you getting all protective. Don't worry; I don't mean literally."

"Fine."

"Although, that sad boy face makes me think maybe I should. You both better hope I don't get tired of your indentured servitude," she says before slamming the door.

"Fuck!" I yell at no one in particular. I want to tear my hair out or put my fist through her door, but I don't do either of those things. I do my best to shake it off before going downstairs.

"Am I in trouble?" Ivy asks. "Are we going to have Girls' Day?"

"No, you're not in trouble," I tell her. I'm the one who's in trouble. I should have thought about this—and I *should* tell Ally that she knows, too. "But no. Darci has homework, so no Girls' Day. You're stuck with me. Do you still want ice cream?"

She looks a little disappointed, but nods. My phone vibrates in my pocket as I lead her into the kitchen.

Ally: Grace is home. I'm turning this off now. I'll text you again before I go to sleep. Have fun babysitting. <3

Me: Okay.

Shit.

Me: I love you.

I shake my head and shove the phone back into my pocket.

What I should have said is that I fucked up. And I'm sorry, Ally. But more stress is the last thing she needs. I can shoulder this for both of us—it's only for a couple of weeks.

Between the stress of what's going on with Ally, Darci finding out about us, Parks, and doing both my own and Darci's homework, I didn't get much sleep the last two nights. My alarm goes off, but I struggle to pull myself out of bed. I must sink back into some half-awake/half-dream state because I swear I feel a warm body next to mine. I reach for Ally and wrap my arm around her waist, hearing the click of an iPhone camera when I do.

I force my eyes open and see that it's Darci lying next to me, and *Darci's* bare stomach my hand is resting on.

"What the fuck are you doing?!" I scream. "Get out of my room!"

"Relax," she says, climbing out of my bed and crossing her arms over her bare chest. "Just a little extra insurance. I need to be sure you'll do what I want."

"You are fucked up," I tell her. "Delete it, now!"

"Hmm...no, I don't think I will," she says. "And if I think for even a *second* you've told Ally what I know or anything about this arrangement, she'll be the first one to see it."

She smirks and walks out the door.

I need to do something about her, and I know that. I'm just not sure what that something will be yet, and I have a lot of other stuff on my mind.

For instance, I need to get to school early...which means I need to be out the door in all of ten minutes.

I spend five of those in the shower, throw on some clothes, and race out the door. The student lot is practically empty when I arrive. After parking the car, I run to the front door, then down the hall to Parks' classroom.

"Mr. Parks, can I talk to you for a minute?"

"I have to get the weight room opened up, Devon. I was just on my way out of here. If there's something you want to talk about, you can shoot me an email," he says.

He starts to get up from his desk when I drop the papers in front of him.

"I think this is a chat you'll want to have."

He picks the papers up, scanning them, the fear visible in his eyes.

"Where did you get this?" he asks. "Did you hack into my computer? Did you take this from my house!?"

"Doesn't matter where I got it," I tell him.

"It sure as hell does! This is a violation of my privacy. I should call your parents!"

At this, I laugh. "Yeah, and tell them what? I should call *their* parents."

Some sense of awareness washes over him, and he gets up from the desk, walks over to the door, and closes it.

"Most of those girls are in college now. And Maisie and I are in a relationship. She'll be eighteen next month."

"I don't really care," I tell him. "And I don't think the school board or anyone else in the community will, either."

"What do you want, you little shit?"

"Five thousand dollars," I tell him.

He laughs. "Five thousand...look around, mother fucker! I'm a teacher. I don't just have five thousand dollars!"

"Well, figure it the fuck out! It's that, or everyone is going to find out about those messages."

He picks the papers up off the desk again, then leans over and turns on his paper shredder, smiling as it chews them up.

Is the guy really this dumb?

"You really think I don't have digital copies saved everywhere of that stuff? That I just handed over everything I have?" I laugh, wiping the smile right off his face.

"Fine," he says. "Go ahead and show these to whoever you want. Who do you think they'll believe—an esteemed coach and teacher or some degenerate kid who's apparently part of some satanic cult?"

I shrug. "I guess we'll find out."

I throw my bag over my shoulder and head for the door, calling his bluff. As suspected, he stops me.

"Okay, okay...wait. Wait a second. What about two thousand?"

"Five. You have until Friday," I tell him.

"I don't have that kind of cash!"

"Not my problem," I tell him. "Figure it out. Take out a loan on a credit card, sell that douchey small-dick truck in the parking lot; I don't really give a shit where it comes from."

"You're going to regret this," he says. "I'll make sure of it."

"If it makes you feel better, the money isn't for me. It's for a good cause."

"Fuck you, kid. Get the fuck out of my face."

"Friday," I tell him. "Don't forget. Oh, and for the record, I think you're a pussy, but if you were thinking of doing anything to me, I have told people about this. They'll know."

I flash him a smile as I leave the room, hoping he hadn't noticed my hands or my voice shaking. I take a deep breath and try to steady myself.

He deserves it, I remind myself.

Still, there's a part of me that feels guilty—not for doing it for him, but because he'll keep doing this when it's all said and done, and he'll keep getting away with it, too. *That* part weighs heavily on my conscience.

I make a mental note to do something about it, but that will have to wait until Ally and the money are long gone.

15

School feels different for me now. It feels like the night of Darci's memorial or that first week all over again—the week after Devon was arrested and Mark and Grace let me go back to school. I feel their eyes on me. I hear them get quiet, but I don't know what they want from me. I don't know what he wants from me, either.

Before volleyball practice last night, I submitted a request for a schedule change, and I was surprised to see how quickly it was completed and without asking any questions. Maybe they knew about what happened in art, too.

So now I'm in seventh period art and first period PE with Mr. Parks. And I shouldn't need to worry about running into Devon in any of my other classes because...well...

One of us is stupid, and it's me.

I hope that makes him feel better—that maybe it brings him some peace when he realizes he won't have to look at me for the next few days, and then I'll be gone.

But I also hope—just a little bit—that maybe he'll miss me.

I'm reminded of just how much he won't miss me when I run my hands through hair that isn't there and again in the lunchroom when he walks in with Audrey. His arm is around her waist; she leans into him and laughs at something. *Nails on a chalkboard.* That's what he always said her voice sounds like. I notice his hand is inside the back of her shirt before they part ways, and she sits beside me at the table.

"Hey, Ally," she says.

I can't even bring myself to fake something nice, to pretend. I've done so much of it, and fuck...I'm just so done now. So, I say nothing.

"What?" Audrey asks. When I still don't answer, she poses the question to the group. "What's her problem?"

"It's probably weird seeing you with Devon," Morgan says. "It's a shit move."

"Why? If all that stuff about them wasn't true, then it shouldn't matter if I am with Devon."

"That's even more reason to stay away from him. What would Darci say?" Morgan asks.

"I don't...I don't care," I say finally. "Devon can do whatever he wants. But...I'm not going to sit here anymore."

"What?" Audrey asks. "What do you mean?"

"Yeah, Ally...just chill," Trevor adds.

"We're not friends, Audrey," I tell her. "I don't want to sit by you. Darci was my friend—I think—but we were *never* friends. And I don't want to be here anymore."

I stand up from my seat and start to gather my things.

"What the fuck?" Audrey exclaims, jumping out of her chair, too.

"Would you both just chill the fuck out? *Chill out,*" Morgan says. "Ally, of course, Audrey is your friend. And Audrey—the last thing our group needs right now is this kind of drama."

"I don't like her," I say. "I don't think I've ever liked her."

"Fuck you, Ally. I should beat your ass."

I laugh before I close the space between us. "You could try."

She doesn't move, but I see in her eyes that I've called her bluff, and she's backing down. I smirk, then grab my tray and leave them there like that. Trevor calls after me to come back, but I ignore him and keep walking. And you know what? It feels good. Maybe I've fucked up a lot since I've been here. I've done things that have hurt people to protect myself. I've had my dignity and self-worth slowly and maliciously stripped from every fiber of my being. I lost my only friend in the most permanent way, broke the only person I've ever loved, and since then, I've just been hiding behind these people who don't even know me, faking it while the vice-grip of regret crushes my insides, and it's eaten away at me until there's barely anything left.

So, the least I can do is leave with a shred of dignity. Maybe it will help me when I try to start over again—to have one less reason to look at the girl in the mirror and feel shame.

At least, that's what I try to tell myself before an arm reaches out and knocks the tray out of my hands, causing milk and mashed potatoes to run down my shirt and onto my shoes.

The eerie silence that falls over the cafeteria tells me precisely who did it. I don't even need to look. I can feel him there just like I always could.

"Watch where you're going, bitch," Devon says.

A few people erupt in laughter—Audrey's, of course, being the loudest—but most of them are quiet, watching and waiting.

I turn to face this new version of Devon—the broken one—and try to muster up the same fucking audacity I had just minutes ago but come up empty-handed. I look at his hands resting in his lap, and I just miss them. I'd do almost anything to go back in time and crawl back into that bed...just to feel them run through my hair again, even if it meant he'd still cut it all off afterward.

When I finally look up and meet his icy glare, all I can manage is, "Yeah. Next time, I'll be more careful."

My eyes fill with tears, and I watch the smirk fall from his face before he quickly replaces it with rage. I ditch my tray and head for the bathroom to try and clean myself up. I take a wet paper towel and do my best to wipe the mashed potatoes from the front of me, but it doesn't look much better when I'm done. All I've managed to do is soak the damn shirt. I scoff, shake my head, and throw the soiled paper towels in the trash. I decide to go to the locker room and change into my gym clothes. I'm about to do just that when I realize I'm no longer alone.

"Devon, what do you want from me?" I ask without looking up. "Whatever you want, you can have it; I'll do it. Do you want me to tell everyone that I lied about us? I will."

"You don't get to do this," he seethes from the doorway. "You don't get to act like *you're* the victim."

"That's not what I'm doing."

"I don't care if you tell people you lied about us or not. I don't care what they think. I want you to tell me the truth—I want to know what the fuck happened to Darci in that woods; I want to know what you two were up to and why you did this to me!"

"Devon...I don't know what you're—"

He crosses the room in three strides, grabbing me by the front of my shirt and slamming my body against the mirror behind me.

"Stop lying! God, would you just fucking stop?!"

"I don't know what you want! I never lied to you! I don't know what happened to Darci! You're the one who was sleeping with her; why don't you tell me?"

"God damn it, I wasn't—" he starts. "You two played me. And whatever you were involved in, *that's* what got Darci killed. And that's what I want. I want to put you in jail."

"Devon, no. Devon, look at me." I reach for him, but he quickly shrugs me off.

"I'm not falling for it," he says. "God, you must think I'm an idiot."

"No," I tell him, shaking my head. "I think you're hurt. I know I did that, but...the stuff you're saying...it doesn't make any sense."

He punches the mirror next to my head, and glass shatters around me. Another girl almost steps inside but quickly backtracks after surveying the scene, and Devon takes that as his cue to leave.

"We're not done," he says. "You know what happened in the woods that night. Maybe it even has something to do with that creepy drawing you made on my back."

"You thought my drawing was creepy?" I feel my lower lip start to quiver.

"Fuck yeah, it was creepy," he says. "Everything about you is fucking creepy."

"Well, you won't have to worry about me for long," I shout at his back. "I'll be out of your way soon."

He doesn't reply or even turn back to look at me.

I shift on my feet, hearing the sound of glass crunching between my Vans and the tile floor. I look at the broken mirror and the shards in the sink, and reality comes crashing down around me. I flee the bathroom before someone catches me in this mess and go through the motions for another day. One more day of this shit. One more weekend of hell.

And then I'll be free...of everything but myself.

After volleyball practice, I take the things I care about from my locker—artwork, the makeup Laurel gave me, and a small tin container with the notes Devon used to slip inside—and stuff it into my duffle bag. I whisper goodbye to the things I'm leaving behind and the person I used to be here.

Then, when I'm sure no one is looking, I cross the hall to Devon's locker and put in the combination. I take out a notebook and flip through it, comforted just seeing his handwriting inside. That's ridiculous, isn't it? To love someone so much you find comfort in their handwriting?

A jacket hangs on a hook inside, and I bring it to my nose and breathe it in. I consider taking it with me, but I've taken enough from him. Instead, I wordlessly say goodbye to Devon, too, and about a million *I'm sorrys* before closing the locker and taking the bus home for the last time.

16

The hallways are busy again by the time I leave Ally in the bathroom. I hate that she got to me—with her sad eyes and her fake fucking bullshit and I almost started to feel bad for her. *Almost.*

And what did she mean when she said I wouldn't have to worry about her for long? Was that a threat? Was she trying to say that...

No.

She wouldn't do something like that. But trying to make me think that she would? That's something the manipulative bitch would do.

I walk in late to calculus and take my seat in the back. The teacher doesn't mouth off to me like he would have last year, demanding retribution for this kind of blatant disrespect, desperate for any excuse to flex his imagined power and stroke his ego. When I look up at him, it looks like resisting the urge is causing him physical pain, and I smirk.

I like being scary.

He hands out a test I didn't know about, but even after missing months of class, I'm not worried. I put my phone in my pocket and take out my scientific calculator as instructed, then write my name and the date at the top of the page.

October 22nd.

Oh, fuck no.

Ally wasn't trying to trick me into thinking she was suicidal; she was referring to her birthday on Monday. Does she actually think that she can just fucking take that money and leave after everything that happened?

She thinks she gets to get out?

I snap the pencil in my fist in half. I look up at the clock—it's almost two. Ally has volleyball practice after school, but Grace will be home pretty soon. I could just tell her. I could go to her house and knock on the door, and maybe she would see me and wouldn't answer it, but I could tell her about the hiding place under Ally's bed. I could tell her about the money, and she'd look, and then she'd take it. Ally would be stuck here, and she'd be pissed.

But that would be so much less satisfying than if she just found it all gone and knew it was me.

So I decide to wait.

I get there early on Sunday and watch the car back out of the driveway. I make sure Ally's in the passenger seat and that her uncle's BMW is still gone, and he's still off campaigning somewhere.

Then, I strut across the street in broad daylight, climb onto the AC unit, and through the bathroom window.

I head through the pristine modern home—the one that still looks like no one lives there—and consider trashing it just for the hell of it. Well, not just for the hell of it, but because this whole fucking family played a part in this and because fuck them, and I barely manage not to. My more calculating side wins over impulse this time. I can't tip them off that someone has been in the house.

Even though I'm almost certain she made up or, at best, exaggerated the abuse, there is something just not right about this house—an ominous feeling. The air is thicker somehow, and it makes it hard to swallow. I wonder how I missed it the first time I was here, but I guess I must not have been paying attention. I missed a lot of things back then.

After taking the stairs two at a time up to the room at the end of the hall without a doorknob, I drop down to the ground and slide under the bed, feeling around for the loose board. I find it quickly, then remove the entire box and set it aside. Then, I dig around in my bag for the present I'd gotten for Ally, remove it from the plastic container, and set it down unceremoniously into the hole before replacing the board. I get up, drop the box of cash inside my bag, and then throw it over my shoulder.

I leave the same way I came in, and I'm back home in under an hour. That was easy.

My dad's new place is a three-bedroom townhouse close to downtown. It's small, but that's okay when you're a twice-divorced guy and your only kid is either going to prison or college, so they won't need much space. There's no pool on the property, and I'm sure that was intentional. He has a cat, he doesn't sleep, and he's lonely. I can tell he misses Lydia. And Darci, too. He misses the life he had before Ally, and so do I.

It was hard enough trying to wrap his head around Darci's death and my inevitable arrest. When the story about the knife came out, and the police found that stupid fucking picture she took, Lydia made up her mind about me pretty fast. She moved out three days later. How could she stay with someone whose son murdered her daughter?

Still, he never really let go. When we'd talk, I'd ask if he was okay, and, of course, he always said he was, but he'd also talk about how everything was going to be better once "they" find out I didn't do this, but I think the only "they" he ever worried about was her. I think he expected her to call once the video came out. Maybe he still does, but it hasn't happened yet.

I close the door to my room on the second floor, dig the box from my bag, and open it. Two envelopes rest on top; I tear open the one stamped and addressed to the school and find her withdrawal form fully filled out, signed, and dated. The other isn't sealed, and there's a bus ticket inside from Seattle to San Diego. It leaves tomorrow night.

Interesting choice. I wonder what happened to Florida. I wonder if that would have been her landing place or if it was just a spot to rest before she moved on because three days on a bus wasn't so appealing when it actually came time to do it.

I also wonder what her plan was. Was she going to try to leave tonight, catch a bus or a ride down to Seattle, and stay the night there? Or was she going to wait until tomorrow after school, skip volleyball practice, then get on the bus and never come back?

Underneath that is the cash. It's all there—*more* than all there. I count out just over $6,300 dollars, which means Ally hasn't completely retired from petty theft or selling drugs or whatever she was up to. There's a handful of third through sixth place track ribbons she's kept for some reason, and some pictures at the bottom of Ally and a woman I assume is her mother. In some photos, she can't be much older than Ally is now. The coloring is different; the woman has light brown hair and blue or green eyes, but the shape of her face, her cheekbones, and her smile are all Ally.

In one of the pictures, she holds a toddler version of the girl who ruined my life in her lap, smiling down at her. In another, they're at a beach together. This one must have been taken right before her mom was arrested because Ally doesn't look much younger than she is now. She's in a bikini, leaning against the shorter woman's shoulder. There aren't any marks on her hips or thighs, and it trips me up for a second.

"Doesn't change anything," I say aloud to myself.

The woman—Ally's mom—looks healthy and normal in all the pictures. Her eyes look clear. She doesn't look like the drug addict she was made out to be.

Maybe that part was true. Maybe she wasn't a user, and she was just desperate.

The only thing missing is the phone. I know someone still has it, but they haven't used it at all. The account is still active. I haven't closed it yet because...what if I need it?

I put the box in its entirety under my own bed. Full circle, I guess. Then, I go back to my new hobby—reading about myself, my ex, and my dead stepsister on the internet. I can't seem to bring myself to do much else. On Friday, I tried to talk myself into going to a party Audrey invited me to, but even knowing how much it would bother Ally, I couldn't bring myself to do it. I did get my Xbox hooked back up, created a new username since even that was on the subreddit, and attempted to play a few times over the weekend, but I can't seem to enjoy it. I tried to pick up where I left off in the Wheel of Time series, too but just stared at the pages.

It's only been a few days, though. Surely, it'll come back, and I'll enjoy things the way I used to. I'll stop thinking about Ally and dead bodies, and maybe my dad won't be so sad.

A knock on my door pulls me out of my head. "Devon?" my dad calls. "Do you want to come down and watch the game with me? I ordered Chinese food."

No, I don't. I don't even like football, and he knows that. I want to sit up here in my room and keep doomscrolling.

"Sure," I tell him. "Be right there."

I join him on the first floor of the townhome, in the dark living room with the curtains drawn shut and no light aside from what's coming from the television screen and the fireplace, and sit down on the couch without saying a word. I count four empty beer bottles on the table before I check the time—just before noon.

"You want one?" he asks as he cracks open another.

"Sure," I say.

He hands me a beer, and I stare at a spot on the wall just above the television, still thinking about Ally and wishing I could be there to see the look on her face when she finds it all gone.

17

"I need to talk to you," Devon tells me in art class on Friday morning. "After class. It's important."

I take in his anxious demeanor, the bags under his eyes, the way he taps his foot nervously under the table. He's been this way for a few days now; we've barely talked at all, and it's been eating away at me.

On top of that, Darci has been shutting me out and taking these little digs at me, and I'm not sure where it's coming from. Mark has been home all week, and he and Grace have constantly fought with each other or me every night.

And I've been lying awake at night with my nerves misfiring, waiting for something bad to happen. That's how Devon looks, too.

"Devon, what's going on with you?"

"I'll tell you before lunch," he whispers. "Meet me in the locker room."

"Are you going to break up with me?" I ask. "I'd rather just know right now. I can't sit around for three more hours—"

"Ally, stop," he says. "I'm not going to break up with you. Are you crazy?"

"You seem unhappy."

"I am," he says. "I'm completely fucking miserable, but that has nothing to do with you."

"That doesn't make me feel better," I tell him.

"Relax," he says. "It's going to be fine."

The space between art and lunch passes slowly, and when the bell rings after fourth period, I rush to the locker room, making it inside while the last gym class is still clearing out. I pretend I need something from my track bag, sifting through my things slowly until the last of them leaves.

Ten minutes pass, then fifteen. I pace back and forth, checking my phone every minute, wondering how long I should wait here and if maybe Devon isn't coming at all.

I feel a hand close around my arm, and I scream.

"Hey," Devon says. "Hey, I'm sorry. That's my fault. I snuck up on you. I forgot and—"

"Devon, what the hell is going on?"

"Get your bag out of your locker," he says.

I put in the combination as he starts talking.

"Remember what I told you about the money? That I'd help you?"

"Yeah," I say, removing the padlock. "You said you'd find someone who deserved it—like a *Dexter* version of stealing."

"Okay, well...I did it."

"What?"

He grabs the bag from my locker and then sets it on the floor. He glances over his shoulder before opening his own backpack, pulling out a manila envelope, and stuffing it into the side pocket of my bag.

"There's $3500 in there," he whispers. "Lock it up, then take it home and hide it."

"What?" I ask. "Where did you get this?"

"From Parks," he says. "He deserved it."

"Oh, my god, Devon."

"It's going to be okay, Ally. You don't have to wait until October anymore. You don't have to stay there. I know someone who can make you a fake ID—he's legit, too; it's what he does. I'm going to wire him the money after school, and he can have everything ready in two weeks."

"Are you serious?!" I ask. "I can leave?"

He nods. "I told you I'd take care of you."

He zips up the bag, stuffs it into my locker, and replaces the padlock.

"You're not kidding?!"

"No, I'm not kidding."

I throw my arms around his neck and jump into his arms, wrapping my legs around his waist. I erupt into some weird mix of excited laughter and tears.

"Oh, my god. I can't...I don't know what to say. I really thought you were going to break up with me."

"You're crazy," he tells me. "I do have one condition, though."

"What's that?"

"No Florida," he says. "No getting on a bus and getting as far away from here as possible. You need to stay close—somewhere I can still get to you. We'll find a small town in the mountains where no one knows you or Mark or Grace, and they won't suspect a thing."

"But—do you really think I can hide in Washington forever, and they won't find me? If I'm a minor, the police will look for me."

"You don't have to hide forever," he says. "You just have to hide for a few months—just until you're eighteen. Then, you can send the police a letter, post on social media, or withdraw from school. You can do tattoos, and when I graduate, we can go wherever you want. Fair?"

"I could never leave you anyway," I tell him. "All I ever used to think about was getting away from here, and for so long, it was the only thing that got me through the day. But now, I can't picture myself happy anywhere without you."

"Ally, you have no fucking idea how happy that makes me."

He leans in, and his lips meet mine. I part my lips to let his tongue in, and he runs his hands over the curve of my ass as he deepens the kiss. I moan against his mouth and tighten my legs around his waist, and he carries me across the locker room until my back hits the wall of a shower stall.

I think we each pour all our collective stress, uneasiness, and whatever else we've been feeling on top of the lust that's always there into that kiss. We taste each other, bite each other's lips, and tear at each other's clothes. Devon grinds his cock into me, and it feels so good that I ignore the way my spine grates against the shower wall. I dig my nails into his back, and drag my tongue and my teeth up his neck, causing him to groan and set me back down on the ground.

"Take off your jeans," he says as he starts on his own. "Be quick about it; we don't have a lot of time."

I unbutton mine and let them drop to the ground, then go for my underwear. Before I can step out of them, he has me pinned again. He hooks his right hand under my knee and hitches my leg to the side, easily driving his thick cock into my wet pussy.

"God, I've missed this," he says as he drills into me. "You feel so good."

"Ahhh!" I let out a moan I'd been trying to hold in.

His thrusts become faster, harder, and I don't bother trying to be quiet—not when the sound of his skin against mine when he drills into me would give us away anyway.

And I don't care at all. Not when it feels this good, and I'm so close to coming on his cock.

"Come on, baby," he says, reaching between us and fingering my clit. "I want to feel you squeezing my dick when I fill you up."

I bring my head into his chest and bury my moan into his hoodie, and he fills me up while I come on his cock, just like he said he would.

"Hey," he says breathlessly afterward. "What do you want your name to be?"

"What do you mean?"

"On your ID. What should I tell him to make the name?"

"Oh," I laugh. "I don't know. Something that would be easy for me to answer to, I guess."

"Like what? Alice? Alissa?"

"Or...Devon."

"You're going to change your name to Devon?"

"Maybe...yeah. Just for a few months. Girls can be named Devon."

"Okay," he laughs. "What's your last name, Devon?"

"North."

He shakes his head. "When's your birthday?"

"The day before your birthday," I tell him as I slip back into my jeans.

He smiles and shakes his head. "So, I guess we'll both be eighteen next week."

"I guess so. We can share a cake."

"What kind?"

"Funfetti."

"Really? Not chocolate?"

"My mom always made funfetti." I kiss him on the lips. "I'm going to the bathroom. I'll be right back."

"I better get out of here," he says. "I can't believe you thought I would break up with you."

"You've been acting weird lately," I tell him. "You said you were miserable."

"I'm just tired, Ally. I haven't been sleeping well, either. I'll text you later, okay?"

I nod, and he kisses me again before he leaves. After I use the bathroom, I walk past my locker and think about the amount of money inside. It gives me this anxious, uneasy feeling, and I'm sure that's what Devon has been feeling all week.

This is *way* different from taking a couple hundred bucks in phones and small bills from teenagers. For the rest of the day, all I can think about is getting home and getting my money safely tucked away in the box under my bed.

It's finally going to happen, though. The finish line has been moved closer.

I'm actually getting the fuck out.

"Ally!" Darci calls after me in the parking lot after track practice. "I'm picking you up. I already talked to Grace, and she said I could bring you shopping for prom dresses with me."

Oh…great.

"Um, okay. Cool."

I'm in my sweats and a t-shirt, my hair still wet after showering. We had to run two miles at the end of practice as a team today. My legs feel like jello, and all I can think about is the money that feels like it's burning a hole through my duffle bag. I'd prefer not to go anywhere without ditching it first.

But I don't want to raise any red flags, as things have been weird enough between us already. And, I guess, I'd still rather not go home.

I climb into her Honda and pull the door closed behind me. She reaches for the volume knob and turns up the latest Taylor Swift album.

"Are we picking up Audrey?" I ask.

"No," she says. "It's been a while since we've spent some time alone together. I think we're overdue, don't you?"

"Yeah," I tell her. "Yeah, that sounds good."

Better, typically. But something is...off. Over the last year, I've spent most of my time on high alert. I've become more attuned to people's moods, their movements, and what to expect next. I can feel when eyes settle on me, whether alone or in the middle of a crowd. As a result, I've learned how to make myself invisible, smaller—someone other people don't want to look at or watch.

Darci is watching me now. She's been watching me all week. It's setting off something in my brain.

Maybe it's just me. Maybe it's my nerves getting the best of me because I'm sitting in Darci's car after track practice, and she's never done this before. And I've got $3,500 in cash in my duffle bag and a getaway plan that involves her brother. I think that would be enough to put anyone on edge.

"Where were you at lunch?" she asks. "We were all waiting for you."

"I'm failing math," I tell her. "I was in the library studying." The first part isn't a lie.

"Really? Huh..."

"Are you sure Grace said this was okay?" I ask as we cross the bridge back to mainland Washington. "It doesn't seem like something she would do."

"Yes, I'm sure. Do you want to see the text?" she asks.

I shake my head. "Not really."

"You know, maybe I could work on her about prom, too. I know Trevor really wants to ask you. That'd be fun, right?"

"Yeah, sure," I tell her.

"Well, don't sound so excited about it."

"I just know she's not going to let me go," I tell her.

"Right," she says. "But if you *were* going, you'd go with Trevor, right? There's no one else you'd want to go with? There's nothing else you're not telling me?"

"What do you mean?"

"You've been cagey," she says. "Distracted. Is it a guy?"

"No," I tell her. "I'm just tired. Mark came back this week, and the house has been...it's just uncomfortable."

"They still fight a lot?"

"Yeah."

"So sad," she says, shaking her head. "I don't know why they don't just get a divorce."

"Well, that's a fresh take from you," I say.

"I'm just saying...we were all a lot happier after my parents got divorced. Even though now I have to live with Devon, and you know how disgusting he is," she says as we pull into the parking lot.

"Not really," I say.

"Not really? You don't think he's disgusting?"

"I mean, I don't really know what that's like," I tell her, getting out of the car.

"Well, it's like if your mom married the dad of some...goth reject loser, and then you had to deal with him being loud and repulsive and perving on you and your friends all day. I can't even walk around my own house without a bra on because he's always there staring at my tits and my ass. The way he follows Audrey around when she's there is even worse. And then he even does it to you."

I feel like I'm going to be sick. She's lying, right? But why would she? Maybe he does watch her like that—he probably can't help it, and I shouldn't be having a fucking anxiety attack over it walking into this department store. I'm sure it's not anything like how she tells it.

Or...maybe he is like that with Darci and the other friends she brings to the house, hoping to get laid, and I'm just the easiest target.

What I want to tell her is that I *do* know what it's like to have to be conscious of what you're wearing and what's showing and eyes on your body when you walk around your own house. But I can't do that.

"I'm sorry you have to deal with that," I say instead.

"Why are you bringing that huge bag inside?" she says. "It looks weird. Why don't you just leave it in the car?"

"Um, habit," I tell her. "Something I picked up from living in bad neighborhoods. I never leave anything in the car."

"Oh...well, that makes sense," she says, accepting the answer.

I follow her around the department store while a sales associate helps her grab a few gowns in her size and takes them to the dressing room.

"What do you think of this one?" she asks, modeling a backless pink gown with sequins around the low v in the front.

"It's pretty," I tell her. "I still like the black one the best."

"Of course you do," she says. "It wouldn't kill you to wear some color yourself."

"It might," I joke.

"I like this one," she says. "I like how it makes my boobs look."

"You look good in everything," I say.

"You should try on the black one."

"Oh...I don't need to do that. I mean, I'll never really be able to go."

"Come on," she says. "Do it for me...for your bestie. Don't you want to make me happy?"

I smile. "Fine. But don't tell anyone. And no pictures."

I step inside the dressing room, lock the door, and strip down to my underwear. I turn toward the mirror and choke back a sob.

I don't have a full-length mirror at home. I've never seen it all like this in front of a mirror before, and definitely not under fluorescent lights.

They look worse than I thought—the scars. If my mom ever sees this, she'll be so hurt.

I turn away from the mirror and take several deep breaths to steady myself. The black dress in question is strapless with a fitted bodice that laces up in the back. It has a floor-length tulle skirt with a high slit on one side, but not high enough for any of them to show.

I hold the dress against my chest with my hands and step out into the dressing room.

"Oh my gosh, yes!" Darci says, rushing over to tie up the back before I can even ask her. "This is why I can't get this dress, Ally. It was made for you."

She finishes the tie and ushers me in front of the main mirror. "You look amazing."

It's perfect.

My eyes well up with tears. I do look pretty. Somehow, the dress fits us both like a glove. I think about what it would be like if I could go to prom—if I could buy this dress and spend the day getting my hair and makeup done with my friends, if I could dance with my boyfriend.

But none of that will ever happen.

I shake my head. "I feel stupid. I'm going to take it off."

"Nuh-uh," Darci says, closing her hand around my arm. "Not yet."

"What? Why not?"

"You need to do something for me first," Darci says. "Twirl."

"What?"

"Twirl first, and then I'll let you take it off."

I feign annoyance and twirl once in front of the mirror for her.

"Satisfied?" I ask.

She reaches out for me and runs her hands down my bare arms.

"You really *are* beautiful, Ally. Does anyone ever tell you that? Does anyone ever touch you? You deserve that."

"No," I reply. It comes out as almost a whisper.

"Ally, I have a secret," she says. "I think you do, too. If you tell me yours, then maybe I could tell you mine, and it would have to be okay."

"I don't...I don't have any secrets, Darci," I lie. "Can you untie this, please?"

She sighs, visibly frustrated. She places her hands on my shoulders, turns me around so my back faces her, and then unties the dress as I asked.

"Thanks," I say and rush back into the changing room.

"I'm getting the pink one," she announces when I come back out, her demeanor changed.

"Good," I tell her. "You'll look great."

"Let's go."

It's tense as we walk to the checkout and even more so once we get back into the car. She starts to drive without saying a word or turning the music back on.

"Can we listen to something?" I ask. "I never get to listen to music at home—"

"Devon's mom lives in that shitty neighborhood over there," she says, pointing toward a familiar exit.

"Oh...does she?"

She doesn't say anything.

"Darci, are you okay?"

"Yeah," she says, wiping tears from under her eyes. I've never seen her cry before, and it's uncomfortable now. I'm not much of a hugger; I don't have much experience comforting other people, so I'm not quite sure what to do.

"I love you, Darci," I tell her. "You're my best friend."

"Am I?" she asks.

"Well...yeah. Of course."

"Sorry, I just...I wish I could go to prom with the person I want to go with. But...it'll be great anyway. I'm glad I'm going with Luke. I mean, it sucks that his girlfriend broke up with him, but we'll have fun."

"Yeah..." I say. "Yeah, I'm sure it will be perfect."

Darci scoffs and shakes her head. She looks like she wants to say something else but stays quiet for the rest of the drive. She never turns on any music.

"Do you want to come in?" I ask her when we pull into the driveway.

"No," she says. "I better not. I'll pick you up tomorrow, though. Around four."

"Okay."

"My parents aren't going to be there; they're going to a concert in Everett, so I'm going to have a bunch of people over. Of course, I didn't tell them that, though."

"Yeah, sounds fun."

"Trevor will be there," she says. I want to scream; I wish she'd stop bringing him up. I don't know why she's pushing him on me so hard, especially when we all know she slept with him a couple of months ago. "I think you guys would make a really good couple. I wish you'd give it a chance."

"There's no point," I say. "I'm not allowed to date. I don't think he's my type, anyway."

"Well, what *is* your type?" she asks.

"I don't really know."

She stares at me like she has something to add, and I wait for just a few seconds before turning and reaching for the door handle.

"See you tomorrow, Darci."

"Yeah...see you tomorrow," she says.

I close the car door and head toward the house; the familiar feeling of trepidation runs down my spine as I force myself to turn the knob and step inside.

"Oh, good—you're back in time for dinner," Mark says. "Did you have fun shopping with Darci?"

"Um, yeah," I tell him. "Thanks."

"I thought you might like that," he says. "Grace didn't want to let you go, but...maybe we could loosen the reigns a little if you keep behaving."

"Her grades are still terrible," Grace says. "She should be studying. Wash your hands and come sit down."

I set my bag on the entryway bench and feel my pulse sky-rocket. All I want to do is take it up to my room and get that money into my hiding place, but I can't think of a good reason to go upstairs and don't want to look suspicious. So, I walk toward the sink to wash my hands and try not to look back at the bag I'm convinced will spontaneously burst into flames at any minute.

"Well, I don't disagree with you there," he says. "You do need to get that math grade up—at least get a high school diploma if I'm going to bring you to work with me in Olympia next year."

He starts toward the dining room but stops behind me at the kitchen sink to run his hand down my back and over my ass.

"And you'll have to start smiling more, too," he adds. "Everyone likes a young girl with a pretty smile."

18

The music is insufferable.

The thought enters my mind, and it's so trivial compared to everything else going on right now that I almost laugh out loud.

That's what I *would* be concerned about if it were just another Saturday night at my house and this was just another one of Darci's parties with her equally insufferable friends.

Now, I have a host of new things to worry about. I blackmailed a teacher. I wired money to some dude I only know because we've been gaming online together for two years to make fake IDs for my girlfriend so she can run away from her abusive foster home.

And Darci knows. And Ally is here. So I have to watch her—watch *both* of them—and make sure she doesn't try something or do anything to hurt her.

"This sucks," Seth says, leaning against the kitchen counter next to me. "Every douchebag in there looks like they want to punch me in the face. None of those girls are going to hook up with any of us. Well, except maybe Isaac if he separates himself from you and me. Tell me again why we can't go somewhere else, Devon."

"They probably do want to punch you in the face. They won't, though. And you have a girlfriend, so just...be a good friend. Get drunk," I tell him, gesturing toward the island where they have almost every type of alcohol imaginable on display. "Chill out."

"Fine, whatever," he says.

He grabs a chef's knife from the cutting board and slices a lime before pouring himself a shot of tequila. He licks salt from his hand, then throws back the shot, bites down on the lime, and repeats the process.

Isaac is on the other side of me, brooding.

"What's your problem?" I ask him.

He shakes his head. "Oh, nothing. I've just got this weird feeling that you're about to do something stupid, that's all."

Of the three of us, I'm not the one known for doing stupid things—that would be Seth. Still, if he knew what I've been up to lately, he'd definitely qualify it as *doing something stupid*, so I don't argue.

"You want some?" I ask, holding out my flask for him to take.

"No thanks," he grumbles. "I feel like at least one of us should keep their wits about them."

"Everything is fine," I tell him.

Morgan comes into the kitchen dragging Ally by the sleeve of her sweatshirt. The two of them laugh when Morgan leans over and whispers something in her ear.

I meet her eyes and smile.

"Hello, ladies," Seth says. "What are you two drinking tonight?"

"Not enough to make you appealing," Morgan says. She grabs two cups and fills one with rum and coke, then pours only coke into the other and hands it to Ally. "And Ally doesn't drink."

"Morgan!" someone calls from the next room.

"Coming!" she answers.

She leaves the kitchen quickly, and Ally looks at me before turning to follow her.

"Hey, you," I say. "Come here."

She turns and tries to hide a smile, then walks around the island, stopping in front of me.

I unscrew the cap on my flask, then grab the wrist holding her cup and splash some whiskey into it.

"You be careful, though," I tell her. "You look like a lightweight."

She smiles. "I will."

I rub small circles inside her wrist with my thumb, and neither of us moves.

"Well, *this* is awkward," Seth says. "Let go of her arm, dude."

I drop her wrist, run my hand through my hair, and laugh.

"Sorry about that," I tell her.

"No problem," she says and turns to leave the kitchen.

"Yeah, sorry, Ally!" Seth says to her back as she exits the room. "He's kind of obsessed with you—it's a little bit creepy."

"Dude..." I shake my head.

"Well, what? You are. You might as well make your move...or at least warn the poor girl."

A couple of Darci's friends walk by us in bikinis, then out the back sliding door.

"I'm going out to the pool," Seth declares. "You guys coming?"

"Nah, I'm good."

"I'll go," Isaac tells him.

They pass Darci on their way out the back sliding door, who scoffs, feigning disgust before marching into the kitchen and getting in my face.

"Did I tell you you could invite your loser friends over here?"

"I didn't ask," I tell her.

"Well, get them the fuck out of here!"

"No, I don't think I will," I tell her.

"Well, then maybe I'll tell Mark and Grace about you and Ally, and you'll never see her again. You should be thanking me for even letting her come over here after she betrayed me—"

"Darci, I'm sick of this shit. I did your stupid essay and your book report *and* your chem project like you wanted. But you don't get to tell me what my friends can and can't do at my house."

"That's exactly what I get to do, Devon. I own you."

"No, you don't. I can't do this anymore. And you're not going to do shit about it. I'm going to tell Ally right now."

"No!" she shouts. "No, you're not. And you're going to keep doing whatever the fuck I want because I *will* tell them, and I'll show her the picture. I'll tell her you fucked me, and she *will* believe it. You *know* she will. She's so weak and insecure and—"

I move fast, and before I can think about it, I'm holding her by her hair with one hand and have the chef's knife at her throat with the other. "I think you're the one who doesn't get it. I'm going to keep doing whatever the fuck I want, and *you're* the one who isn't going to do shit about it because if you do, I will *fucking kill you!*"

"Oh, my god!" someone yells. A part of my brain registers that I have an audience, but I don't really care.

"Do you hear me? I will fucking kill you!"

"Someone get him off me!" Darci yells.

"Devon?" Ally says weakly. I turn and see her standing next to us. "Devon, please stop."

I look back to Darci. She looks fucking terrified...just like Ally.

"Devon!" Ally yells. "Stop! You're scaring me!"

I look at Ally again, then over her shoulder toward the small crowd gathered in front of the kitchen. A few of them hold up their phones, recording.

I stab the knife into the cutting board, then let Darci go and storm out of the kitchen. I look over my shoulder and see her fall into Ally's arms, and the rest of those assholes—her *friends* who were just enjoying the show—start to move in on the two of them. I continue up the staircase to my room and slam the door behind me.

Maybe I fucked up just a little. Maybe I overreacted, but it's fine; it'll be fine. Maybe I scared Darci enough that she won't say anything.

I remember the IDs and check my text messages.

James: Got the money. IDs will be ready soon—give me a week, ten days max.

Well, thank fuck for that. I let the phone slide out of my hands and onto the ground, then the door opens, and Ally quickly ducks inside, closing and locking it behind her.

"What the hell happened?" she asks.

"Ally..."

"Why would you do that to her? What's wrong with you?"

"Allyson, come here."

"No! Tell me now!"

"Ally, please...just come here and lie down next to me. Then, I'll tell you."

She hesitates for a minute before she crosses the room, climbs into bed, and lies down beside me. She looks frustrated instead of comfortable, and it's so fucking cute on her I almost laugh.

I reach over and turn off the light, then roll onto my side and pull her into me so her back is against my chest.

"That's better," I say, leaning into her shoulder and smelling her hair. "You know what? You smell like lavender. It makes me sleepy *and* horny now—"

"Devon, *stop*."

"What?"

"Why would you do that to Darci, Devon?"

"I hate Darci," I tell her. "I want to stab her, that's why. Can we just go to sleep? I never get to hold you like this."

"I can't stay in here, Devon. She'll know."

"She already knows," I tell her.

"What?"

"Ivy came over here last weekend. She told her. She didn't mean to...I didn't think about it."

"Oh, my god..."

"It's okay. We're still okay. I mean, she's been making me do all her homework, and I haven't gotten much sleep, but...that'll all be over soon."

"I'll talk to her," she says. "I'll tell her to stop."

"Ally, no—don't. She'll tell your aunt and uncle. She said she would and that she'd make sure I never saw you again if I didn't do what she said."

"She's just mad. She's my friend. I can talk to her, and she'll stop."

"No, she won't. I don't want to hurt you, Ally—I really don't—but Darci won't stop. I don't know why she's latched onto you so tightly, but it's not because she's your friend. She doesn't care about you like you think she does. If she did, she wouldn't do this; she wouldn't want to hurt you. And she does—she wants to hurt you. She told me she wants to torture you."

It's quiet for a minute, and I regret it. "Ally?"

"Okay," she chokes out.

"Are you?"

Ally nods.

"She was threatening to hurt you. I know I shouldn't have done it, but that's why I did it. I'm so sorry, Ally."

"It's okay," she sniffles.

"I love you so much."

"I love you, too," she says.

If she's trying to hide that she's crying now, she's doing a bad job of it. I wrap my arms around her a little tighter, kiss her shoulder, and bury my head in her lavender hair.

"I promise I'm not going to let anything happen to you again. We're going to get through this. I'm still getting you out of here, Ally."

I hold her there like that until, eventually, we both fall asleep.

"Shit," I hear Ally say before she jumps out of bed.

"What? What's wrong?"

"It's morning," she says. "I shouldn't be in here—your parents are home."

"It's okay. It's early. They're probably still asleep. I'm sure they didn't even come up here last night. Why would they?"

She doesn't acknowledge me and bolts out the bedroom door. I drag myself out of bed and follow her. From the landing, it looks like the evidence of the party has been destroyed. It's messy, but there are no empty cups or bottles of beer or alcohol lying around, and the kitchen has been cleaned. At least Darci was of sound enough mind to do that. The knife I pulled on her still stands straight up, wedged into the cutting board.

"Allyson?"

"She's not even here," Ally says from Darci's bedroom.

"Huh. Weird. She was probably just pissed and went to Audrey's or something."

"Well, that's going to look bad."

I shrug. "There's nothing we can do about that now. We'll be okay."

The look on her face tells me that she isn't so sure. I reach for her and pull her against my chest.

"Hey," I say. "You're still my girl, right? I'm going to take care of you. Don't worry about it."

She sighs. "Okay."

"What do you want to do? Are you hungry?"

"Yeah," she says. "Devon, will you text her?"

"I don't think she's going to want to talk to me, but sure. If that's what you want."

I go to my room, grab my phone, and text Darci, asking where she is. I have one of those inward struggles with myself not to say the shitty thing—like how the fuck could you just leave Ally here, what the hell were you thinking, and why do you suck so bad in every way possible?

"She's not down here anywhere, either," Ally says when I come downstairs.

"Well, she's an asshole." I cross the room to the front door, open it, and look out at the driveway. "Her car is still here. I'm going to make some coffee. Just...try to relax. Turn on the TV or something."

I go to the kitchen and start a pot of coffee, then backtrack to the living room to ask Ally if she wants eggs or pancakes since that's about the extent of my cooking abilities.

She's sitting on the couch, locked in a battle of wits with the TV, her brow furrowed in frustration. I cover her hand with mine and take the remote from her, then lean down and kiss her on the lips.

"This is the remote for the sound system. It will never, ever change the channel."

She pouts. "Help me?"

"I'll help you, but it's gonna cost you," I tell her.

I pull her down flat on the couch and move on top of her, tasting her mouth before moving to her earlobes because I know it drives her crazy.

"Well, it just so happens that I've recently come into some money."

"I don't want your money; I want something else."

I dip my hand down into her leggings, and she arches her back and opens her hips to give me easier access.

"You want to go back upstairs for a few minutes?" I ask.

I hear a bedroom door open nearby and practically jump off the couch just before my dad and Lydia walk into the room.

"Uh, here's the remote," I say quickly, handing the right one to my very flustered girlfriend. "Just hit the guide button there."

"You're up early, and you made coffee. What a nice surprise," Lydia says as she enters the room.

"Uh, yeah."

She fills a cup and then sits on a barstool.

"Are you going to join us for church, too?"

I grab two more cups, filling one for me and then for Ally before I answer. "No, I just woke up hungry. I was going to make something—unless you guys were planning on cooking."

"I was going to fry up that bacon and some eggs," my dad says. "Darci up yet?"

"Darci's not here," I tell them.

"What?" her mom asks. "Well, then, where is she?"

"I don't know. She was here when I went to bed, but Ally said she was gone when she woke up, and she hasn't seen her. I texted her, but wherever she is, she's probably asleep. Audrey and Morgan were over here, so I'm sure she probably left with one of them."

"Well, why would she leave Ally here alone? She shouldn't have done that," Lydia says, shaking her head. "I'll go get my phone—see if she has sent a text or anything. Then, I guess I'll start calling the girls' moms."

"This your fault?" my dad asks when she leaves the room. "Did she leave because you two got into it over that girl?"

"No...I don't think so."

He shakes his head.

"It wasn't because of me," I say, but my eyes dart to the knife, and I'm not so sure. "I'm going to take this to Allyson."

I walk back into the living room, hand Ally her coffee, and sit down on the chair next to her.

"Thank you."

She smiles at me, then takes a drink. I look over at the TV and see she's settled on one of those HGTV shows—in this one, they're looking for bargain cabins.

"We're going to find you a place like that," I tell her quietly. "A place in the woods where no one will be able to find you except for me. And then I'm going to fuck you in every single room, and we're going to be as loud as we want. And you'll just be naked—all the time."

She laughs. "Okay."

"I'm one hundred percent serious. No clothes ever, Ally."

"I want a dog, too," she says. "I've never had a pet. I think I would feel better being out there alone if I had a dog."

"I'll get you a dog. I'll get you seventeen dogs if that's what you want."

"That seems a little excessive," she says, laughing again quietly. "And irresponsible. I should probably just start with one and go from there."

"Well, that's weird," Lydia says, making her way back over to the kitchen. "Both Morgan and Audrey haven't seen her since last night, and Darci's phone is going straight to voicemail. I'm starting to get worried; what do you think we should do, Jeff?"

My dad groans and walks toward us.

"You two—what the hell happened here last night? Where's your sister?"

"Dad, we really don't know where she is."

"I'm about ten minutes away from calling the police, so if you *do* know something, now is the time to speak up."

"I'm sure she's fine; she's just a shitty friend. But go ahead and call them if that will make you feel better."

"Well, when did you last see her?"

"Um, I saw her last," Ally says. "It was a little after midnight. But there were still other people here when I went to sleep."

"Other people? How many people?"

Ally looks over at me, wondering if she should tell the truth because it might help Darci or lie so that she doesn't get both of us in trouble for throwing a party.

"A lot," I answer. "Twenty? Twenty-five?"

He sighs and heads back into the kitchen; Lydia starts rattling off names of other people they could call.

"Devon, I'm scared," Ally says. "What if she's not okay? What if she got in the car with someone who was drunk and got hurt, and it's our fault?"

I don't want to admit it, but I'm starting to get nervous, too. Fear is contagious—I can feel it in the air coming off of my dad and stepmom and from Ally, too. The hair on my neck starts to stand up.

"She's going to be fine, Ally. They'll find her."

She doesn't look convinced.

"Hey...it's not your fault, okay?"

"I love you, Devon," she whispers.

"Okay, you know what, Lyd? You go ahead and start calling the kid's parents since you know them a lot better than I do. I'm going to call the hospital, and then I'm calling the police."

He opens the back sliding door and steps outside. Then, he wails.

"Oh, god no!" he yells before I hear a splash.

We run for the back door, and when I step outside, I see my dad trying to drag Darci's bloody, lifeless body from the pool.

Ally screams and sinks to the ground, and I run to the other side of the pool to try to help my dad. By the time I reach the staircase, he's cradling her against his chest, rocking her back and forth, weeping, and it's obvious by the tone of her skin that whatever happened to Darci happened hours ago.

"No!" he screams over and over. "Not my baby, god, why?!"

"Oh, god!" Lydia screams as she runs to his side. "HELP! Someone help! Help her! Jeff, do something!"

I see Lydia fall to the ground next to my dad, and she begins to stroke Darci's hair away from her face, begging her to wake up. Tunnel vision starts to set in, and suddenly, I'm unsteady on my feet, too. I double over and vomit into the pool, and everything else happens in slow motion.

Neighbors run over from all sides. Someone calls 911, and the police and an ambulance arrive; they have to pry Lydia from Darci's dead body, and she howls in the front yard when they take her away.

And after that, none of us are ever whole or the same again.

19

Sleep must have come for me at some point last night because my alarm wakes me up now. It's still dark, which is typical for this time of year and usually makes it difficult for me to get up and move, but as soon as my eyes open, I remember what day it is, and my heart drops into my stomach. A surge of adrenaline pulls me out of bed, my hands already shaking in anticipation.

It's been exactly one year since I made this plan. I'd felt so utterly hopeless at the time, and having something to look forward to—a set date, a starting point for the life I wanted, an end to this nightmare—was just about all that kept me going. My box of secrets, my great escape.

"Happy birthday, Ally," I say aloud to the girl in the mirror. I feel kind of stupid for doing it, but no one else is going to, and for some reason, it still feels good to hear it.

I dress for school like everything is normal, grab my bag, and head downstairs. I don't even bother to stop in the kitchen or say a word to Grace.

Once outside, I walk past the bus stop and a few blocks over to a small, rocky beach at the edge of the neighborhood. I watch the time on my phone, waiting for her to be gone and wanting so badly to say something to him. But I can't, and I can't do this today. I can let regret crush me tomorrow, but I have to leave today. It's the nicest thing I could do for Devon, anyway.

I wait until 8:50 AM to start walking back to the house. After climbing through the window, I head straight up to my room to pack. I couldn't risk her finding the bag before, but I'd set it all aside in a drawer—all the things I decided I'd need. I place them inside the bag quickly, then crawl underneath the bed, remove the loose board, and reach inside.

And I feel...nothing.

The room starts to spin. Suddenly, it's a thousand fucking degrees, and I feel like I'm in a literal instead of just a figurative hell. It must have shifted, right? That's what happened. I reach to the right but find nothing. I feel around the other side, and there's something...damp? Spongey?

Against my better judgment, I grasp the wet thing, pull it out, and...

It's a cupcake.

A mother fucking cupcake.

Covered in ants.

I scramble out from under the bed and toss it onto the floor, frantically trying to get them off my arms. I scream and cry, and then I scream some more. I let my body sink to the floor and wail like I'm in pain—like I've had my guts ripped out because it feels like I have.

Devon.

You didn't.

How could you?

I punch the floor and tear at my hair and sob until my voice goes hoarse, and I have nothing left anymore.

And then I lie there, face down in my own snot. I look at the mashed-up funfetti cupcake on the floor and the pink icing on the wall, and my stomach growls.

I pick up the piece closest to me, turn it over in my hands, and once I convince myself not to eat it, I cry again.

Then, I go down to the kitchen and open the fridge. I pull out a gallon of milk and chug it straight from the carton for a good minute before replacing it. I take a block of sharp cheddar cheese from the drawer, open it, take two huge bites from it, and then toss it haphazardly back onto the shelf. I dig around for something else and find two giant ribeye steaks.

I take them out, hurl them onto the counter, and then pull a pan from the cabinet below. I toss it on the stove, turn on the burner, and melt butter in the pan.

Because it's my mother fucking birthday. And now I have nothing to look forward to except this goddamn steak.

I laugh hard at that realization, then decide I need music. I ask Alexa to play Everclear because that's what my mom would be listening to if she were the one in the kitchen cooking for me on my birthday. I toss the steak in the sizzling pan, and my eyes settle on Grace's wine rack.

"Don't mind if I fucking do," I say aloud.

So, I pour the wine and cook my steak, and I drink and I cook and then I drink some more. I finish off the steak and make another one. I polish off a bottle and open a fresh one.

I lie on the sofa, put *Teen Mom* on the television, and cover myself with a blanket. I think of Darci and how she'd watch this every night before bed and how, even though I was only over there once or twice a month, it always seemed to be the same three or four episodes that were on TV. I miss that house. I miss Darci's white down comforter and the smell of their fabric softener. I miss Devon's eyes on me and cedar and sandalwood.

I miss swimming.

My eyes flutter closed, and the wine bottle slips from my hand and spills all over the carpet.

And I laugh. And I stay there. And I don't really care what happens next.

I wake up to hands in my hair, and not in a good way.

Grace pulls me from the couch, and I crack my head on the coffee table on my way down to the floor.

"What do you think you're doing?" she snarls. "You think this is *your* house, and you can just do whatever the hell you want?"

I force myself up onto my knees, head pounding from the wine.

"You forgot to say happy birthday," I say right before her fist connects with the side of my face.

My head whips to the side, saliva and blood dripping from my mouth. I wipe it away with my forearm and turn back to face her.

"I don't care what you do to me anymore," I tell her. "I don't care what happens to me. And that's *your* fault. This is all your fault because you let it happen." I attempt to pull myself to my feet. "You're fucking pathetic—look at you. Everyone acts like you're some kind of saint. You're a *monster*."

She hits me again, and I lose my balance, just barely managing not to fall again.

"You stand next to him on stage—on TV and in front of everyone when you know what he's doing."

"Shut up!" she yells. "Shut up, you disgusting little—"

Her hand shoots out and digs into my hair again, pulling my face into hers, her breath hot against my cheek.

"Just kill me!" I scream. "Do it! Get it over with!"

We stay locked like that for a while, and I wait. I see the wheels turning in her head and wonder if maybe she will kill me this time. Maybe she's wondering if she could and if she'd get away with it, or maybe she's trying to figure out what she would do with my body afterward.

It occurs to me that she probably has no fucking clue what to do with me now. And then, I laugh.

Rage flashes in her eyes as she drags me by my hair through the living room and over to the staircase. I try and fail to wriggle free, and between that, the force pulling me up the staircase, and my unsteady equilibrium, I lose my balance fairly quickly. She drags me the rest of the way up the steps, each one painfully grating against my spine until we finally reach the landing.

She pulls me down the hall and into my room and leaves me there, slamming the door hard enough behind her that, not having any latch, it just springs back open.

I hear her scream, something excruciating, before she starts to sob, too.

Eventually, she slams her own bedroom door. I don't leave my room the rest of the day, so I don't know if she ever leaves hers, either.

I stay there on the floor for a long time, falling in and out of a hangover-induced sleep, staring at the space underneath my bed and through it to the other side where the remnants of the infested cupcake lay on the floor. At some point, I wake up and vomit on the hardwoods. All my heavy body and spinning head can manage to do is turn and face the other way and go back to sleep.

When it starts to get dark, I finally peel myself off the floor. I grab a dirty towel from my laundry basket and clean up the semi-dried puke, gagging again at the smell. Afterward, I creep down the hallway and into the bathroom.

I turn on the shower, letting the hot water run down my aching body. Then, I drop down to the bottom of the tub, dig the razor blade from my bar of soap, and examine the tattered canvas of my body, trying to find the right place to add to my collection. I settle on a spot just above my hip, right where the soft flesh of my stomach begins. I dig in the tip and drag it horizontally across my skin three times, just enough to let it out and leave a mark.

I watch the blood run down my hip, turning pink as it spirals down the drain, and stay there until the water goes cold and finally runs clear.

Then, I crawl into bed, defeated.

When my alarm wakes me the next morning, I'm not quite sure what to do. Do I go to school? Do I...stay in my room? Do I try to make a run for it with no money and nowhere to go? I could take a bus to Seattle and stay there for a while—sleep in the streets and hope that no one recognizes my face.

But the nights are getting colder. And I wouldn't be safe there, either.

In the end, I get ready for school. I pull on a pair of loose-fitting jeans, a black t-shirt, and my Vans. I dig the makeup Laurel gave me last year from my bag and start applying black eyeshadow to my lids, then mascara to my lashes, and the cherry red color to my lips. I run a brush through my thick, dark hair, which aches at the roots, and examine the bluish-green bruise on my jaw. She's never left a mark on my face like this before. I wriggle my jaw left and then right, wincing at the pain.

Then, I go downstairs. When I pass Grace in the kitchen, something flashes in her eyes as she takes me in—the makeup I'm not supposed to wear, the mark on my face, maybe the fucking audacity. I go straight for the freezer and take out a breakfast burrito, then toss it in the microwave, set the timer, and wait. She doesn't try to stop me.

I see a half-empty bottle of whiskey on the table and stuff it inside my bag. She doesn't look up, not even when she speaks.

"If I wanted to kill you, you'd be dead already, you know," she says. "I could sneak into your room at night; do it while you sleep."

"Trust me, I'm fully aware I'm not safe in my room at night here."

Her posture stiffens, but she still doesn't look up from the newspaper. The microwave dings, and I take my burrito with me out the door and to the bus stop. It hurts when I chew.

Other than that, I feel nothing.

20

Ally never did show up at school on Monday. I worried that maybe she left anyway and I wouldn't get to see the look on her face, but there she is, just across the hall, rifling through her locker. I look around Audrey, who hangs on my arm going on about Halloween parties and costumes and shit I'm not really listening to and don't give a fuck about, and watch her. She leans against the open locker door, looking sick. I close my own, throw my arm around Audrey's shoulders, and start walking in that direction, bringing her along with me. She doesn't even stop talking to take a breath.

"But then, I heard Sofia say she was going as a pirate, and obviously, I don't want to show up dressed like her. She probably heard me say it first..."

"Hey, Ally," I say when we get to her. "How was your birthday?"

She puts her bag inside the locker and slams it shut, the force drawing the eyes of the people around us.

I smirk as she turns to us...until I see the huge bruise on the side of her face.

"It was super great," she deadpans.

"Oh, look, she decided to try makeup for the first time," Audrey says. "And it *looks* like the first time. You look like a raccoon. Here's a hint: less is more."

She doesn't react, keeping her eyes trained on me.

"How could you?"

"I think it looks good, Ally," Trevor says, coming up behind me. "Fuck them—both of them. Let's go to P.E."

She stuffs her hands in her pockets, and they walk around us, disappearing together down the hall.

Something about that was so much less satisfying than I expected, and it pisses me off.

"God, did you see her?" Audrey asks. "She has to be the only person on the planet who actually looks *worse* with makeup."

"Fuck off, Audrey."

"What?"

"I don't want to hear one more fucking word from your mouth about Ally."

"But you—"

I turn into the art room, leaving her there alone. I sigh as I make my way down the aisle to my seat—the one behind where Ally *should* be sitting right now—and get back to work on my project for the art fair.

I thought I was just about finished, but I got new inspiration this morning. I darken the eyelids, make the lashes look thick and matted, and add a dark bruise to the side of the face.

At lunch, I sit with Isaac and Seth and watch Ally sit alone in a corner and eat, then leave the cafeteria. When I can't take it anymore, I leave them at the table and start looking for her. I check the gym first, surprised to find it empty, then the bathrooms, scanning the halls as I go. I stop when I hear her voice coming from Mr. Parks' classroom.

"Yeah, I'm eighteen now," she says, "and so I wanted to start looking for a job, something easy. My aunt and uncle don't want me working, but I could really use the money, you know? I want to save up to buy a car. You said you lived downtown, right? Do you know of anywhere down there that's hiring?"

"You're eighteen, huh?" he asks.

"Yeah, my birthday was yesterday."

"Hmm, well. There is something you could do to help me out if you're interested. It'd be easy money; we'd just have to keep it between ourselves because of who your uncle is, and you know...since you're a student."

"Yeah, that sounds great," she says. "What is it?"

"You may not know this, but I'm actually an amateur photographer."

"Oh, that's so cool."

"Yeah, and you look...very photogenic. If you could come by my place sometime this weekend, I'd love to take some pictures of you. There's a big window in the back bedroom that lets in a lot of light and um...I think you'd be perfect for it." He rips a small square of paper from the corner of his calendar, writes something down, and hands it to her. "You just give me a call when you can get away."

"How much?" she asks.

"Two hundred," he says.

"Fine," she tells him. She stuffs the paper in her pocket and leaves the room.

"What the hell do you think you're doing?" I ask as she rushes past me.

"That's none of your fucking business!"

"You're feeding yourself to him," I say. "Why would you do something like that?"

"I'm out of options," she says. "You said you don't give a shit what happens to me. Guess what? I don't care what happens to me anymore, either. You did that. So, thank you. It's freeing in a way. And you know what else?"

I have a feeling I don't want to know, but I don't stop her, so she keeps going.

"Maybe now, I can finally hate you. Everything that happens to me now can be because *you* let it happen—because you *wanted* it to happen. If I hate you, then maybe I'll finally be able to move on."

She opens her locker, pulls a bottle of whiskey from her backpack, and takes a long, hard pull from the bottle.

Holy shit. She really has lost it.

"No," I growl, grabbing her by the arm and backing her into the doorway of an empty classroom. "You don't get it, Ally. You don't get to just leave."

"God, Devon, would you stop?" She laughs, and it makes me want to break her in half. "I get it, I really do. I ruined you, and that's my fault. But I don't have whatever it is you think I have—whatever you think you're going to get out of me if you keep doing whatever the fuck it is you're doing."

"Stop fucking lying!" I shout.

"I'm not lying!" she yells back. "Give me my money back, Devon! Please. Please give me my money back."

"It's not your fucking money, Ally."

"I hate you," she hisses. "I wish we never met."

She puts both hands on my chest and pushes me hard. I stumble just a little bit before she spits in my face, and I'm back on her. I pull the knife from my pocket, flip it open, and hold it at the base of her throat.

"The feeling is fucking mutual," I tell her. "And you're going to pay for it."

"Oh, yeah? And how exactly are you going to do that? Another haircut? Are you going to parade Audrey around the school some more? Please," she scoffs. She wraps her hand around my wrist that holds the knife. "You're going to threaten me with the only thing that's brought me any kind of relief over the past few months? Huh? Make sure it leaves a mark, Devon, or it doesn't count."

She leans forward until the knife digs into her skin, causing blood to run down her throat and pool at the collar of her black t-shirt. "That's better. There's nothing else you can do to me, Devon. I have nothing left. The sooner you figure that out, the sooner we can both move on."

Shocked, I lower the knife. "You're lying."

She reaches out and places her hands on either side of my face. "You know I'm not. You *know* me."

I shake my head. "I don't."

"You've *seen* me."

She lifts onto her toes, and her lips barely brush against mine. The scent of whiskey on her breath assaults my nostrils.

"Stop," I tell her.

"I'm not doing anything." She fists my shirt and buries her head in my neck. "I just want to smell you," she says, breathing me in. "You smell so good. I dream about it sometimes, you know? Your scent, your hands on me."

"You're insane," I tell her, shaking my head. "And you're drunk."

I shrug her off me and feel something warm and wet against my skin. I look down at my gray t-shirt and see a deep, red blood stain on the front.

"Oops," she says. "Sorry about that."

But something about that blood stain does something to me. I push her up against the wall and cover her mouth with mine, kissing her hard enough that our teeth knock together. Her tongue dips into my mouth as she kisses me back just as desperately, teasing my lips with her teeth.

I reach my hands down and lift her up by her ass, and she wraps her legs around my waist. I carry her like that into the classroom and kick the door closed, then I bring her over to the teacher's desk and set her down on its edge, kissing her mouth, sucking on her neck while I grind my hard cock into her pussy.

"Devon, fuck me," she pleads, going for the button on my pants.

"Fuck," I groan. "You let anyone else do this to you while I was gone?"

"No," she moans. "No one. *Never.*"

"If I find out you're lying, I'm going to beat your ass raw," I say as her hand dips below my waistband. My dick jumps when she wraps her hand around it and strokes the length of me.

"Fuck, that feels good," I tell her. "Touch yourself. Get your fingers wet."

I pump my dick in my hand while she opens her jeans and reaches inside of her underwear. I see it in her eyes when her fingers dip inside her. She rolls her hips while she moves them in and out, watching me watch her, and a tiny moan escapes her lips.

"Do you want to come?" I ask.

She nods.

"Don't. Not yet."

She looks pained when she stops herself, but she does it anyway and wraps her wet fingers around my dick, running them over the tip and mixing my precum with her own. I'm just about to put her on her knees when the bell rings, and it's like an alarm goes off in my head, and I remember what I'm doing and who I'm doing it with.

I take a couple of steps back and shove my dick back into my jeans.

"You almost fucking got me," I say, shaking my head. "Fuck."

"Devon!" she calls after me when I flee the fucking scene as if the entire goddamn room is on fire.

I turn into the bathroom and quickly into a stall, locking the door behind me. I spit in my hand, then take my painfully hard cock out again and start to stroke it, not caring that other people in the bathroom might hear me. I grunt while I pump my dick into my fist, picturing Ally on her knees with her pink tongue out and tears clinging to her eyelashes.

She was a liar, but she was always such a good little slut for me, and she was ready to let me do whatever I wanted to her in that classroom. I could have beat her ass raw like I said and then fucked it, and she would have enjoyed every minute of it.

I think of her little red ass bent over the desk while I fuck my fist until white hot cum shoots out into the toilet and all over my hand.

I clean myself up, then stay there for a while, catching my breath and trying to get a handle on what the hell just happened, trying to figure out how the fuck I let her get in my head. Old habits—that's what it was. The version of the girl I thought I knew is still somewhat fresh in my mind, and seeing her in pain affected me. And she *was* in pain, not because of the cut or even the bruise on her face.

I'm not lying. You know me. You've seen me.

I start to wonder if I have fucking lost it because she sure as hell isn't living up to the evil genius who lives in my head. I thought I wanted to kill Ally, but from the looks of it, Ally's been dead for a while, and I don't feel any better.

By the time I leave the restroom, the previous class period has let out, and the hallway is full again. I have to pass Ally's locker on the way to mine, and she's there, laughing with Morgan, Luke, and Trevor.

"No fucking way," I hear Morgan say. "Ally Hargrove, why do I feel like I'm just meeting you for the first time?"

Ally laughs, and Morgan discreetly takes a swig from the bottle of whiskey in her locker, then Trevor does the same.

"I'm enjoying this new side of you," Trevor says.

"So am I," Morgan adds. "Ally! You should come to Luke's party this weekend. I'll pick you up. I can even bring one of my old costumes for you to wear."

"Yeah, I'll go," she says.

"Really?"

"Yeah, fuck it. I can do whatever I want now."

"Thank you, god! Finally!" Trevor says.

I scoff, accidentally locking eyes with her when I do, then shake my head and turn back toward my locker. I grab my books and head down the hallway to history, finding a seat in the back and slipping into my new normal—the one where everyone is always looking at me either because they're scared of me or because they think it's cool that I went to jail for murder.

I prefer the former. I need to bring back the satanic book covers.

I don't notice Ally at her locker for the rest of the day, and I hate that I even look for her, but I can't help it. I wonder if she's getting drunk under the bleachers with someone else...or in a classroom begging them to fuck her. Maybe she's even with Parks.

I get my answer when Morgan walks into physics with Luke seventh period, and they're both huddled over her phone laughing.

"Dude, she's completely wasted," Morgan says. "I don't even think she can get up off the bathroom floor. There's no way she's going to be okay for volleyball practice tonight. Her aunt is going to be pissed."

"Oh, my god," Luke says. "That's hilarious."

"Right? I don't know what happened to her, but she is spiraling, and I'm kind of here for it. Oh, and did you see her back? It's covered in bruises, and she says she has no idea where they came from."

Luke laughs again.

"So you just left her there, then, Morgan? Am I hearing this right?"

She rolls her eyes. "No one was talking to you, Devon. Mind your own business."

"You're an awesome friend. Good job," I tell her. "I bet you feel great about yourself."

"Who are you to judge anyone's character?" she scoffs.

Normally, I'd argue, but at this point, I'm not sure I can.

I manage to stay in the classroom for maybe about two more minutes until, once again, I can't resist the urge to go and find her.

It isn't hard. I duck into the tiny bathroom across from the gym—the one that's almost always empty because there aren't any lockers in this hall—and see someone crumpled on the floor of the furthest stall. I push the door open and find her slumped against the bathroom wall with her eyes closed. I shake my head and sigh.

"What do you want?" she asks. "Do you believe me now? That there's nothing you can do to me?"

She gestures at the scene she's set.

I lower myself onto the floor next to her and run a finger over her bruised cheek. "What happened to your pretty face, Ally?"

"Part of my birthday beating."

"Hold out your hand," I tell her, opening my bag.

She does what I ask, and I place two small brown pills in her palm.

"Take these," I tell her, then hand her a Powerade and a chicken salad sandwich from the lunch room. "With these."

She pops the pills in her mouth, then washes them down with the Powerade.

"You're not even going to ask if those were poisoned?"

"I told you," she says. "I don't care."

"I don't either, so don't read this wrong. I'm not doing this because I care about you; I'm doing it because no one else does."

"Devon, please, can I have my money back?"

"No," I tell her. "Just...eat. And get off the damn floor. At least *pretend* like you're better than this."

I leave the bathroom, then go to her locker, put in the combination, and take the whiskey bottle from her bag. I've never heard of the brand, but it looks expensive, and there's still a decent amount left.

I do myself a favor and toss it into my bag before returning to class.

When I get home that night, I finish the bottle's contents and go for my daily dose of doomscrolling, but I can't stop thinking about what happened to Ally and what might be happening to her now. I take the pictures out of the envelope under my bed—the ones of baby Ally and the teenage Ally who doesn't have any scars—and I can't stop staring at them. I can't stop looking at the one of her smiling on the beach in a bathing suit.

I bet that version of Ally would have done better.

That's why I end up looking up Adam Hargrove instead. He's made himself a little harder to find since Reddit found him. Still, it isn't that difficult—not for someone who's determined.

I'm drunk enough that I have to close one eye to do it, but I manage to send that massive piece of garbage a scathing email letting him know exactly what the fuck I think about him before I go to bed.

And resign to take out some more trash in the morning.

21

There are police cars in the parking lot when I get off the bus.

The flashing red and blue lights set something off inside me—at a cellular level. I feel it rolling through me, and suddenly, in my head, I'm on my knees on the cold concrete near the deep end of the pool, watching Devon's dad pull Darci's body from the water.

I barely make it through the parking lot, moving like cinder blocks are attached to my legs. Once I reach the sidewalk, I stop moving forward and stay there frozen, just trying to keep myself from dropping to the ground.

What if they're here about Darci? Maybe they found out who killed her, and it's another student. Or maybe they didn't, and they're here to arrest Devon again.

"Ally?" a voice next to me calls. "Ally, let's go."

A hand closes around my arm, and I react, shoving the person off me and screaming.

"Hey! What the hell is wrong with you?" Morgan shouts as she stumbles backward.

"I'm sorry!" I say. "I'm so sorry. Are you okay?"

"Yeah, are you?"

"What's happening?" I ask her. "Why are the police here?"

"I don't know. Do you think it has something to do with Darci?"

I shrug.

"Let's go," she says. Morgan places her hand on my arm again, and this time, I let her guide me inside the building.

Upon entering, I find the walls covered in photocopied papers. Students linger in the hallway with cell phones out, trying to get pictures and videos of it all while a couple of teachers move up and down the hall, yelling at them to put their phones away while ripping the papers from the walls.

"What the hell is going on here?" Morgan asks.

I narrow my eyes and push my way through the crowd to try to get a better look. Transcripts of text messages and emails cover the walls.

"I guess all that stuff they say about Parks is true," Trevor says, walking up behind me.

The collective volume lowers, and I turn to see police marching Mr. Parks down the hall and out the side doors.

"Sorry, Ally," Devon says from beside me. "I guess you'll have to get a real job."

I turn to face him but say nothing.

"See you later," he says, then walks away.

"Oh, my god," Morgan says. "Do you think they'll send us all home? This seems like something we should all go home for."

I'm about to agree, but then a voice comes over the intercom and proves us both wrong.

"Attention, students," the voice says. "You have one minute to clear the hallways and report to your first period class. Anyone still in the hallway will spend the evening in detention."

"Fuck that," Trevor says. "Let's go."

"Oh, I brought a couple of costumes for you to wear to the party this weekend," Morgan shouts after me as she speed-walks in the other direction. "I'll bring them to you at lunch!"

"At lunch?" I ask. I've been avoiding our table and the cafeteria in general as much as possible after my fight with Audrey, not wanting to see her or Devon. We have math class together, and usually, we sit together, but after that day at lunch, she moved to the other side of the room—and made a huge scene about it, too. "But—"

"Don't worry about Audrey," she says. "She hasn't been sitting with us anyway. I'm going to tell you the same thing I told her, though."

"What's that?" I ask.

"Apologize and get over it. I already lost one best friend, and you're both making it so much worse."

I know on some level that she's right. I also know that if anyone is going to apologize, that burden will fall on me, but that doesn't mean I'll do it.

"That was awesome," Trevor laughs as we make our way toward the gym. "I wonder who's going to be teaching class today. Not Parks, obviously."

"Yeah, obviously not," I reply. I wonder if I should feel bad about that, too.

It turned out the principal was the one who taught gym class, and Morgan was right that I didn't have to worry about Audrey. She split her lunch hour between sitting with the other cheerleaders and on Devon's lap. I tried on the costumes she brought for me after school and settled on a black cat costume that at least had a leather skirt long enough to cover the tops of my legs.

I stuff it into my locker, then prepare for our first volleyball game since the memorial. I head onto the court to warm up with my team until the buzzer sounds for the match to begin. I take my place on the sidelines while they introduce the players, then step into the outside hitter position alongside Morgan.

The other team serves first, and the ball goes deep into the back row. It's bumped up to Morgan, who sets me up for an easy point.

"Miss it, slut!" someone yells from the crowd before I hit the ball. It catches me off guard enough that I barely make contact with the outside of my hand, and the ball sails far too slowly over the net and is recovered easily by the other team.

I glare over my shoulder and see Audrey laughing on the sidelines, hanging all over Devon.

"Ally Hargrove is a whore!" she yells.

I grit my teeth. Fuck saying sorry. I'm going to fucking kill them both.

The next two times, I'm ready. Maybe I overstep a little, taking a hit that should have been my teammates, but I drill the ball straight into the ground on the next two plays and step in to serve with our team in the lead.

"Come on, Ally! Do what you do best! Choke!" Audrey yells as I step back from the line.

"Are you going to do anything about this!?" I yell at Coach Davis.

She shakes her head but walks over and says something to Audrey that I don't hear, who only laughs. When she steps away, she grabs Devon by his shirt, pulls him into her, and kisses him on the mouth.

And I see red. And nothing else.

I spike the ball hard, but not toward the net, hitting her right in the face, and the next thing I know, I'm in the stands, swinging at her. Coach's arms circle around my waist and attempt to pull me back while I fight against her, desperately trying to claw at any part of Audrey I can get to.

"Get out!" Coach yells. "Get out of here, Ally. Go home. You're done."

"But she—"

"Look at her!" she says. "Look what you did to her face. Look at your team! You're *done,* Ally. Hit the showers and turn in your jersey."

Turn in my jersey? *No.*

No, I can't.

"Please don't kick me off the team," I beg. "This is...it's all I have."

"You should have thought about that before you attacked another student in the middle of a match!" she says. "Don't embarrass your team more than you already have. Go now and go quietly."

I look out at the court and see them all staring at me—the other team, too. I see the silent plea in Morgan's eyes for me to just go before I make it any worse, so I do. I pick up my bag and try to hold my head up, not letting the tears fall as I cross the gym to the locker room.

I strip down, cover myself with my towel, and head to the showers. I close the curtain behind me, turn on the water, and wait until it's hot against my hand and steam billows off the cold tile floor before draping my towel over the shower wall and stepping under the stream. Once I do, I let myself cry.

I was wrong when I told Devon I had nothing left to lose—I had one more thing.

I let myself sob under the water long after it goes cold—letting it run down my face, wondering what the hell I'm going to do now and how I'm supposed to crawl out of the grave I've dug for myself.

I don't think I can do this anymore.

I open my eyes, confused, when I realize the water has shut off and turn to find Devon standing in the small space next to me.

I scramble to grab my towel from the wall and wrap it around my body, clutching it to my chest and doing my best to cover myself.

"Looks like that water was cold," he says.

"Get out, Devon! Now!"

"No, I don't think I will," he says, closing the space between us. He runs a finger down my left cheek. "I didn't want you to get kicked off the team. I don't know what to do with you. I want to hurt you, but I don't want anything else to hurt you. Can you understand that?"

"No, I can't. *Not at all.*"

I never want him to hurt. Ever.

"Is this *that* shower?"

"*No,*" I tell him. "I don't go in that one."

He frowns, and his eyes run down my body, lingering on my chest and then on the exposed skin near my center. I'm suddenly aware of just how poorly the towel covers my body. I attempt to clutch it tighter, even though his gaze floods my core with warm, wet heat.

"Have you been hurting yourself?" he asks.

"Please, just go away."

He pushes the towel open and runs his hands over my hips, stopping to trace the freshly scabbed-over lines near my waist.

"Ally..." he says and shakes his head.

"No," I say. "You don't get to judge me. Leave me alone."

I try to walk around him, and his arms pin me in place.

"Is that what you want? Yesterday, you were begging me to fuck you."

"That was before I knew you were fucking Audrey. I wouldn't touch you now," I sneer.

He laughs—as if anything about this is funny. "I never fucked Audrey."

One hand rests on my hip just under the cuts, and with the other, he grazes his knuckles against the exposed skin on my stomach. He traces lines up and down my core, dipping low enough to cause me to suck in a breath through my teeth.

"Don't," I force out.

"Don't what?" he asks. "Touch your pussy?"

"Yes," I say weakly.

But he dips his hand lower anyway and starts rubbing my clit in slow circles with two fingers.

"You know, for a girl who doesn't want it, you're slick as fuck for me."

My breath heaves as he picks up speed, and my mind loses the battle with my body not to give in.

"Open," he says, coaxing my clenched thighs apart with his knee. A soft moan escapes me as I give in and open up for him.

"There you go," he says. "That's better."

His hand dips lower, pushing two fingers into me, moving them in and out while working my clit with his thumb. I whimper and arch my back against the shower wall while he works my pussy.

"God, listen to how wet you are," he says.

I squeeze my eyes shut and start bucking against his hand, so close to the edge and desperate for more friction.

Just as my legs start to shake, his hand stills, and I almost scream.

"Drop the towel, Ally," he says. "Let me see your tits, and I'll let you come."

I hesitate for only a second, my willpower long gone by now, before I let the towel fall to the wet floor.

"Fuck..." he says.

He dips down and sucks my nipple into his mouth, then goes back to work pumping into me with his fingers, edging me closer again to my orgasm. With my own hands now free, I pull his sweatpants down over his hips and start jerking his cock. He groans as his tongue flicks back and forth over my nipple, and he curls his fingers inward, increasing his speed.

"Oh, my god," I moan. "I'm going to come. Fuck!"

My pussy clenches around his fingers as the spasms wrack my body. I ride it out with one arm hooked around his shoulders to keep me on my feet and the other hand still wrapped around his dick.

"Devon!"

"That's it, baby. Keep saying my name," he says, still fucking me with his fingers while it rolls through me. "Let them all know what a slut you are for me. I bet you think of me every time you come, don't you?"

"Yes..." I tell him breathlessly, finally starting to come back down. "Oh, my god."

He pulls his fingers out and shoves them into my open mouth.

"Suck," he instructs.

I close my lips around his fingers and suck them clean as he drags them back out, staring straight into his darkened lust-filled eyes while I do.

He smiles just a little. "Get on your knees, Ally."

I drop to the tile floor without wasting any time and run my tongue up and down the length of his cock, feeling it jump in my fist before licking and sucking the tip into my mouth. I take him deep into my throat, moaning around him when he threads his fingers through what's left of my hair, gripping it hard at the still-sore scalp.

"Fuck, that's good," he says. "Look at me."

I look up at him through watery eyes and lashes, and he thrusts forward, fucking my mouth while I choke on his cock. He's never been this rough with me, but I don't really give a shit—the sight of him losing control and fucking my mouth until I choke has me wet and squeezing my thighs together all over again.

"Keep looking at me," he says as the tears start to spill over. "I'm going to come. And you...are...going...to...take it...all."

He thrusts into my mouth hard and groans. One hand stays wrapped up in my hair, holding my head firmly in place, while he braces himself with the other against the shower wall. His dick twitches as cum coats the back of my throat.

"Fuck..."

Once he stills, I swallow, grab my towel, and storm out of the shower. I rush over to my locker and, with shaky hands, start dressing myself, unsure how to process what just happened. I don't think he did what he did because he loves me. I don't think it's going to make anything better at all.

I'm stepping into my jeans when I hear footsteps, and he sits on the bench behind me.

"Ally?"

I don't answer. My shaky hands don't cooperate with me as I attempt to button my jeans. Eventually, I give up and go for the t-shirt hanging in the locker and pull it over my head.

"Allyson?"

"What?!" I snap.

"Did I hurt you?"

"No," I say, still refusing to look at him. I slip into my Vans and see my jersey draped across the bench. I remember I'm not on the team anymore and have to turn it in before I leave. Sad and angry all over again, I start to empty the contents of my locker, aggressively throwing it all into my bag.

"Ally?"

He grabs my hand, and I start to cry all over again.

He buttons my jeans for me, then stands and pulls me into his chest, and I let him, wrapping my arms around his back and burrowing my head in under his chin.

"I don't want to give my jersey back," I cry.

"I know."

"You didn't hurt me," I tell him through tears. "I just...I sleep in your hoodie—the black one with the skull on the front. And I *miss you*... all the time. Every moment of every day, I miss you."

The buzzer sounds, indicating the end of a match, and the locker room won't be empty for much longer. I don't want to still be here—to have to face my former teammates after what happened—and I know he doesn't want to be seen here, either, so I let him go.

"I'll wait for you in the hall, okay?" he says. "I'll take you home."

I nod and throw my bag over my shoulder, then walk through the rows of lockers and over to the office. I leave the jersey on the desk and linger for a few seconds. Darci was the one who convinced me to try out for volleyball. I think it surprised both of us when I was actually good at it. Some of my only good memories here are from being out on the court with her and Morgan or on the bus rides home from away games. It was more than just a sport for me. It was an escape, a comfort. It was something to look forward to when I couldn't find a reason to get out of bed. I had this, and then I had him.

And then we found her body, and my knees hit the concrete, and it was all gone.

Devon is waiting in the hall like he said he would; I follow him out to his car, both of us silent and unsure of what to do with each other now.

Once he leaves the parking lot, I decide to break the silence in the most awkward way.

"Have you ever been to her grave?" I ask.

He sighs. "No. My dad hasn't either. He wasn't allowed to go to the funeral."

"Yeah, neither was I," I tell him. "I feel like...I still can't go. Like if someone found out I was there, it would hurt her family all over again."

"I've seen pictures of it online," he says. "It looks nice. There's a volleyball with her number on it."

"I think about her all the time. And I feel so bad—not because I did anything to her like you think I did—but because I miss her, and sometimes I'm so fucking mad at her. I'm mad at her because if she really did just stage that picture like you said to hurt me—"

"That *is* what she did."

"Then that means that in the end, she wasn't my friend. She didn't care about me. And I'm mad at her for dying and *ruining everything*. I know that's not fair, but I am."

"Ally, I think she cared about you. I just think Darci was bad at caring for people in general. I'm not really sure why."

"The day before she died, she told me she had a secret, and that if I told her my secret, she would tell me hers. I think about that a lot; I wonder if I had just told her, if it would have saved her."

Devon ignores me, staring straight ahead at the road. He thinks I'm lying; he thinks I did something.

"Do you really like Audrey?"

He scoffs and shakes his head. "What do you think?"

He pulls the car to a stop on Cypress, and we both just sit there.

"Devon, my picture wasn't supposed to be creepy. It was just supposed to be you...or what you were to me anyway: light in a very dark place. I'd go back and do it differently if I could. When I try to picture a version of my life where I'm happy—which is getting harder and harder to do—I still picture me with you."

He sighs, running his hands over his face and then through his hair. "What am I supposed to say to that, Ally? I'd do it differently, too, but probably not in the way that you'd want."

"Right...okay."

I unbuckle my seatbelt and get out of the car.

I trudge back to the house through wet leaves. The neighborhood is quiet, aside from the cool October breeze rustling through the trees. The scent of saltwater hangs thick in the air, the way that it always does here when rain is inevitable, but it isn't raining yet. The houses are all decorated for Halloween, and it makes me miss my mom.

Grace and Mark don't celebrate Halloween, and when she was growing up, my mom wasn't allowed to, either, but the two of us always did together. My dad, too, when he was around. It was my favorite day of the year—more so than Christmas because we didn't need money to get candy, and it didn't make my mom sad. It didn't remind her that we were alone the way the other holidays did. We could just pick up an old costume and a couple of plastic bags, knock on some doors and eat candy, watch scary movies and tell ghost stories.

Now, Halloween is the holiday that reminds me I'm alone.

When I walk inside, the house is dark, and there's no sign of Grace, same as the last couple of days.

But there is a padlock on the refrigerator. That's new.

I sigh, grab a couple of pieces of bread from the cabinet and some peanut butter, and make a sandwich before I head upstairs. I slip out of my jeans and t-shirt and into some sweatpants, then remove Devon's hoodie from under the mattress, pull it over my head, and crawl into bed.

How much longer can I keep doing this? Everyone has a breaking point, and I feel I'm far past my own. I try to argue with myself that maybe I could stay and make things right with Devon, that he was kind to me. But what does it say about me that my bar for kindness has been lowered to driving me home after getting me kicked off the volleyball team and coming down my throat? I'm disgusted with myself. That isn't kindness, it's something else. Pity, at best.

I'm not doing this because I care about you. I'm doing this because no one else does.

I can't live in this never-ending nightmare anymore.

22

I'm losing track of time. I know it's been a couple of days since they found Darci because the sun has come and gone, but I've been in my room ever since. They haven't let me go to school, and Grace watches my every move. I haven't been able to sleep because I see her bloodied body floating in the water every time I close my eyes.

And I've barely been able to move or breathe since Grace called me down to the living room yesterday to show me the picture of Devon and Darci in bed together on the TV screen. The way she smirked when she saw the look on my face...

On the one hand, it makes a lot of sense. It explains Darci's weird behavior toward me over the past week, the secrets, the things she said about her secret boyfriend, and how she'd never be able to go to prom with him. And if she knew about us like Devon said, it explains why she'd try and push me onto Trevor.

But I can't wrap my head around the idea that Devon would do that to me. He loves me. We made plans.

But she was prettier than me. And just...better.

I hear someone push my door open and then Grace's voice. "Come downstairs. Now."

I drag myself out of bed and follow her down the staircase and into the dining room.

"Sit down, Ally. You have a phone call," Mark says.

I sit down at the table across from him. Grace leans against the wall behind him with her arms crossed in front of her body.

He slides the phone across the table, and I stare at the screen: *Oregon Department of Corrections*. Tears spring to my eyes as I bring the phone to my ear.

"Mom?"

"Hi, baby. Oh, my god, it's so nice to hear your voice. I miss you so much. How are you? Are you good?"

"Yeah," I lie. "Yeah, I'm good. Are you okay?"

She chokes back a sob. "It's hard. I hate it here. I'm not..."

"No, you're not," I tell her.

Not a criminal, not a bad person, not someone who belongs there.

"I think about you every day," she says. "Are they treating you okay? Do you like school? Do you have a lot of friends? I'm sorry; I just know we don't have a lot of time."

"Yeah, Mom. Everything is great. I like school, and I have a lot of friends. I'm on the volleyball and track teams. I was thinking of sending you some of my ribbons."

"I would love that so much. And some new pictures—maybe some of your art. I miss it."

"Yeah, I can do that."

"Mark was just telling me that he would look at my case and see if he could get me up for parole early. I'll still miss your eighteenth birthday," she sobs, "but maybe I can take you out for a drink when you turn twenty-one."

I look across the table at him, my brows furrowed in confusion. Why would he do that?

"Time's up," he says and reaches for the phone. I hand it to him, and he ends the call without notice.

"I've made an appointment for you to talk to the police about what happened last weekend. I'll be going with you as your attorney. If you do what you're told, you can go to school tomorrow."

"What does that mean?"

"It means that you've humiliated us!" Grace yells. "And you're going to fix it!"

"Leave the room, Grace," Mark says.

She sulks but does as he asks, casting a stony glare over her shoulder before passing through the doorway.

"This is an election year, Ally. And I cannot express to you how important it is that I don't have a niece living with me who is wrapped up in a goddamn murder investigation."

"Devon didn't do it."

"Don't!" he yells, hitting the table with both fists. "Don't even say his name. He's told police that he was with you all night. That better not be true."

I stare straight ahead, unsure of how to respond.

"You're going to tell them it's not true," he says. "You're going to take their eyes off this family so I can get my campaign back on track. This falls back on *all* of us."

"I don't care! I can't just let—" I pause before I say the name. "I can't let him go to jail."

"I don't think you understand how bad this can get for you," he says. "And just so we're clear, what I'm saying is that I don't think you understand how bad I can make this for you."

"What do you mean?"

"Well, if you behave and do as you're told, I can help your mom like I told her I would," he says. "But if you don't..."

"Then...what?"

"People die in those prisons all the time," he says. "There are a lot of violent, dangerous people in there who are never getting out. It'd be very easy for someone like me to make it so you never see your mom again."

"What?" My god, is he really threatening to kill my mom? "You can't..."

"No one cares about the people in there, Ally," he says. "If you want to see your mom again—if you want to go back to school—then you'll tell them you were asleep in Darci's room. We're a nice Christian family. I can't have people thinking my niece is some murderer's whore."

"He didn't kill her."

He shrugs. "Then he has nothing to worry about. The police will do their job. This boy doesn't care about you, Allyson. He had a relationship with his stepsister. Don't ruin your life for someone who's made a fool out of you. Go shower and get dressed, and then we'll head down to the station."

I push my chair back and leave the table, unsure of what the hell I'm going to do next.

"Ally?" Mark calls after me.

I freeze but don't turn around.

"You do the right thing. Your mom's life depends on it. And you know, if I can't trust you, you might have to start sleeping in my room at night so I can keep a better eye on you."

A chill rolls down my spine, and a sob catches in my throat. I grit my teeth and drag myself back up the staircase to my room.

It's a risky move, but I crawl under my bed and remove my phone from its hiding place. I take it with me to the bathroom, power it on after I turn on the shower, and watch the text messages come in.

Devon: Ally, please call me when you can. I love you. I hope you're okay.

Devon: I'm scared. Are you okay? Please say something.

Devon: Ally, that picture…I should have told you about it. Darci staged it. She said she needed it as collateral to make sure I did what she said.

Devon: I went to school today. I wanted to see you, but you weren't there. I miss you so much.

Devon: I think I'm fucked. I think my dad knows it, too. Everyone on the news and online is just angry that they haven't arrested me yet. I just wish I knew where your head was. I just want to talk to you. Please? I love you.

Me: They're upset. I'm afraid they're going to hurt my mom. I'm scared, too. I miss you, too, but I don't know what to believe, and I don't know what to do. The police will do their job, Devon. You'll be okay.

I turn off the phone, shower, get dressed, and head downstairs. Then, I get in the car and prepare to tell a lie that will change everything.

23

It's been three days since they found Darci. The news vans have been parked on our street ever since. I look out my bedroom window and see one of them filming in the backyard, trying to get the now-empty pool in the background of his video.

I throw open the window. "This is private property," I tell him. "You can't film here."

He gestures to the cameraman to turn it on me, and I immediately regret it.

"Technically, I'm on your neighbor's property. They've permitted us to film here. Devon, can you tell us why you killed your sister?"

I slam the window shut and lie back on the bed. It was only hours after Darci's death before the videos my classmates took of me threatening her at the party went viral and made their way onto the news, making me suspect number one.

The next day, they found the picture Darci took of us together in my bed and pulled it from the cloud on her laptop.

And it looks bad—really bad. I know that. I also have an alibi—someone who was with me all night and knows that I couldn't have killed Darci, someone who knows I'd never hurt anyone.

Aside from one text, she hasn't spoken to me since that day. She hasn't been at school, either. I talked my dad into letting me go today, hoping I could see her, and it was awful. Students and teachers cried in the hallways; there was no actual classwork. It was like no one had the energy to do anything other than mourn.

No one bothered to offer me condolences for my loss or express any kind of sympathy for what I went through that day; they're all waiting for me to be arrested...just like I am.

I stare at my phone and consider calling or texting her again, but I don't know what to say that hasn't already been said. I know she's mourning, too. I know she was traumatized that day in my backyard, and she's seen the picture; I know they're watching her, and she's scared. Over the past few days, I've left so many messages and sent so many texts that have gone unanswered.

And I've been over and over what the fuck could have happened to Darci so many times in my head. I've listened to my dad and Lydia fight and cry like they are now.

I've cried, too.

"Please, Lydia," I hear my dad say, "don't do this. Please don't go."

"How could I stay here, Jeff? Your son *murdered* my daughter."

"He didn't do it, Lyd. You know him—you've lived with him for years. Devon isn't a violent person. He's not capable of something like this."

"Did you see the video?" she screams. "Did you? Of course, he's violent. Look what he was exposed to in that house with his mother! I should have never let him anywhere near my daughter."

"She was my daughter, too," my dad cries. "I'm mourning her, too. Please, stay. They'll find who really did this."

"You *know* who did this!" she shouts.

I open my door and step out onto the landing. "You don't have to go, Lydia. I'll leave now. I'll go stay with my mom, and I won't come back. Just...please don't go."

"Oh, you're going to leave," she says. "But the only place you're going is straight into a prison cell, and you're never getting out."

"Lydia, please..." my dad starts before we hear a horn honk in the driveway.

"That's my ride," she says. "I'll send someone for the rest of my things. And I don't want to see either of you at the funeral. I can't...I can't even look at you. I *never* want to see you again."

She leaves the house, wheeling her suitcase behind her, and I'm just stuck there, feet glued in place and unsure of what to do.

"Dad, I'm so sorry."

He sighs, wiping tears from under his eyes. "Come here, Devon. Come sit down."

I force my leaden legs to move down the staircase and sit beside him on the couch.

"You're not going to school tomorrow," Dad says. "There's no point now."

"What do you mean?"

"I talked to the lawyer. They already have the warrant, and they're going to arrest you tomorrow."

Of course. On my birthday. They've been waiting for me to turn eighteen. I bring my elbows to my knees, drop my head into my hands, and cry like a fucking baby.

"I'm so scared," I tell him. "Dad, I really didn't do this. I know it looks bad, but everything I've told you is true."

"Is there anything you want to do before they take you? Do you want to go down to the pier? What do you want for dinner?"

"I just want to see Ally."

He shakes his head. "I don't think that's an option."

"I don't want to go anywhere," I tell him. "They'll just follow us. They were in the parking lot at school, too. Do you think Mom would come over? Do you think she'd make lasagna?" I ask.

"I'm sure she would do that." He moves over until we're side-by-side and puts his arm around my shoulders. "It's going to be okay. They're going to find out who really did this to your sister."

He holds me, and I cry into his shoulder. That's the other thing—my sister. I was always so adamant that no one ever called her that, but we were family whether I liked it or not. As far as my dad is concerned, she was his little girl.

"I'm going to go give your mom a call," he says.

"Yeah," I sniffle. "That sounds good."

I head to my room, close the door behind me, and call Ally one last time. It goes straight to voicemail like I expect it to.

"Hey, Ally. I'm just...um. This is the last one, I promise. They're going to arrest me tomorrow. And...look, I don't know what's going through your head right now, but I really need you to tell them you were with me when they ask. It's really important, Ally. This is bad. I know you're scared. I know you're afraid of them, and you're worried about your mom. I know you're hurting and...confused, but I have never lied to you. I would *never* hurt you. I love you so much, Allyson. I just...fuck. I wish I could see you. I wish I could hold you and tell you in person. And...that's it. Be good, okay? Take care of yourself. I'll see you soon...I hope."

I lie back down on the bed until I hear the doorbell ring. I walk downstairs just as my dad lets my mom and Ivy inside.

"Let me take that for you, Steph," my dad says, taking the grocery bag from her hands and carrying it to the kitchen.

"Hi, Mom."

She looks over at me and bursts into tears.

"I'm okay," I lie as she pulls me into a hug.

"You will be," she says. "We're going fix this. But first, I'm going to make you dinner. And I brought a birthday cake."

"Okay," I tell her.

Mom kisses me on the forehead and walks past me into the kitchen.

"Hey, Ivy."

"Get away from me!" Ivy yells and runs after my mom.

"Ivy, wait! What's wrong?" I call after her. When I enter the kitchen, she's all but hiding behind my mom's body.

"Her babysitter let her watch the news," Mom says. "I'm sorry, Devon. I was furious when I found out."

So, my sister is scared of me...because she believes I murdered my other sister. That's perfect.

"Can I help you, Mom?"

"That's okay, sweetheart. Just relax."

"I can't relax. I need to help. I have to do something."

"Okay," she says. "Come over here."

I help my mom make the lasagna, then we all sit down at the table and eat in silence. The mood is somber, heavy. I eat like it might be the last time I'll ever have a decent meal because it very well may be, and everyone else mostly pushes their food around on their plate.

Ivy refuses to look at me.

Afterward, my dad clears the table while my mom prepares the cake.

"Um, should we sing?" she asks.

"No," I tell her. "I don't want to do that."

I think that the only thing that could possibly make this worse—that could make this eerie scene more like a Lovecraftian horror show than it already is—would be if we were to gather around the table and sing "Happy Birthday."

It's almost comical when she sets a slice of funfetti cake in front of me—on the day that would have been Ally's new birthday, no less.

Afterward, we all watch *Lord of the Rings*. It was my dad's idea, and I humored him by pretending it was a good one and that I'd actually be watching instead of lost in my own thoughts for the duration of the movie.

Mom and Ivy end up staying the night. Ivy falls asleep on the couch, and my mom sleeps on the floor in my bedroom.

In the morning, the police take me away in handcuffs before my dad even finishes making breakfast.

24

Light in a dark place. I sleep in your hoodie.

God damn it, Ally.

And fuck me, too, for following her into the locker room.

That's what's been playing in my head on repeat since last night and still is now as I try to make it through the day.

I've been avoiding her because I don't know what to do with her, but I think she's avoiding me, too. As much as I want to hate her—as much as I want to be mad at her, and I want to know what happened to Darci, and I want that answer to have something to do with her—I can't. Not all the time. I see a bruise on her face or pain in her eyes, and it hurts me, too.

I told myself that I wanted her to hurt, but that was when I didn't think that was what she was already doing. That was when I was sure that she was fine, that she was glad that she did what she did, and that she never really cared about me at all.

I'm not sure about anything now.

I have no idea what I want or who I am anymore. I have nightmares all the time, and nothing feels good—nothing feels the same. But holding Ally felt good. Sitting in the car talking to her felt the same. It's the only time anything has felt that way in months. And god, I miss her.

Also, fuck. Because I hate it.

I loved her so much, and it has been months—that's it—only *months* since it all happened, not years, even though it feels like it sometimes. I loved her so much, and she left me there, and, maybe even worse, she actually thought I could cheat on her. I can't wrap my head around any of it.

I meet her by her locker after school.

"Hey," I say.

It still feels weird—like I shouldn't be talking to her at school, or we're going to get caught.

"Hi," Ally says sadly.

"I wanted to give you these," I tell her.

I hold out an envelope, and she takes it from my hands. Inside are the pictures of her with her mother and the track ribbons she kept inside the box under her bed. She eyes me suspiciously as if she expects the envelope to hold something sinister before opening it just enough to assess its contents.

"Thanks for giving back the pictures you stole from me," she says.

"Um, I thought maybe since you don't have volleyball anymore, we could go somewhere."

She shrugs. "What do you mean *go somewhere*?"

"I mean that...I want to take you somewhere."

"Why? Do you want a blow job again?" she says, closing her locker and walking the entire wrong way.

I mean, yeah. I'd love to fuck her mouth again like that. I came twice again in the shower this morning thinking about it.

But...

"That's not what I meant."

"No, I don't want to go somewhere. I'm going to go check out the art fair, and then I'm going home."

The...what.

"That's today?"

"Yeah, and I thought I would miss it because of volleyball and well...I didn't even plan to be here, but you ruined that for me. Grace won't expect me home for a while anyway."

Fuck me. I'd pay her to fucking leave right now. I try to think of anything that will make her turn the other way but come up with absolutely nothing and instead end up silently following her to the art wing, hoping maybe I can distract her.

It's a small event, but still, there's a table with flyers that act as a map, labeled with each student's name, the title of their work, and where you can find it. Ally picks one up and scans it for her own name, then heads in that direction.

I look for mine, too, and find that it's a little too close for comfort.

We stop in front of a charcoal drawing that's textbook Ally; I could pick something she made from any line up...a mile away.

It's a car parked next to a beach. There's a girl and her mother standing at the outdoor showers—the ones they always have so you can wash the sand from your body before you leave. It looks like she's washing the girl's hair.

"What is this?" I ask.

"Home," she says. "Remember when I told you my mom and I lived in her car for a while? This is the car."

"I'm sorry, Ally."

"Don't be sorry," she says. "You know, I never minded it. Before the car, there were a lot of very temporary living situations that never felt like home. The car was a constant. I felt like every day was an adventure. We spent the entire summer outside at parks or on the beach, and we'd shower in our bathing suits like this, and I thought it was fun. I only knew it was something to be embarrassed about because I could feel it coming from my mom. She still tried to make it fun, though."

I catch her off guard when I move closer and hook my pinky around hers, but she doesn't pull away. She looks over at me with just her eyes through thick, dark lashes, her head still straight forward.

"It's beautiful," I tell her. "You're an amazing artist; you know that."

I hear a couple of guys laughing, and sure enough, when I glance over my shoulder, I see them in front of my drawing, taking pictures with their phones.

Fuck.

"Yeah. Yeah, I like this one. It's kind of a reminder of...how sometimes we don't notice how good things are when we're in them. We're too focused on what's wrong or what we don't have to enjoy what we do. I didn't know that car was the safest home I'd ever have."

"Is that what happened with us?" I ask before I have a chance to think better of it.

She pulls her hand away and crosses her arms in front of her chest.

"No...I knew it was good. I just...knew I didn't deserve it. It was *too* good. That's why I wasn't surprised when...I saw that picture."

"Allyson, there's no way you still think I did that. How *could* you?"

"I don't know. I guess maybe I don't; maybe not now. But I did. Everybody wanted her."

"Not me, Ally. Not under any circumstance."

She holds my eyes for a moment, and I wait for her reply, but it's only, "I'm going to go try to check out the rest of this before my bus comes."

Ally turns and walks directly toward my contribution to this shit show.

"Hey," I say, stepping into her path. "Or...we could go now. I thought maybe we could go see Darci's grave like you said."

She shakes her head. "I don't know, Devon. I don't know if I could handle that, and I don't know if it would feel right if we were there together."

She tries to step around me again, and I grab her shoulder. "We could go to a drive-thru. I could get you something really greasy and a giant soda. You want to?"

"Yeah, but..." she pauses, narrowing her eyes. "What did you do, Devon?"

Fuck. "Nothing!"

"Move!" she says.

She shoves me aside and rushes right over to my fucked up display, shouldering her way through our peers until she has a front-row seat to take it all in.

Nearby students snicker and take out their cell phones as I walk up behind her, holding my breath. Ally takes in the Ally on my canvas, which is essentially a modern take on a caricature, exaggerating all the things I know she hates about herself—her nose, her neck, the bags under her eyes. I left a hole in the place where her heart should be, the word liar where she should have a mouth, gave her a bag of stolen money and cell phones, a bruise on her cheek, and festering cuts down her arms.

"It turned out you were ugly on the inside, too," she reads aloud from the page.

"Ally..." I start, not sure of where to go next. Was I sorry? I was sorry that other people saw it; I didn't really mean it. But it was cathartic at the time. That's what art is supposed to be, right? Sometimes, you have to get it out—that's what she always says.

The woman stays still as a fucking statue.

"Everyone is watching us, Ally. We should go."

She turns and looks at me over her shoulder, her expression seething, then grabs the canvas in her hands.

"I hate you!" she screams, and—before I get a chance to react—she brings the whole thing down over my goddamn head. I stumble backward and desperately try to grasp anything to keep myself on my feet, and that something ends up being the sleeve of Ally's hoodie. I pull her down with me as I careen into the refreshment table, causing it to flip onto its side, and the entire assortment of food and punch comes down on top of us.

We both flail on the ground for a minute in the mess. I struggle to get the giant canvas off me, and just as I do, Ally makes it to her knees and starts pummeling me with anything she can get her hands on. Cupcakes, cookies, celery and carrot sticks, plastic cups, wet fucking napkins—all of it.

"I fucking hate you!" she yells again. "You asshole!"

"Stop!" I yell. "Stop it, Allyson!"

She's crying again when I finally get ahold of her arms and make her stop.

I look up when I feel Mr. Ames and the principal both standing over us, and so does Ally.

"Both of you need to go to my office—now," Principal Coleman says. "Get up. Start walking."

Her voice seems to snap Ally out of her rage-induced blackout. She looks around at the mess and the crowd, then pushes to her feet and walks wordlessly toward the principal's office, trying not to make eye contact with anyone along the way.

"Have a seat," Coleman says, ushering us both inside. "And don't touch each other. Don't talk to each other. I'll be right in."

Ames appears next to her just as she closes the door. I try to make out what they're saying but can't quite hear anything.

“Ally?”

“Shut up,” she says. “She said no fucking talking.”

“Ally, I’m so sorry.”

“You’re sorry?” she says and laughs before grabbing my bag from the chair next to me and raising it over her head. I attempt to shield myself with my arm while she brings it down on me over and over again. “You’re fucking sorry!?”

“Yes!”

“How.” Swing “Could.” Swing. “You.” Swing. “You mother.” Swing. “Fucking.” Swing. “Asshole!”

“Stop! Fuck! She said no touching!”

“I’m not touching you!” she grits through clenched teeth, throwing the bag at me one last time. “You called me ugly.”

Her lower lip starts to quiver. She crosses her arms over her chest and turns to face the front of the room.

“I didn’t mean that. You’re beautiful, Ally. You know I think you’re beautiful.”

“Shut up!” Ally looks down at the floor and sniffles. “You drew my cuts, Devon.”

“Okay,” Coleman says as she steps inside the office. “Well, you two ruined the art show.”

“It was my fault,” I tell her. “Ally didn’t do anything. I shouldn’t have...drawn that.”

“No, you shouldn’t have,” she says. “And to be honest, Ames probably should have realized what he was putting on display, but he’s new here and didn’t.”

“So, can Ally go?”

“I don’t need your help, Devon—” Ally starts.

"No," Coleman says. "Regardless of who started what or what happened between the two of you, Hargrove escalated it to a physical altercation. You'll both have detention after school for two weeks. And honestly, Hargrove...between this and what happened in the gym yesterday, you're lucky you won't be expelled. On top of all that, with the way your grades are, you're in danger of not graduating. I'm *very* concerned about you. I am going to talk to the counselor, and we'll find a regular time for her to meet with you during the week."

"Ally, I'm so sorry."

"Don't."

Coleman shakes her head before continuing, "Anyway, Ames has a project for you two—a way you can make it up to the school. He's recently started adding a mural to the wall in the main gym. And now...you get to do it. Starting tomorrow."

"With him!?" Ally asks, appalled.

"Sorry. I'm unable to arrange special separate punishments for you two. You're just going to have to try your best to behave like the adults you're supposed to be now and not like the toddlers I saw a few minutes ago in the hallway. I don't know what happened between you two, and—quite frankly—I don't care. Finish the damn mural, and then...stay away from each other for the few months you have left here. Got it?"

"Can I go now?" Ally asks. "I'm going to miss the bus."

"You can go," she says.

We both start to get up and grab our things, but she stops me.

"Not you, West. I'm giving her a two-minute head start."

Ally narrows her eyes at me as she heads out the door, and I sink back into the seat, nervously tapping my foot.

"You've been through a lot, Devon," Coleman says.

"Yeah, you think?"

She shakes her head. "Do you want pity, or do you want your life back? What happened to you was terrible. But it was just that: *something that happened to you.* It doesn't have to define you. What you do now...*that* will."

"More good news. Thanks."

"Get your shit together, Devon. You can go now."

25

"Ally!" Devon shouts, jogging across the parking lot to catch up with me. "Wait!"

"No!" I yell back.

"Let me take you home," he says.

"NO!"

I look over just in time to see my bus blow past the stop.

"Was that it?" he asks. "That was your bus, right?"

"...No," I lie.

"Yes, it was," he says. He grabs me by my arm and turns me to face him. "Ally, I didn't mean it."

"You called me ugly. Inside and out. And I know—I know that's my fault. I made you like this. I broke you, and I hate myself for it. But you *know* me. You've *seen* me. How could you?"

"Ally, you left me to rot in jail, remember? I was mad at you. I'm still so fucking mad at you."

"You stole my money!" I shout. "You left me to rot in jail, too! A *worse* jail. I shouldn't even be talking to you."

"Ally...wait..." he says.

"Give me my money back, Devon!"

"I can't!" he shouts. "I don't have it! I used it to pay the lawyer. It bankrupted my dad!"

He attempts to grab me by my arm again, and I shake him off. "Let go of me!"

"Hey," someone says from behind me. "Is everything okay?"

I turn toward the source of the voice and see a redheaded girl with a cast walking with another guy from our class.

"Yeah, everything is fine," Devon says.

"No. It's not," I tell her.

"Hey, cool party, guys," Tristan says. "I don't normally have a good time at stuff like this, but if this is what I have to look forward to, I'll see you at the next one."

"God, would you shut up?" the girl says. "Can we give you a ride home?"

"We?" Tristan repeats.

She shoots him a glare.

"Yeah, fine, Mila. Whatever you want."

"No, we're good," Devon tells them.

"We are *not* good," I tell him. "A ride would be great."

"It's the Jeep," Tristan says.

"Cool," Devon says, shaking his head. "That's cool. Hey Tristan, maybe I'll give your girlfriend a ride sometime."

"Oh, Devon." He laughs as he opens the driver's side door. "Yeah, okay. Hey, Mila? You want to go anywhere with Devon?"

"Uhh...no," she says as she climbs into the passenger side.

"Sorry, Devon. Mila doesn't like you, either. Nice try, though. Also, you have pink frosting in your hair—looks super douchey."

He closes the door, and I look back at Devon one more time before getting into the back of the Jeep. He stays there, staring at me, as we back out and leave him alone in the parking lot. I lean against the cold window, trying to keep my tears from spilling over again.

The girl—Mila—turns around in her seat. "Are you okay?" she asks. "I'm new here; I don't really know Devon, but he seems like an asshole. That drawing was fucked up."

"He wasn't always like that," Tristan says.

She shoots him another glare.

"What? He wasn't."

"No, he's right," I tell her, drying my eyes. "He used to be...nice. It's my fault."

"It was *still* fucked up," she says. "I'm sorry."

"Yeah...it was. Thanks."

"Where do you live?" she asks.

"She lives in our neighborhood," Tristan answers before I can. "I remember the news vans."

"Tristan...Jesus."

"What? It was a traffic issue. I can't recall a traffic issue?" She rolls her eyes at him and turns back around. "You live on Cherry, right?" he asks.

"Yeah, but...can you drop me off at the bus stop on Cypress? I'm not really supposed to be in the car with..." With who? Guys? Strangers? Anyone, really. "...people."

"With *people*?!" he asks. "How were you planning to get home if we weren't there, then? A flying saucer?"

"I missed the last bus."

"Ignore him," Mila says. "He has problems."

Tristan pulls up to the bus stop and puts the car in park. "You sure you don't want me to drop you off closer? It's raining."

"No, this is good," I tell him, opening the door. "Thanks."

Even though it's pouring when I get out of the car, I don't bother hurrying. I drag myself the short distance home and slip my shoes off before I enter the dark house, closing the door softly behind me. I'm relieved Grace is already asleep, even if she is passed out on the couch in front of the TV. Quietly, I creep upstairs, eager to get out of my clothes and wash away the evidence of what happened. I'm pretty sure I've got pink frosting in my hair, too.

I don't put on the skull hoodie before I lie down in bed.

I don't think I slept at all last night.

I get off the bus, walk into school like a zombie, and head straight for my locker. The smell hits me before I see it—the greasy brown paper bag sitting on top of my books. My stomach twists and pangs with hunger, reminding me again how long it's been since I've eaten.

Biscuits and gravy. My favorite.

I want to cry. And I do.

I grab the bag, head to the restroom, then sit down on the toilet and let the tears fall while I scarf the bag's contents. My body is so painfully empty it hurts when the first couple of bites hit my stomach, but by the fourth, it adjusts.

I skip P.E. and head straight to the computer lab, finding a spot near the back and logging in using Devon's student ID and password. I'm pleasantly surprised it still works. I open the search engine and look for women's shelters in Western Washington and write down the phone numbers inside my sketchpad.

I stuff my shoe into the door when I step outside the building and start dialing the numbers. The third place I call—in Everett—tells me they have space for me on Sunday. I give them a fake name and head back to the computer lab to look up a bus schedule and find a route that gets me close.

I make it to second period just a little bit late. My eyes flutter open and closed from the lack of sleep and lack of drive to pay attention.

I'm doing it. I'm getting out. It's different than what I planned—hell, I don't have a plan at all. I have no money, it won't be smooth or easy, but it will be better than this. It *has* to be.

I get to lunch a little bit later than I want, and Audrey approaches me in the line.

"What you did was really fucked up."

"Which thing?" I ask, not looking at her.

"Ummm...the one where you attacked me! Look at my face!"

"You look fine," I tell her, paying the cashier. "And Devon doesn't like you, Audrey. I'm not saying that to hurt your feelings—it's just true. He was just trying to make me mad. Surely, you realize that."

I linger only for a second, waiting for a reply, and when I don't get one, I leave her there and look for somewhere else to sit.

"Hey, Laurel," I say. "Can I sit with you guys?"

"Of course," she says. "Scoot over, Mila."

The two other girls eye me suspiciously—like I'm a disease—but ultimately say nothing. They return to their conversation—something about cheerleading and the bus that I don't really pay attention to. When I see Devon come in and start scanning the cafeteria, I pull the hood of my jacket over my head and hunch down over my food. If he sees me, he doesn't say anything. I know I'll have to see him after school for detention. I also know it will be the last time I'll ever see him.

It helps that I'm mad at him; that makes it easier to leave, but I won't be able to forget. The vile things we've done to each other and the way we loved each other are seared deeply into my brain, both as raw as they ever were, and I don't see that changing. I don't think these are the kind of things you can just forget about or cut out. They're the kind of things that haunt you when you're old, the kind that will keep you up at night, squeezing your heart while you ruminate over all of the ways you could have done things differently and wonder how it could still—after all this time—possibly hurt so much.

The kind of things that will become the dark circles under your eyes. The scars you don't wear, the ones that no one sees unless they know exactly where to look. And I'll never show anyone again.

"Ally?" Laurel says, pulling me out of my thoughts. "The bell rang. Did you hear it?"

"Oh...sorry. I didn't."

"Are you okay?"

"Yeah, I'm fine," I tell her, following her to return my tray. "I just...didn't sleep much last night."

"I'm not surprised," she says. "I'm not trying to be a dick, but...Mila told me about what happened at the art fair. Do you want to talk about it?"

"No...I don't. Thanks, though."

Were we friends? Not really. But she's shown me kindness when I was vulnerable—when I couldn't trust many of the people I've called friends here to do the same.

"Hey, Laurel?"

"Yeah?"

"I know we haven't talked much. But you helped me...a couple of times when I really needed it, and it made a difference. It mattered to me. I won't forget it. I want you to know that."

"Anytime, Ally. Really. I'd give you my number, but..."

"Yeah, I don't have a phone. Anyway...thanks. I'll see you around."

26

I look around the cafeteria, but I don't see Ally anywhere. I know she's here...somewhere. I checked her locker, and the food was gone.

I take a tray and grab a seat next to Isaac and Seth.

"Dude, I heard about what happened at the art fair. Fucking awesome," Seth says. Isaac scoffs and shakes his head. "Isaac disagrees, but I think the bitch deserved it."

I practically leap across the table and grab him by the collar of his shirt. "Don't fucking call her that. Ever. Do you hear me? I'll fucking..."

Kill you, I almost say. I let go of his collar and sink back into my seat.

"Jesus, man. What the fuck?"

"It was fucked up," Isaac says. "I'm not talking about what you just did to Seth, either. What you did to Ally was fucked. I don't care how much you hate her. I saw the drawing, Devon."

"I sat in jail for over four months because Ally Hargrove was insecure and scared. I drew a picture."

"Devon, I know you don't want to hear this, but I don't really care: Ally is not the reason you were in jail. You get that, right? You went to jail because twenty people saw you put a knife to Darci's throat and tell her you were going to kill her a few hours before she was murdered. Even if Ally would have said she was with you, who saw her? How could Ally account for your whereabouts if she was asleep?"

"Even if you are right, she still shouldn't have done it."

"No, she shouldn't have. But...you said she was scared, right? You said that they hurt her. I don't know what it's like to be scared of someone like that. Do you?"

Yeah. I do.

I think about when I was thirteen, and I got in the middle of my mom and Jack when they were fighting in the kitchen.

I thought I was a lot bigger than I was. I grabbed a pan from the counter, thinking I could sneak up behind him and hit him over the head, and he'd pass out and fall to the ground the way they always do in the movies. But my mom spotted me and yelled, "Devon, no!"

Jack spun around so fast I didn't stand a chance. It wasn't the first time he beat me, but it was the worst. He took the pan from my hand and clocked me square in the jaw. I fell to the ground, choking on blood, spitting teeth, and scrambling to get to my feet so I could run. I did get to my feet, but I didn't run. He grabbed me, slammed me against the wall, and strangled me until I passed out while my mom screamed for him to stop.

The next time I heard them fighting, I stayed in my room...scared.

The next week, I went to my dad's, and he said I was never going back. My mom didn't even try to argue. I didn't see her for months.

"I could have kept her safe. She should have trusted me," I tell him.

"You know what? I believe that you believe that."

"What's that supposed to mean?"

"It means you have a hero complex."

"All right, whatever. I'm not hungry, anyway," I say.

I push out of my chair and leave the cafeteria, forced to contemplate the quiet part I'd done such a good job ignoring, the one thing that, throughout this entire ordeal, has been the most impossible to swallow.

Maybe it's not Ally's fault.

"Hey," I say to Ally when she walks into the gym for our shared detention. "I have all of the stuff here. I thought maybe you skipped."

"Nope."

"You weren't at lunch."

"Yeah, I was," she says.

"Oh. Okay...well. The outline is already up, so we just have to fill it in."

"Fine."

"I'm sorry, Ally," I say.

She doesn't answer.

"Are you going to talk to me at all?"

"No. Not if I can help it."

"Well...we kind of have to talk to finish this. We need like...a plan."

"A plan? Okay, fine. Here's the plan: you do the shitty eagle, I'll do the shitty flowers, and we can split the stupid fucking letters and the mountains down the middle."

"Okay, fine," I tell her, climbing the ladder. "You're not going to...push the ladder over or anything, right?"

"Don't give me any ideas," she says.

I take the brown paint pan and climb to the top while Ally kneels to paint the rhododendrons. We work like that—in silence—for the first half hour. Until I absolutely can't take it anymore.

I look down and see her bent over on all fours, adding more paint to her tray. Her white scoop-neck t-shirt falls away from her body, and I get a pretty good view of her tits. Between that and her ass up in the air, I feel my dick go rock fucking hard.

My feelings for Ally are...complicated. I'm mad at her. I don't know if I can trust her, but I don't want her to leave. I know we're not done; I'm not sure what that means, but it's true.

And I didn't want to hurt her like I hurt her with that picture. Also, I'd sell my soul to pull those jeans down and fuck her just like that right now.

"You know, I like this arrangement," I tell her. "I can see right down your top."

"Yeah, well. Not much to see."

"You've got plenty to see—trust me. A good handful is plenty."

"Would you stop? We aren't talking."

"Your haircut is nice, too."

She turns and looks at me for the first time today, outraged. "You did *not* just say that to me."

"What? I can't like it?"

"No!"

"Why not? I always thought you'd look nice with short hair. And I was right—look at you. You're like a midnight pixie."

"What the *fuck* is a midnight pixie, Devon?"

"It's like Tinkerbell, but...from hell. In a hot way." She turns away, but not before I catch her smiling. "You're laughing."

"No, I'm not."

"You have to forgive me, Ally."

She shakes her head. "You won't forgive me."

"I'm coming around to the idea," I say honestly.

"Well, I don't need you to," she says.

I sigh, at a loss, and she goes back to work.

"I kept your hair," I tell her.

"You're joking."

"No, I'm serious. It's in my desk drawer at my mom's house."

"Well...*throw it away*, Devon."

"No way; I need it. I've been practicing braiding. I'm going to make it into a necklace, wear it to school when I'm done."

She laughs. "Devon...no."

I climb down the ladder and sit on the floor next to her.

"Don't be mad at me."

"Why not? What's going to happen if I'm not mad? You're mad at me."

"Yeah, I am. But...it's us, Ally. What am I supposed to do?"

"Try to forget," she says softly.

"Is that what you're doing?" I ask. "Do you have any tips? Because it's not fucking working out like I expected. How do I forget you?"

"I ruined your life," she says. "I guess I know how to make an impression, but—"

"You left a mark, Ally. A deep one. You can't blame me if it made me a little crazy."

"Devon..."

I place a hand on her cheek, brushing her hair away from her face and behind her ear. "You said you missed me. I'm right here. When they came to get me, do you know what was the worst part of the whole thing?"

She shakes her head.

"It was knowing that whatever happened—if I got out the next day or not for months or years—when that happened, I wouldn't have you anymore. It crushed me. Why couldn't you have just trusted me?"

"Because I'm an ugly person. Inside and out."

"Ally..."

"It's past four thirty," she tells me. "We can go now."

I follow her out into the hallway. "Well, we have to clean up the paint!"

"You do it. I'll do it on Monday."

"Ally, maybe we could—"

"I can't do this, Devon. Not in any way. I can't be here anymore or...I won't be *anywhere* anymore...at all. Do you get that? Do you hear what I'm saying?"

"What are you talking about?"

"You don't have to feel bad for hurting me. I don't want you to. You don't have to be sorry because I forgive you. Is that what you want?"

"Well...yes. But—"

"I'm always going to forgive you because...it's us. Okay? I have to go."

I watch her leave, then head back inside the gym to clean up the paint and return it to the art supply closet. I'm still folding the drop cloth when the basketball players begin filing in for practice.

"I mean, she practically said we were going to hook up," Trevor says.

I know he's talking about Ally. I feel his eyes on me, waiting for a reaction, and sadly, I can't resist. I laugh just a little and shake my head.

"Is that okay with you, Devon? If I fuck your girlfriend?"

"It's kind of weird that you'd want to fuck your mom, but I guess, man. As long as it's consensual."

A couple of the other guys laugh, and I feel the rage dripping off him.

"Dude, Ally was never with him," Luke says.

Isaac comes out of the locker room, dribbling a ball. He looks over at me, and I roll my eyes, tuck the drop cloth under my arm, and pick up the paint caddy with the other hand.

"Hey," he says, jogging over to me, "are you okay, man?"

"Your friends are douchebags. Are you going to the party tomorrow with these idiots?"

"I wasn't planning on it," he says. "And you shouldn't either."

"He said Ally is going to be there," I tell him. "I hurt her—with the picture. It was too much; you were right."

"Well, isn't that what you wanted?"

"I thought so, but...I don't anymore."

His coach blows the whistle. "Nguyen! Get over here!"

Isaac glances over his shoulder before turning back to me and saying, "Don't go to that party, dude. Ally probably won't even be there. You guys need to give each other space. Focus on yourself; get your fucking head right."

"Yeah, okay."

"I'm serious," he says, then jogs over to meet his teammates.

I walk back to the supply closet and take Isaac's words to heart only for a minute before deciding I'm not going to listen to him. Ally and I are different. He doesn't get that. He doesn't get how we work.

Once home, I go straight to my room, ready to spend another evening getting drunk alone and doomscrolling Reddit until night comes. I open the app and prepare to start dumpster diving, but I surprise myself. I set my phone aside and grab a pencil and some paper from the nightstand. I start to draw Ally again—*my* Ally, the way I've always seen her. Beautiful and resilient, fierce but vulnerable, introspective and passionate. I don't expect it to fix everything, but she always loved it when I'd draw for her, so maybe that's a good place to start. At the very least, maybe it'll get the other one out of her head. Even if we do both forget and move on, she needs to know that I don't see her like that.

It occurs to me as I start to sketch her hair that this is the first thing I've done since I got out that wasn't motivated by some kind of spite and it's the stillest my underlying anger has been in months. I wouldn't say that I feel good or better even, but it's a start.

27

I wait until Grace passes out on Saturday to leave through the window, not bothering to try and be quiet. She hasn't left her room much over the past week except to go to work. Sometimes, I wonder if she's planning something. I wonder if maybe she's just satisfied now that she's won or if she's less satisfied knowing that I've all but lost the will to live, and she can see in my eyes that nothing hurts anymore.

Luke's house is only a few blocks away, so I decided to walk. Trick-or-treating ended a couple of hours ago, but there are still a few older kids out walking the neighborhood—enough that I'm not worried about being alone or looking out of place. Toilet paper adorns some of the trees and sidewalks, likely having been picked up by the icy late October breeze.

I walk into Luke's packed house and start scanning the room for one of my friends, finding Morgan quickly, thanks to the pink wig she showed me at school. I don't recognize the person she's talking to as Audrey until it's too late.

"Hey," I say.

"Oh, my god...she actually came," Audrey bemoans. "Great. I'll have to warn Devon before he gets here."

She makes sure to look me up and down, her face expressing her obvious disgust, before turning and marching off toward the front of the house.

"She's lying. Devon isn't coming here," I scoff. "He doesn't like Luke, and he doesn't like Audrey. And she doesn't like him either. She just likes that he's notorious now or whatever. She doesn't care about him."

"You know, for someone who wasn't involved with Devon, you sure seem to care a lot."

I look at the only friend I have left—the only person who maybe really cares about me—and I almost tell her the truth before we're interrupted.

"What's up?" Trevor says, pulling off his ghost face mask. "It's me."

"Yeah..." Morgan says. "We know..."

"Right....okay. Well, get a beer, ladies. Luke has a keg in the kitchen. We're playing beer pong in the loft. You ever play beer pong, Ally?"

"In another life," I answer.

"That will work," he says. "You're my partner then. I'll come find you when it's our turn."

I lose myself for the next hour—drinking, dancing, laughing with Morgan and a couple of other girls from the team. They talk about the county tournament and how they'll probably lose without me.

No one mentions the reason I'm not on the team or what I did. They don't ask me about Devon.

And I almost feel normal.

Then I think about the last time I was at a party like this—months ago with Devon when he loved me. I try not to scan the room for any sign of him or Audrey, but I can't stop myself. I never spot him, and Audrey is on the couch hanging on some basketball player a year below us, so maybe she was lying about him coming here.

Or maybe she did warn him about me, and he decided not to come.

I realize that should be a relief; seeing him here with her would be gut-wrenching. Just thinking about it brings back that vice-grip feeling in my chest that I only ever barely get rid of.

But also, I want to see him. I want him to see me and tell me I look pretty. I want to catch his eye from across the room and try and hide my smile. I want him to text me that he loves me before he goes to sleep, and I want to hide under my covers and read it over and over.

But I know that won't ever happen again. This version of Devon—the one I have to leave here—would do things differently if he could do it again, too, but not in the way I want.

"Hey," Morgan says. "I'm going to go get another beer. Do you want one?"

No, I don't. I should probably go, but not without saying goodbye. If this is the last time I'm going to see her, then I should do a little better.

"Actually, do you think we could go outside and talk for a minute?" I ask.

"Right now?" she asks. "Can it wait? Eagan just got here."

"Well, I was actually just about to leave, so—"

"Oh, okay! I'll see you on Monday, then!" she says. She sets her beer down on the counter and blows past me.

Right. I laugh just a little and shake my head. I don't know what else I can expect, really. I've never been honest with her. She has no reason to think I'm anything other than what she sees at school: a little aloof and over-sheltered but otherwise just like her. She hasn't seen me. She doesn't know about the scars or the stealing or the box I hid under my bed. She doesn't know about Devon or what Darci did before she died.

She doesn't know that it might have been my fault that she left that night—that maybe I am at least a little bit responsible for what happened to her, just not in the way people thought I was before.

If I'm honest with myself, if she knew all of that, she never would have stuck by me like she did. She would never choose me over Audrey.

I pick up the cup she left on the counter, throw back its contents, and silently wish her well as I head for the front door.

I step out into the night, the light breeze now a fierce wind that takes my breath away when it hits me head-on. I duck my head down and run my hands over my bare arms, hoping to take the edge off.

"Hey, Ally. You look really pretty."

I look up and see Devon in front of me on the sidewalk.

"Didn't Audrey warn you I would be here?"

He gives me one of those half-smiles and runs his hands through his dark hair. It's starting to look a little shaggy now, but still much shorter than I'm used to—just another reminder of how he's not the same.

"Yeah, she did," he says.

"Well, the good news is I'm leaving," I tell him. "The bad news is I think she got tired of waiting on you and moved on to someone else."

He shakes his head. "I just wanted to see you, Allyson."

"Well, I can't imagine why."

"You said you'd do things differently if you could. Don't make this hard again."

"What do you mean?" I ask.

"You miss me. I fucking miss you, too. Being there fucked me up, Ally. It fucked with my head, too. I know I'm not the same; I feel it all the time. The only time I don't feel it is when I'm with you. I don't want to be at this party. I want to go somewhere with you."

I hesitate to reply. I look into his pale blue eyes, and all I want to do is go swimming, but that will make it harder to get on a bus tomorrow night.

"They're showing *Halloween* at the theatre. You love that movie. You said it was one of your mom's favorites, and you watched it every year."

"You remember that?" I ask.

"Of course I do. I remember everything you've ever said." He pulls his hoodie over his head. "You're freezing. Here—arms up."

I hold up my arms, and he pulls the sweatshirt down over my head. Cedar and sandalwood, just like always. But no hint of the fabric softener I always associated with his and Darci's home—that must have been all Lydia.

"Better?" he asks.

I nod. "Yeah, that's better."

"Do you want to go with me?"

"Are you fucking with me?" I ask. "I mean, is this a game?"

He throws the same question back at me. "Are *you* fucking with *me*?"

"No, Devon. I never—"

"You know what? I don't care," he says. "If this is just a game, then I want to keep playing. I don't know how to do anything else."

I smile. "Are you bored with everyone and everything again already?"

"*Perpetually*," he says. "Come on, let's go." He hooks an arm around my waist. "I parked just down the block."

We walk like that until we get to Devon's car and climb inside. No music blares through the speakers at a decibel you can both feel and hear the way it always did before when he'd start his car. I buckle my seatbelt, then bring the collar of the sweatshirt over my nose and breathe it in again.

"Are you going to talk to me, or are you just going to look at me like I'm about to catch on fire?" he asks.

"I guess I didn't realize that was what I was doing," I tell him. "I think maybe I'm trying to reconcile the version of you I know and the one who drew that picture."

"Ally—"

"I know, I know—I'm terrible, and it's my fault. But...can I ask you something? You said that you're different now—that you *feel* different. How do you feel?"

"Bad, mostly," he says. "I'm angry all the fucking time. I don't care about my classes or my grades. I listen to Seth and Isaac talk about their lives, but I don't really care about anything they're saying. It all just seems so...trivial. I don't enjoy reading or gaming anymore. That picture I drew of...you is the only thing I've started and finished since I got out. And I didn't do it because I was inspired; I did it to hurt you. I'm angry with everyone, and I can't make myself give a fuck about anything other than how mad I am."

"My mom has been in there for a long time," I tell him. "A lot longer than you. Do you think she's..."

"She's not okay, Ally. Probably not at all. She's going to be different, too. People can't...they can't live like that, you know? Not good ones, anyway."

I nod and turn toward the window so he doesn't see the tears spill over. A few seconds later, he turns into the theatre parking lot and stops the car. I unbuckle my seatbelt, and he reaches under my chin, turning my face toward his.

"I know that's not what you want to hear, Ally, but I'm not going to start lying to you now because I *do* care about you."

"Yeah. I wouldn't want you to," I say, then get out of the car.

He meets me around the back of the vehicle and grabs my hand, lacing his fingers in mine, and we walk up to the theatre together. He buys our tickets, then we get in line for food and drinks. My stomach growls when we step in line, and I breathe in the scent of distinctly movie theatre buttered popcorn.

"What do you want?" Devon asks. "Popcorn?"

I nod. "And nachos."

"Is that it?"

"And a giant soda."

"Soda? Are you sure? Not a slushie?" he asks as we step up to the register.

"I'm sure," I tell him.

One of our classmates works the register, eyeing us like it's the spookiest thing he's seen all fucking night. He looks like he wants to say something about it, but I know he won't—not to Devon.

Devon pulls me in close to his side, orders the food, and pays the kid, who says nothing aside from our total and watches us over his shoulder while he gets our food.

"We scare people," Devon says. "Did that happen to you at all when I was gone?"

"Were they afraid of me? Um, kind of. There was a good mix of pity and fear. They all knew there was something wrong with me. They knew I was a liar."

"Are you worried about them seeing us now?"

Now, specifically? Not at all. I couldn't really tell him why, though.

I shrug. “I don’t know. Not really. I don’t expect to see any of Mark and Grace’s friends here.”

“Have you ever googled us?” he asks.

“No...have you?”

“Oh yeah,” he says. “All the time. It’s all I do. I wouldn’t recommend it, though.”

The kid wordlessly sets our food down on the counter and walks away. Devon smiles at me; I snicker a little, then grab the nachos and soda and follow him down the hall to the theatre.

“When was the last time you went to the movies?” he asks after we find seats.

It takes me a minute to remember. “It was before I moved here, obviously. It was one of the new *Exorcist* movies, but I don’t remember what it was called.”

“Was it with a guy?” he whispers as the movie starts.

I nod. “It was a date.”

“Was he better than me?”

I shake my head. “What do you think? Watch the movie, Devon. Let me eat my nachos.”

Devon slouches further into his seat and throws his arm around my shoulders. He’s different but the same. He’s still the only person who can touch me like this without making my skin crawl. Even though I stare at the screen for the entire two hours, I don’t think I really watch the movie; I’m too aware of him. I lean in and just feel him there, and that’s enough.

It’s after one when the movie lets out, and it must have been the latest showing of the night because there are only a handful of cars left outside when we silently make our way through the parking lot.

Once inside, Devon puts the keys in the ignition but doesn't start the car. He sighs and leans back in his seat, staring up at the sunroof.

"Ally, why didn't you write to me?" he asks. "I know why I never called or wrote to you—because I knew it wouldn't get to you anyway—but I wanted to. I wanted to see you. My heart was in my throat whenever I'd dig through my piles of hate mail looking for your handwriting, but there was never anything."

"I was ashamed," I tell him honestly. "There was nothing I could say that would make it better. I would have told the truth in court, though, Devon. I was going to. I even thought maybe I'd get lucky, and they'd put me in jail for lying. It'd be a better place for me."

"I don't know about that, Ally," he says. "Do you want to see something? Look."

He lifts his shirt and reveals two large, angry scars near his hip.

"I got stabbed a couple of times with what I think was a rusted-off piece of a bedframe. I thought I was going to die. I wasn't very popular there, to say the least. I spent a lot of time in solitary for my own safety."

I lean over into his seat and run my fingers over the rutted, jagged lines of skin on his hips.

"Now we're both carved in scars," he says. "I won't be able to forget, either."

I shake my head and bite back a sob. "And it's my fault."

"It's not," he says. "It's not your fault. You couldn't have saved me, Ally; I realize that now. That fucking video was the only thing that was ever going to save me."

"I'm so sorry, Devon."

"Come here, pretty girl," he says. "Don't cry. I hate it when you cry."

I climb into his seat, wrap my arms around his neck, and bury my face in his shoulder.

He runs his fingers through my hair, and it reminds me of the first time I was in this car with him—when I laid my head down on the center console and cried while he did the exact same thing because I'd forgotten what it was like to be touched out of kindness.

He leans down and kisses the top of my head. "I really do like your hair like this."

"Devon...don't do this again."

"I'm going to kiss you now, okay?"

I nod and watch him lick his lips, then he leans in slowly until his mouth finds mine. I suck in a breath and moan against his mouth before parting my own lips and letting him in. It's different than when he kissed me in the classroom—when I was drunk and he was angry and kissed me like he hated me. He kisses me like he needs me to breathe, exactly the way I need him, and all the other stuff melts away. I forget about the dark place I'm in and give into this feeling, letting it pull me under and replacing the hopelessness and regret that's consumed me all this time. The vice that's constantly squeezing my chest lets up, and I feel alive again. Maybe he is different, but *this*...this feels the same.

I drink it all in, telling myself to catalog this feeling, too. *This* is what it's like to love someone else. Even in the shittiest of circumstances, I'm glad I got to feel it at least once.

I tighten my grip around his neck and move to straddle his lap.

Devon grips my hips in his hands and pushes the leather skirt up to my waist, and grinds his cock into me while he drags his tongue up the length of my throat. The feeling of him hard against my clit through my silk panties already has my breath heaving as I roll my hips over him, and his mouth finds mine again.

"I haven't been with anyone else," he says. "Okay?"

"Uh-huh," I whimper as I roll up and down his cock.

"Fuck, Ally," he says. He leans the seat back a little, then reaches between us and pulls his pants down over his hips. He moves my panties to the side, then wraps one hand around the base of his cock and guides my hips toward him with the other. I gasp as the head slides over my clit before slotting against my opening, then I sink down onto him.

I groan when he finally fills me, then go back to working my hips over him, chasing the orgasm I'm so close to.

"That's it," he says. "Make your pussy come on my dick, baby."

"It feels so good," I force out breathlessly as I pick up the pace. "I'm already gonna...oh, my god, it feels so good..."

He raises his hips, and I come down harder on him in just the right spot. I ride him a little harder for just a little longer before the spasms start to roll through my body. He holds my ass in place and thrusts up into me while I come apart, digging my nails into his biceps and muttering profanities until my head falls onto his chest.

"Get in the backseat, Ally," he says. "On your stomach."

I do what he says, and then he gets into the backseat behind me and positions himself between my legs. He lifts my hips, and I bring my knees under them, then he slides his cock inside me.

"God, I missed this," he says. He thrusts into me hard and then pulls out torturously slow, repeating it over and over again, making it last—making my clit throb again. "I love seeing you like this. You should see how wet you've got my dick, Ally."

I moan at his words, and he picks up the pace, drilling into me. I arch my back and push back against him.

"Shit. Just like that," he says.

I reach between my legs and rub circles on my swollen clit and come all over again, the sensation almost too much as he continues to fuck me hard and fast through it all. My legs go limp, and he spreads me wide, thrusting into me a couple more times before he stills and his cock jerks inside me.

"Fuck..." he groans as he comes.

He pulls out, and when I turn to face him, he comes down on top of me and kisses me on the mouth. I run my hands through his hair, but there isn't much of it. Then, I run my finger over his ears, but there aren't any plugs, and I start to panic.

"Get off me," I tell him, and I try to roll out from under him. "I can't...I can't breathe. Get off me."

"Yeah, okay," he says. He sits back onto his knees and then starts pulling his pants back up over his hips as I move as far as I can get against the window.

"Allyson? Are you okay? Do you want me to...roll down the windows or something?"

I shake my head. "No."

He moves over until he's right next to me. "Ally, look at me."

I look at him from the corner of my eye, then he reaches out, puts a hand on my cheek, and turns me to face him.

"I love you, Allyson," he says. "I love you so much. You're okay."

I don't say anything, just stare straight forward.

"They made me take them out...when they arrested me. I can put them back in if you want. I'm sure it's healed some, and I'd have to get smaller ones, but I could do it. Would that help?"

I nod. "Can you keep talking?"

"Yeah, okay. What about this one?" he says and points to his septum. "Should I put that one back in, too? Or did you not like it?

"I did like it," I tell him. "I miss it, too."

"Great, we can go right now if you want. You can pick them out for me."

"Really?"

"Yeah...I mean, maybe. Those places are open super late, but...probably not this late. Tomorrow, though. Okay? Or the next day after we paint the wall."

"Okay," I say. I realize my heart rate has steadied and remember that I won't see him tomorrow or any other day ever again. "I love you, Devon."

"I love you, too. Are you okay?"

I nod and lean against him. "Yeah, I'm okay. I need to go back, though."

"Is it any better there?"

"No."

"Then I don't want to take you back."

"I don't really have another option right now, Devon."

"Just five more minutes," he says, wrapping his arms around me. "Okay?"

"Okay," I tell him.

I decide to rest my eyes...just for a minute.

28

"Shit. Ally, wake up. The sun is starting to come up. We have to go."

I open my eyes and take in my surroundings—the interior of the car, the fog on the windows, the warmth radiating from Devon in direct contrast to the chill in the air and over my body anywhere we aren't touching.

"God, it's fucking freezing," he says. He climbs into the front seat, starts the car, and turns on the heat. "I'm sorry, Ally. I fell asleep. It's almost 7:00 AM."

"Shit. We need to go."

I climb into the front seat as he pulls out of the parking lot.

"What do you want to do?"

"Um, just drop me off near the house, but away from the camera. She may still be asleep."

It won't really matter after today, anyway. I don't tell him that.

Devon turns down my street a few minutes later and parks about two houses down.

"Text me when you can, Ally. Let me know that you're okay," he says.

I suck in a breath. "I will. It might...be a while. But I *will* text you. I'll let you know when I'm okay."

He leans in, brushes some hair away from my face, and kisses me. "I love you, Ally."

"I love you, too. And I want you to be happy...all the time, no matter what that means. Even if it's without me. I'd be okay with it if you wanted to move on. I wouldn't blame you."

He furrows his brow. "Ally, what are you talking about? I don't want that. We're fine. We're going to be fine; don't talk like that."

"Right...okay. I just wanted to say it. I'll text you when I can."

I throw my arms around his neck, then pull back and study his face, looking into his eyes. I take it all in, committing it to memory as best I can so I'll remember that, at one point, I had something good—a light in a dark place. And I took the time to realize how good it was while I was still in it.

I'll remember a cold October night in a dark, empty parking lot and hope the memory will keep me warm enough to get through all the others.

My lower lip starts to quiver; I bite down on it and try to hold back the tears.

"Bye, Devon."

"Bye, pretty girl. I'll see you tomorrow."

I force a smile, then get out of the car and head for the side of the house and the half-bathroom window. I climb inside, close it behind me, then slowly open the door and peer out into the living room. It's still dark and quiet. I don't hear a TV or smell any food. I step out into the room and hold my breath as I cautiously make my way up the staircase. Once I get to the landing, I can't stop myself from running to my room.

I close the door behind me and let out the breath I've been holding.

He'll be fine—probably better even. He'll understand.

But, god, I'll miss him. I can't imagine letting anyone else touch or hold me ever again, not when the thought alone makes me sick.

I hear Grace's bedroom door open and dive under the covers, pulling them up to my chin and turning to face the wall. I hear her bare feet against the hardwood floors until they stop in front of my bedroom door. She stays there for a few seconds before it flies open.

"Get up," she says. "Get dressed. We're going to church."

"Okay," I reply. I stay there under the covers, hoping that she'll turn around and leave instead of stepping into the room, ripping the covers from my body, and pulling me out of bed as she's been known to do. She'll see my makeup, and she'll see my clothes, and then what?

I breathe a sigh of relief when she does leave, then throw on something else and stash the costume and Devon's sweatshirt under my bed before running into the bathroom and closing the door. I shower, scrubbing the makeup from my face and washing the scent of smoke and stale beer from my hair, then I dress in one of the outfits Grace has deemed church-appropriate and get into the car without eating or bothering to complain about my empty stomach.

I sit quietly through church and the ride home, then go to my room and don't bother to leave it for the rest of the day. I lie on my bed with my sketchbook, and I draw something new—not the people without faces, not dark forests or a body floating in a pool with wet, matted blonde hair, not a girl in a black tulle skirt grimacing while another girl asks her to twirl.

I try to picture myself happy alone and imagine what that would look like. I draw a girl on the beach with her toes in the sand and a body etched in ink instead of carved in scars—a girl with a memory to keep her warm at night and stave off the nightmares.

When night comes, I wait patiently until I hear the TV turn off, then footsteps on the staircase and the slamming of a door, indicating Grace has gone to bed. Then, I pull the almost-packed duffle bag from my closet and add some toiletries and just a few of the important things I want to take with me. I find the envelope with the old photographs and my track ribbons, my sketchbook and my pencils. I pack my makeup and the small amount of cash I have for the buses, Devon's sweatshirts, and the cell phone.

I pack every note he's ever slipped into my locker, every picture he's ever drawn for me, and wonder if he will keep my hair.

It's a ridiculous thought.

And then I wait until I'm absolutely certain she's asleep and prepare to catch a bus downtown, then to Anacortes, and then to Everett. I think about how taking public transit alone at night should worry me a little, but I'm not afraid at all. Whatever might happen to me out there can't be much worse than what will continue to happen to me in this house if I stay.

After throwing the duffle bag over my shoulder, I head for my bedroom door, my hands shaking with adrenaline from the rush, not fear.

At least not until I hear the front door open and close. Then, I hear the whistling.

And I freeze.

No.

He wasn't supposed to be here. Not until Wednesday. I saw it on the calendar.

But he is.

My heart thuds in my chest, and my mind reels, going through my options. I can't stop now; I can't miss my chance. But I won't make it out the front door, either.

I hear footfall on the staircase and make a decision. If I jump out the second-story window, it will hurt, but I won't die. I may break a bone or sprain my ankle, but I've had worse. I can ease my way out the window, hang from the ledge, then drop down into the shrubbery below, and it won't be that bad.

The whistling gets closer to my bedroom door, and I cross the room in two steps, throw open the window, and toss the duffle bag out.

Then, my bedroom door creeps open.

"Going somewhere?" Mark asks.

I hoist myself onto the ledge and prepare to dive out head first, but my movements are sloppy, and his are fast. He darts across the room and quickly brings the window down on my torso once, twice, then three times, and holds it there. Pain radiates from my ribcage, and I can't move or breathe.

"I heard you've been a problem, Allyson. I'm very disappointed in you."

He opens the window, pulls me back inside, and throws me down on the bed. I pull myself up and try to run to the door, but the pain in my ribs makes it almost impossible to move, and Mark catches up to me quickly. He grabs me by the back of my shirt and pulls me back into the room, laughing as I swing my fists and kick at him weakly.

"I think I need to remind you how things work around here," he says. "First of all, you know I like it better when you fight."

After that, everything goes dark.

29

I don't see Ally come to her locker at all on Monday morning. And I watch just like I always do. I check all of her hiding places and don't find her there, either. Once the hallway clears at lunch, I open her locker, look inside, and find the picture I drew and the breakfast burritos still sitting on top of her books. Her bag isn't there.

I sigh and pull out my phone, hoping she's not avoiding me, but then...maybe hoping that she is. At least if that's the case, it means she's okay. It's not like it would be out of character.

Me: Ally, where are you?

I take the bag of burritos, sit at the table next to Seth, and fold my arms across my chest.

"Whoa, the nose ring is back," he says.

"Yeah, it's back," I reply. I fiddle with it with my thumb and first finger; it's an anxious habit I've apparently kept even though I didn't even have one for months. The hole closed up, too. I had to get it re-pierced yesterday, and it's a little sore now.

I was able to get some of my smaller gauges in, though. I have to admit that I feel a little more like me.

But I did it for her. I wanted to show her and see her smile.

"Hey, Devon. Do you know if Ally is here today?"

I look up and see Laurel Lindley leaning against the table in front of me.

"Apparently not," I tell her. "Why? What do you want from Ally?"

"So defensive," Seth says.

I shrug.

"Well, I'm just kind of worried about her. She said some stuff to me on Friday—nice stuff; I didn't think much about it. Then, I went home, and over the weekend, I couldn't *stop* thinking about it."

"What do you mean?"

"It just that—and I don't want to freak you out—but it sounded like she was saying goodbye. In a very final way."

And I want you to be happy—all the time, no matter what that means. Even if it's without me. I'd be okay with it if you wanted to move on. I wouldn't blame you.

Shit.

"I have to go."

I push my chair back with enough force that it topples over on its side, throw my bag over my shoulder, and race out of the school and through the parking lot. I jump into my car and drive until I'm parked right in front of Ally's house because fuck it. Fuck them, and fuck the camera.

She better be here. She better be okay.

After I try the doorknob and find it locked, I head over to the same bathroom window I've climbed through before.

"Ally?" I call out. "Are you here?"

But there's no answer.

I take the stairs two at a time, then run down the hallway to Ally's bedroom and push the door open.

"Allyson?"

I pull the covers back and find her there in a pair of sweatpants and a t-shirt. Dried blood covers a split in her swollen lower lip.

"Come on," I tell her. "Let's get out of here."

I reach down to help her sit up, and she wretches in pain.

"I can't," she says. "I can't move. It's my ribs. I think...I think they're broken. It hurts to breathe."

I lift her shirt to her bra, revealing a purple and green stained torso. And that's how it looks—stained, like someone dipped her in ink.

"We have to get you to a hospital, Ally."

"I can't walk, Devon. It hurts so bad."

"You're going to have to let me move you. It'll hurt, but we don't have a choice, Ally. I'm going to pick you up now, okay?"

She nods, and I reach under her body and lift her from the bed. She grunts in pain and buries her face into my chest.

"It's okay," I tell her, carrying her quickly from the room and down the hallway. "You're going to be okay. You're doing great."

She grits her teeth together and screams as we descend the staircase.

"I'm going to set you down so I can open the front door, okay? Then we're going to go. My car isn't far."

"The cameras—" she starts.

"—have already seen me," I tell her. "It's okay. You *never* have to go back."

I put her down in the living room as I said I would, unlock and open the front door, then carry her through the yard and over to my car and set her in the front seat.

"Devon," she almost wheezes, "my bag...it's in the side yard under my bedroom window. Can you get it?"

"Yeah, I'll get it."

I run back toward the house, then over to the side yard and find the duffle bag resting on top of the shrubbery. I grab it by the handles and race back to the car, climbing in and starting it quickly.

She jumps when I reach across her and buckle her seatbelt, then resumes her slumped position against the window. I fly through the neighborhood toward the bridge and pull into the hospital parking lot about twenty minutes later.

"Stay here, Ally," I tell her. "I'm going to grab a wheelchair. I'll lock the doors, okay?"

She shakes her head. "No. Don't leave me here."

I point out her window. "Look. You can see the front door from here. I'll be right back, I promise."

I get out of the car and hear a second door slam a few seconds later. Ally clutches her stomach and leans against the side of the vehicle as she shuffles forward.

"I think I'm dying," she says. "It hurts so bad."

I rush to her side, lift her into my arms again, and carry her toward the building. I get her into a wheelchair at the front door; they hand me some paperwork and take her straight back to a room. A medical assistant lifts her into the bed and starts asking her questions she doesn't want to answer.

My mind takes me back to when I was fourteen, and my mom was in the hospital looking small and frail and terrified just like this. She dragged herself over to a neighbor's house after Jack beat her one night, and they called 911. My grandparents came to get Ivy. It took the police days to find him.

"We'll get a nurse in here soon," the man says. "They'll get your IV in. I'll order some pain meds and X-rays. They'll assess your oxygen levels, and we'll find out if you need some help breathing or if you're doing okay on your own. Do you have any questions, Allyson?"

She shakes her head.

"I want to talk to a police officer," I tell him. "A family member did this to her—her aunt."

"Devon, no."

"I'll let them know," the MA says before he leaves the room.

I cross the room to the dark-haired girl lying on the bed, staring up at the ceiling. She looks so much smaller than she normally does like this.

"Hey," I say. "Can I lie down with you?"

She nods, and I climb into the bed next to her. I take her hand in mine, and she stares straight ahead, not speaking.

"Ally, what happened?"

"It wasn't her," Ally says. "It was *him*. I was going to leave; I found a shelter, packed a bag, and then...he came home and caught me. I was halfway out the window, and he brought it down on my ribcage...multiple times, and then he...he..."

She shakes her head and turns away from me again.

"Allyson..."

"Okay," a young woman says, pushing the curtain aside. "I'm Melody. I'm going to be your nurse. Can you confirm your last name and date of birth for me?"

I wait while the nurse gets Ally's IV in and watch the relief wash over her as the pain meds start to do their job. The nurse listens to her lungs and checks her oxygen, then makes the determination that she's breathing well enough on her own and won't need a respirator.

They ask her if she has any other serious injuries other than the ones to her torso. She hesitates before answering no, and then the nurse tells her someone will be down to take her to radiology when they're ready and leaves the room.

But rage runs through my veins because I'm afraid of how she would have finished that sentence.

"I'm going to kill him," I mutter through clenched teeth.

"Didn't you learn not to go around saying things like that?"

"I mean it this time," I tell her. "Allyson, did he—"

"Don't say it," she begs. "Please, don't say it."

"You need to tell the police, Allyson. And the nurse—you need to have them do a...rape kit."

"No," she cries. "No, I don't want to. I just want to leave. If it didn't hurt to move, I'd run right now. It won't matter, Devon. If you love me, please don't make me."

"Has this happened before?"

She nods. "This is the third time. The first time was...right before my seventeenth birthday. I told Grace, and...that was the first time she hit me. She called me disgusting. She said it was my fault."

Tears sting my eyes, threatening to spill over, and I swallow hard. "I lied about the money, Ally. I didn't use it to pay my lawyer—I still have it. It's under my bed. I'll give it back. You can go."

She looks at me like she's ready to fight me—like she wants to be angry about it but simply doesn't have the energy for it. I'd deserve it. She said everything that happens to her in that house is my fault now because I took her money and wrecked her plans. So...this is my fault, too.

"Okay," is all she whispers.

And after she goes...I think I really will kill him. Because Ally is right—it wouldn't matter. And if that's the case, then what's the point of any of this? Jack gets to try and kill me and my mom, and then he gets to spend all the time he wants with Ivy. Mark gets to rape his underaged niece and be a congressman. Ally's mom sits in prison because she was desperate and had no one to help her. Whoever really killed Darci will probably never pay for it, and our parents suffer every minute of every day for it.

It's not fucking fair. And I think maybe I should level the playing field a bit. And I *could* do it. Maybe I wouldn't have been able to a year ago—maybe I wasn't a violent person *then*—but like I told Ally, I'm different now.

A radiology tech comes into the room and tells Ally they're ready for her upstairs. I start to get up to follow, but she tells me I'm not allowed to go with her. I watch her go and pace the room, nervously waiting for what feels like an eternity for her to return.

The nurse steps back inside with a police officer behind her.

"Did you ask to speak to an officer?" he asks.

"Yeah, I did," I tell him. "My girlfriend was attacked by her uncle. She probably won't talk to you, but I want to file a report."

He sits down in the chair in the corner, a clipboard and pen in hand.

He asks for some basic information about Ally, the date and nature of the attack, and then he asks the question I've been waiting for.

"And what is the name of the attacker?"

"Mark Harris."

His brows furrow, and he looks up at me. "Mark Harris? The congressman?"

I nod. "Yes, that's the one."

"Wait a minute, aren't you..."

"Yeah, I am. Devon West, the one you guys falsely arrested for my sister's murder."

When they bring Ally back, she refuses to say much to the police officer, only nods. She's angry with me—I can tell—but she's also too tired from being in too much pain for too long to care. She falls asleep, and a few hours later, the doctor comes into the room and tells us that Ally's lungs appear to be intact and there isn't any internal bleeding. They send us home with a prescription for pain pills and tell us there's nothing more they can do with fractured ribs; she just needs to rest and wait for them to heal.

I pull the car up, and the MA wheels her out the front door and helps her inside.

"I'll take you to my house," I tell her. "We can pick up your pills on the way. I'll stay with you, and then when you can walk better again, we'll get you out of here, okay?"

"What if they come for me?" she asks. "We went through the door. They'll know that I'm with you."

Then they'll get what they deserve.

"I'll call the police," I lie. "They can't make you go with them now, Ally."

After spending about half an hour in the pharmacy drive-thru, I finally get Ally back to my dad's townhouse. I help her up the stairs, then into bed and under the covers.

"Can I get you anything else?" I ask. "Are you hungry?"

"No," she says.

That's a first.

"It's starting to hurt again, though."

"They said you can't have the pills until five, Ally. I'll set an alarm, okay? Do you want me to turn on the TV?"

She nods.

I open the Netflix app and flip through the suggested viewing, stopping on *Chilling Adventures of Sabrina.*

"Have you seen this? I think you'd like it."

"I haven't seen it," she says. "That's fine."

"I love you, Ally. I'll be right back, okay? I just have a couple of things to do downstairs. I'm not leaving."

I close the door behind me and make my way back down the staircase. I lock all of the windows and doors and then go to my dad's closet, open the safe, and remove and load one of the three guns inside.

I've never used one before. Neither had my dad—not ever in his life. He hated the damn things.

Then, he found his daughter's body in the pool in the backyard, and everything changed. Now, he goes to the shooting range every weekend.

I shove the gun into my waistband, close the safe, and head back out to the kitchen just as the front door opens but is stopped by the chain lock.

"Devon?" my dad calls. "Are you here? Why'd you chain lock the door?"

"Yeah, hold on a sec," I tell him.

I make sure the gun is hidden under my shirt and then go to the door, push it closed, remove the lock, and let him inside.

After he passes through, I quickly bolt the door again and put the lock back in place.

"I have to tell you something. You aren't going to like it."

"What? What's wrong? Did something happen at school? Is it...is it about your sister?"

"No, Dad. Um...Ally is here. She's upstairs."

"Oh, hell no," he says. "No fucking way. Get her out of here—now."

"Dad, listen. It isn't what you think. She's hurt."

"I care just about as much as she cared about you."

"Lower your voice...*please*. Let me explain. And then, if she has to go, I'm going with her," I say.

"There had better be a good goddamn reason why that girl is in this house."

"Sit down," I tell him.

He shakes his head. "I'd rather not."

I explain the entire situation to him. After Darci died, I told him that Grace had hit Ally in the past and that she was afraid of them, but that was about it. Now, I tell him about her mom, the hospital, and what Mark did. And afterward, he just stares at me.

"How do you know she's not making this up?" he says. "Grace has been friends with Lydia for about a decade now. She and Mark have always seemed like such nice people. Ally is...a kid who has had a rough life."

"She's not lying. Rib cages don't shatter themselves. They hurt her. And he raped her. If you want us to leave, we'll go, but it's hard for her to move right now. I'd at least rather wait until morning."

He paces the floor for a few minutes. "She can stay for the night, but that's it. And if they show up here looking for her, I'm going to tell them the truth."

I bite back the words I want to say and instead tell him, "That's fine."

I go to the kitchen, grab a glass of water and some snacks, and return to my room.

"Hey, you're awake," I say.

"The show is good," she tells me.

"Um, you can take your pill now. You have to take it with food and water, so I brought all this. What do you want?"

"Oh, um...I guess the granola."

"Good choice," I say, handing her both the bag of granola and the water. "It has dried cherries."

Ally forces a smile. "You *are* the same," she says.

I shake my head. "I'm really not," I tell her. "I just love you. That's the only thing that's the same. Can I sit with you?"

"Yes," she says.

I sit down next to her, and she leans against my shoulder. I'm nervous to wrap my arm around her, but I do it anyway.

"Is this fine? Am I hurting you?"

"No," she says. "I like it. I like your gauges, too, by the way."

"Anything for you, baby."

"I'm so sorry, Devon. I meant to leave. I didn't mean for either of us to have to deal with this anymore."

"You have nothing to be sorry for, Ally. But I'm sorry, too."

Shortly after she takes her pill, she falls asleep. I turn the TV off and don't sleep at all. I lie awake in the dark, waiting for something bad to happen.

And it does.

30

I wake up in a dark room to a distant sound of thudding. I shoot straight up, forgetting where I am and about the broken ribs, but the sudden movement gives me a sharp, painful reminder. I groan and reach toward Devon, wrapping my hand around his bicep.

"Devon, did you hear that? What was it?"

"It's nothing, Ally. Don't worry about it. Just stay here, okay?"

"Was it the door?" I ask. "Do you think they're here?"

"I'm sure it was nothing," he says. He places his hand on my cheek and kisses me on the forehead. "But I'm going to go check...just to make sure. Don't leave this room."

I hear him rifling around for something in the dark, and then he leaves the room and closes the door behind him. I stay there, seated in the bed, my pulse racing, and then I hear the sound again.

Like a fist against a wooden door.

I throw my legs over the side of the bed and bring myself to stand; the pain isn't quite as excruciating as before, but my legs are still unsteady. I shuffle out of the bedroom and then to the staircase. After descending about halfway, I get a clear view of Devon standing in front of the door.

"Devon, I can hear you in there," Mark says through the door. "I need to talk to your dad for a minute, if that's okay. I think there's been a misunderstanding."

Devon doesn't answer. He watches through the peephole and reaches slowly for the waistbands of his pants.

"No, I think I understand just fine," he says.

"Jeff, are you in there, buddy?" Mark's voice calls. "I just want to talk to my friend for a minute."

"Sorry, Mark. I'm the only one here," Devon says.

"I know she's in there," Mark says, his tone noticeably changed. "You think you can lie to the police about me and then just hide?"

I see a gun in Devon's hand, and he starts to unlock the door. Fear consumes me as I struggle to find my voice.

"Devon, no!" I shout. "Please don't open it! Don't do this!"

"Go back upstairs!" he yells back.

"Ally, is that you?" Mark says through the door. "Go ahead and open it; I just want to talk. I think we can all work this out. I think you'll be very happy with what I can offer you both. What do you want? Five thousand? Ten thousand?"

"Yeah, sure. I'll let you in, and we can talk. But you don't talk to her. Don't look at her. You talk to me, okay?" Devon bluffs with his finger on the trigger.

"Devon, don't!" I plead, gritting my teeth as I slowly and painfully descend the remaining stairs.

But he doesn't listen. He turns the deadbolt and goes for the chain lock at the top.

"Help!" I yell, hoping to wake Devon's dad.

As soon as the lock falls away, Mark pushes his way through the door, causing Devon to stumble backward, and he launches himself at him.

Devon, who had hoped for the element of surprise, loses his footing and falls to the ground, bringing the shorter but heavier man down on top of him. The gun slips from his hand and slides across the hardwood floor.

"No!" I yell. I fall down the remaining steps and land at the bottom of the staircase. I'm in so much pain I can barely move except that I have to. I *have* to get up. I grab the railing and scream as I pull myself to my feet, and the two men wrestle in front of me on the floor.

Devon ends up on top, punching Mark several times in the face before he reaches out and grabs a decorative vase next to the fireplace and smashes it against Devon's head. He falls back, and Mark is able to get out from under him. He picks up a six-inch shard of glass and buries it in Devon's back.

"Ahh!" he yells in pain. He pulls the bloody shard from his back, shouting again as the glass is removed and digs into his palm.

"Leave him alone!" I scream.

Mark looks over and flashes me a bloody grin...then I see his eyes go for the gun, and he begins crawling toward the weapon.

Adrenaline rolls through me, and I run toward him. I grab a fire poker, bring it over my head, and back down on his back.

"God damn it!" he screams. "You nasty little bitch."

I pull it out, the end dripping with blood, and bring it down on him again and again until he gets ahold of my leg and pulls it out from under me.

The fire poker lands next to Devon, who is now on his feet but clearly unsteady and losing a lot of blood. He grabs it and swings at the man, knocking him off balance again and causing him to roll across the floor.

And he lands right next to the gun.

Mark grips the handle, and Devon comes down on top of him. They struggle with each other for control over the weapon wedged somewhere between them.

"You know, I wasn't going to do this," Mark says as they struggle. "Now, there's something I've said before. I was just going to take the girl and take care of her the same way I took care of your sister. You could have walked away from this."

"The only one who isn't going to be walking out of here is you, you sick fuck!" Devon yells.

Then, the shot rings out. Blood and brain matter paint the walls and the front of my body. I fall to my knees and scream.

"Devon!"

31

"Are you sure you don't want me to stay? You seem upset, and what Devon did was crazy," Audrey says. "Are you going to tell your parents?"

"Enough people have already posted it online; I'm sure they'll see it," I tell her.

But I wasn't planning on telling them. I haven't decided what I'm going to do about my best friend's betrayal quite yet.

For the most part, I'm furious, but there's a small part of me that's sad, too, because we *were* friends. Maybe it started as a favor to him, but that isn't all it is now. And I gave her a chance to tell me the truth, and she didn't do it. I know I haven't been entirely honest with her, but that's different. This is serious.

Devon is a mistake. A convenient choice, and one she will live to regret.

"Where's Ally?" Audrey asks.

I purse my lips and shake my head. There's a question I don't want to answer—and an answer I *really* don't want to picture in my head.

"Probably sleeping," I tell her. "You know how boring she is."

She laughs. "Okay, well, text me tomorrow if you want to hang out. Maybe we can go down to the boardwalk or something if you don't have to babysit Ally."

"I'm off duty tomorrow; I'll let you know."

She closes the door behind her, and I sigh as I take in the disaster around me.

"Devon should be cleaning this shit up," I mutter. I pull a trash bag from the pantry, aggressively shake it out, and start tossing in empty cups and beer bottles. I clear out the living room first, then the kitchen. I stare at the knife still wedged into the cutting board.

I think I'll leave that there for our parents.

"Just so you know—I hate you both!" I yell, not knowing if they can hear me or not, and also not really giving a shit.

I shake my head as I clear away the last of the trash and wipe down the counters. I'm done with Ally Hargrove. Fucking *done*. I hope she enjoys being a social pariah for the rest of high school.

After I finish and the house is back to its normal level of messy, I dig my phone out of my back pocket and stare at my unanswered text messages.

Me: I can't believe you're spending the night there with her. You're not going to have sex with her, right?

Me: YOU SAID YOU LOVED ME. WHEN ARE YOU LEAVING HER? YOU PROMISED ME.

Then, a few hours later...

Me: STOP IGNORING ME. I HAVE PICTURES. I WILL TELL EVERYONE.

I collapse on the sofa and stare at the screen while my fingers hover over the keyboard. I don't see what the big deal is—people get divorced all the time. We're in love, and I'm going to be eighteen soon. I'm getting sick of the excuses.

I'm about to say just that when my phone dings with his reply.

Mark: I'm here. Meet me out back.

I smile and shake my head, then shove my phone back into my pocket. He wasn't ignoring me; he was trying to find a way to see me. I should have known better.

I run upstairs to my room, brush my hair out, reapply some lipstick, and head out the back sliding glass door.

"I should have grabbed a jacket," I mutter as the cold air settles onto my skin. But who am I kidding? I look amazing in this top. It's worth a little suffering for my tits to look this good. And maybe I went a little crazy in my text messages earlier, but I had to get my point across. I'm not the type of person you can just cut off and throw away. People don't get to ghost me and reappear whenever they want, like nothing is wrong.

I'm the mother fucking prize. I make these rules.

The walk through the woods to the spot where we normally meet is about ten minutes. I emerge from the tree line next to a dark two-lane road and see the silver BMW parked in the usual spot with its lights off. Mark sits in the driver's seat; I see him there, wearing a hat like he only does when we meet like this.

My heart jumps in my chest. He looks so good in a hat. It makes him look young.

It's been two weeks since I've been alone with him. I've seen him sitting beside her at church, but that's it. I've volunteered in the nursery and listened to her go on about the baby they're still trying to have while digging my nails into my fists to keep myself from scratching her eyes out.

I can't wait for the day when it's me by his side at these events. My parents might have a hard time with it at first, but they'll have to get over it. They like Mark; they think he's a great person. I don't see why that would have to change.

And Ally...I don't care what she thinks anymore. It was a nice idea, though—that we'd be family in *this* way, not because she was fucking my loser stepbrother.

I cross the road and climb into the car.

"I missed you so much," I tell him as I close the door behind me. I climb onto the center console, lean over, and kiss his lips.

But he doesn't kiss me back.

"What's wrong?" I ask.

"We have a problem, Darci. You've been threatening me, thinking you can tell me what I can and can't do," he says. "This ends *now*."

"What ends now? What do you mean?" I ask.

"We're done, Darci."

My eyes fill with tears. "No...but...you said you loved me. You said we were going to be together for real."

He laughs. "I wanted one thing from you. And it was good, but you've become a liability."

"You're lying!" I shout. I start hammering his chest with both of my fists. "You love me. You want to be with me! Stop worrying about them! Man the fuck up and tell her the truth, or I will."

I feel something cold and metal jut into my chin.

"No, that's not what I want," he says. "You know what your problem is, Darci? You're smart, but not conventionally smart—you're smart in the way that makes a woman dangerous. You're cunning, and I should have known better. There are so many more Darcis out there with fewer brain cells to rub together who would be a lot easier to control. *That's* what I want."

I hear his words, and I feel the barrel of the gun under my chin, but I can't make sense of any of it.

"You don't want some stupid girl, Mark," I tell him. "You want me. You want what we have together." I swallow hard and reach for the waistband of his pants, but he only pushes the gun harder into my throat. I sink back into my chair.

"You're going to give me your phone, Darci. And you'll never mention any of this to anyone, or it will be the last thing you ever do. I won't lose everything I worked for over some needy little whore."

"I'm pregnant!" I lie. I stopped taking my birth control, but it's way too soon to know. "We're having a baby. That's what you wanted, right? You've wanted a baby for so long. We can have that together."

He laughs, but not like he usually does. His eyes stay hard and dark. "You stupid little girl," he says, pulling the hammer back. "You are not having this baby. We're going to take care of this now—right after you give me that phone."

No.

I will not go down like this—tossed aside and ashamed. He won't get away with it. If he wants to do this to me, there are going to be some fucking consequences, damn it.

And he's smart. He won't just shoot me...I don't think.

My eyes dart to the driver's side door. I try to make out the status of the lock in the dark. The car is off, and I never heard it click when I got in; as far as I can tell, it's unlocked.

"Okay," I tell him. "I'll give you the phone."

I reach behind me but go for the door handle instead, then throw myself out of the car. I tumble down into the ditch, hearing him screaming after me, but the words are muffled as if I'm hearing them through water. Once I stop rolling, I pull myself onto my feet and break into a run back toward the woods and the safety of my home.

But I don't even make it across the road.

I never see the other car coming. I don't know if it's from the tunnel vision caused by adrenaline and fear or if maybe the driver was drunk and had their headlights off, but the next thing I know, all I feel is pain. I'm rolling over the hood of a car, and it's almost surreal how slowly everything is happening.

My body hits the pavement, but I don't feel it. I don't feel anything. I try to get up, but I can't move my legs.

My eyes flutter open, and I see Mark step out of his vehicle. He stands over me, emotionless.

"Help," I tell him. "Help me, please. I can't feel my legs. Call my mom. I want my mom."

"What a fucking mess." He shakes his head. "Darci, it's important that you know I was never going to do this. I just wanted to scare you enough to make you stop. You really are such a pretty girl." He kneels beside me on the road and smooths some hair away from my face. "What a waste."

"What do you mean? You're going to help me, right? Mark?"

He rolls me onto my side, checks my back pockets, then turns on the flashlight on his phone and starts searching for something on the road. A few minutes go by before he finds it.

"There it is," he says, holding up the cell phone.

I hear his car door open and close, and then he's back at my side. I'm relieved when he picks me up and throws me over his shoulder. I expect him to take me back to the car and then to the hospital, but he walks toward the woods instead, taking me home.

"Mark? Did you call an ambulance? I can't feel my legs. I can barely move my arms. I'm scared."

"I didn't call an ambulance, Darci," he says.

My head starts to swim as I hang limply over his shoulder. I'm beginning to lose consciousness; I can feel it. No longer able to feel my arms, I try to focus on the bracelets lining my wrists and the sounds they make as we move. I need to stay awake.

"Can you carry me differently?" I cry. "I think...I think I'm going to pass out like this."

"Go ahead and let it happen," he says. "That will make it easier on both of us. I really did care about you, Darci."

"What are you talking about? What will it make easier?" I ask.

He's not going to hurt me. He's not going to shoot me, or he would have done it already.

Right?

I fight against my body to remain conscious as Mark hauls me back to the house. Relief washes over me when we emerge from the woods, even though I can't quite see where we are. Then, the ground changes from grass to the pavers of our back patio. I see my mom's rhododendron bushes. I smell the chlorine of the pool.

And then I'm in the water, unable to fight my way to the surface. I panic, thinking I'd become too heavy for Mark and he'd dropped me by mistake. Then, I open my eyes and see the silhouette of his figure standing at the side of the pool, looking down at me, watching with his hands in his pockets. He makes no moves to help me, and I finally realize what's happening.

For once in my life, I don't even try to fight. I just wait for the lights to go out.

32

Devon's dad runs across the living room with a gun in his hand. He rolls Mark's lifeless body from Devon and onto the floor, then starts punching what's left of his face over and over again.

"You son of a bitch!" he cries. "You killed her? You killed my daughter?"

"Dad, stop!" Devon groans, attempting to pull himself into a seated position. "He's dead, Dad. He's already dead. You got him. It's over."

The man falls into his son's arms and weeps.

"He was our friend," he cries. "We trusted him."

"I know," Devon says. "I know. Dad?"

He doesn't answer.

"Dad, you need to call 911. We need to get the police. I...I need to go to the hospital. I'm bleeding a lot. It's my back. He got me."

Jeff moves to get a look at Devon's back, lifting the shirt soaked in dark blood, and snaps back to reality. "Don't try to move," he tells him. "I need to get my phone. I'll be right back."

He leaves him and runs back to the bedroom, and Devon lies on his back on the hardwood floor.

"I'm okay," he says to me. "You should see the other guy."

I shake my head, still in shock.

"Come here, Allyson," he says.

I force my aching body to move over Mark's lifeless corpse and lie on the floor next to Devon, resting my head on his chest. I squeeze my eyes shut as fingers run through my hair, and Devon says softly, "It's all over now. It's going to be okay."

Still unable to speak, I lie there and wait. I don't think much time goes by before Jeff comes back and announces they're sending an ambulance and the police are on their way. I don't move—not until the lights from the sirens are streaming through the windows and police are coming through the ajar door with guns drawn, ordering us to put our hands in the air. I sit up and do what they asked, but Devon doesn't move. I watch them cuff his dad and march him out the door before the paramedics wheel in a stretcher. They move Devon onto a backboard, and a female police officer kneels beside me and asks me if I'm hurt.

I nod. I've been hurt, and I want to go with Devon. I *have* to go with Devon.

Another paramedic joins her at my side.

"What's your name, Sweetheart?" the woman says.

But nothing comes out. I still can't form words.

"Can you stand?" she asks.

I nod and reach for her with shaking hands.

"I need a space blanket over here!" she yells out the front door.

She covers me with a metallic-looking blanket, then she and the officer help me to my feet, supporting me on either side. They lead me into the back of the ambulance. With Devon.

Another paramedic straps me onto a bench seat, and I look at my boyfriend, whose eyes are closed and skin is so pale it almost looks green, and sob.

"He's just sleeping," the paramedic tells me. "His vitals are really good, considering all the blood he's lost. His lungs are still strong. He's going to be okay."

I allow myself to relax just a little as the tears continue to fall. Someone gives me a shot of something on the way to the hospital, and the rest of the night is kind of a blur.

I wake up in a white room, the sun streaming through the windows. I hear footsteps behind me and whip around, ready to attack the source.

"Whoa," a nurse says. "Take it easy. You're awake, that's good. Ally Hargrove, right?"

"Yes," I say, surprised when I hear my own voice again. "Where is he? Where's Devon?"

"He's in the ICU. He needed surgery, and he's still sleeping. You can't see him right now, but he's going to be okay. Okay?"

"Can I...can I leave?" I ask.

"The police need to talk to you before we can discharge you, and you'll need to be checked out by a doctor, but I'll let them know you're awake, and we'll see if we can get you out of here today. How are you feeling? We've got you on something for the pain from the broken ribs, but does it hurt anywhere else? How is your vision?"

"Um, it's fine. I feel okay. I don't feel any worse than I did before."

"Okay, good. That's good. Are you hungry?" she asks.

The mention of food makes my stomach rumble. "Yes."

"Do you like sausage and eggs?"

"I like everything," I tell her.

"Okay, I'll order you some breakfast, and we'll get a doctor in here as soon as possible and see what we can do for you, okay?"

I nod, and she flashes me a smile before leaving the room.

I look out the window at the bare trees and the sun streaming in, and everything looks and feels different. I'll be able to check out of the hospital today, and then I wonder where I'll go. It occurs to me that...I can go wherever I want. I don't have to be afraid anymore. I'm *free*.

Everything *is* different.

I drop my head into my hands and laugh—and it's a kind of laugh that consumes me, one that I can't make sense of, and it only makes me laugh harder. It hurts my ribs, but I can't bring myself to stop. Minutes go by like this until someone comes in with a tray of food, and I do my best to stifle myself.

"Knock, knock," a woman calls in a sing-song tone. "Ally Hargrove? I'm Cristina. I come bearing breakfast."

"That's...excellent," I tell her, laughing again.

"Everything okay?" she asks.

"Yeah," I tell her. "Yeah, everything is...it really is going to be okay."

"Well, that's great to hear," she says. She laughs a little, too—not because it's funny, but it must be just a little bit contagious. "I didn't know if you wanted coffee or orange juice, so I brought both."

"I want both," I tell her as she sets it down in front of me.

"You know, you can turn on the TV," she says. "There's a remote probably stuffed into the side of the bed somewhere."

"Oh, my god, yes," I say through a mouthful of eggs.

"You know, you're in a pretty good mood for someone who came in last night with half a dozen rib fractures and blood splatter all over your sweatpants."

I shrug. "It's a new day."

I start flipping through channels and stop when I come across a local news station with a photo of Mark in the top corner. The smile falls from my face as I try to focus on what they're saying.

"I heard about what happened to you," Cristina says. "I want to tell you how brave you are. You're a survivor; I am, too. And I want you to know you're not alone—there are *millions* of us. Our stories matter. Someday...they're going to have to pay attention."

I nod and choke back a sob. "Thank you."

"That monster got exactly what he deserved," she says. "I'll bring down your lunch around noon if you're still here. You call #16 on that phone if you need anything else from the kitchen, baby."

"Thank you," I tell her.

I learn a lot from the newscast. Devon's dad was released from police custody this morning. Apparently, the man's paranoia after the death of his daughter paid off in a big way. There was an indoor security camera in the kitchen that, though it didn't pick up much footage from the struggle, picked up a lot of the audio, including the Mark's confession to killing Darci. The video of the man carrying Darci's body from the woods and through the yard to what would eventually be the family's pool runs repeatedly, too. They compare the man's stature to Mark's, and even though he's wearing a hat and a sweatshirt like he never does, the figure is a match.

It's still hard to watch, and even though I'm glad the family finally knows who was responsible for her death, it brings me no peace.

They mention that the family has declined to comment at this time.

I change the channel minutes before the police arrive to interview me. The doctor discharges me about an hour after lunch. The nurse brings me some scrubs to wear and tells me no, Devon isn't awake yet, and I can't see him, but I can call and check in whenever I want.

"I don't know where I'll go," I tell her after she helps me into the wheelchair.

"There's someone here to pick you up," she says.

My heart stops. I feel the color drain from my face as I expect to see Grace at the other end of the hallway.

"No!" I tell her. "I won't go with her. You can't make me; I'm eighteen. Make her *go*."

"Her?" she asks. "I'm pretty sure they said it was a man."

"What?"

She pushes me into the hallway leading to the main entry, and I see Devon's dad waiting by the front doors.

"You ready to go, kid?" he asks.

All I can do is nod my head.

We made national news.

I watched our local police department give a press statement earlier this evening. They said they found evidence on Mark's computer that suggested he and Darci had a sexual relationship.

After I let that sink in for a minute, I realized that the older guy she was seeing but could never talk about was never a college student. It was always Mark.

They haven't officially closed the case yet. Still, between that, the report Devon filed about what happened to me a day earlier, and the recorded confession, they do expect to render him the one responsible for her death soon.

They're still hoping to find physical evidence or Darci's cell phone. Grace is being held for questioning while they try to figure out if she knew about it or was involved in any way. I'm not sure if she did, but I hope she gets what she deserves.

Meanwhile, I'm sitting on Devon's computer googling us like he said he always does, and he's right—it's terrible but addicting. I can't stop reading.

I also can't believe how many pictures of me playing volleyball exist on Reddit. Some people even wrote fanfiction about us—extremely violent, extremely sexual fanfiction. Who does that? And has Devon read it?

A knock on the door makes me jump. "Ally?"

"Yeah?"

"Can I come in?" Jeff asks.

"Yes," I tell him.

"He's awake," he says. "I'm going to go see him now. Do you want to come with me?"

"Oh, my god, yes. Thank you," I tell him.

I close the laptop, swing my legs over the edge of the bed, and slip on my Vans before forcing myself to stand.

"Do you need some help getting down the stairs?"

I meet his eyes and lie. "No, I'll be okay."

I can tell he knows I do, but he nods and starts down the staircase in front of me, checking over his shoulder to ensure

I'm doing okay as I try to put as much weight as possible onto the handrail.

The ride to the hospital is quick and quiet. We take the elevator up to the fifth floor, and Devon is there, sitting in bed watching TV. I expect him to look frail and broken, but he doesn't. He even smiles when we walk through the door.

I let his dad go to him first; he holds him and tells him how glad he is to see that he's okay. Then I fall into his arms and try my best not to start crying again.

"Are you okay?" he asks.

"I should be asking you that," I tell him. "I'm better now."

His dad solemnly updates him on everything we've learned over the past twelve hours, and he nods and listens, but mostly, he's just watching me watch him.

Like I'm the only person in the room—like I'm the only thing that matters.

Afterward, Jeff tells him he's going down to the cafeteria to get some coffee and something to eat, but I think maybe he just wanted to give us some time to talk alone.

"That's my hoodie," Devon says when he leaves the room.

I look down at the black skull hoodie and shrug. "I told you I sleep in it every night."

"Come here. Lie down with me."

"I don't want to hurt you," I tell him.

"I'm not that fragile, Ally. People like us don't break easily."

I climb onto the bed, and he wraps his arms around me and kisses my forehead.

"Your dad was there to get me when they discharged me this afternoon. He said I could stay as long as I want."

"Will you?" he asks. "Stay?"

"For a little while...if that's okay. Until we're both better."

"And then what?"

"And then...I'll have to go. I don't know how to be part of Black Rock now. To be honest, I never really did. I'll find a place in Oregon—somewhere close enough for me to see my mom when she's allowed to have visitors. It's been such a long time."

"That sounds really nice, Ally," he says. "You're not getting rid of me, though. You realize that, right? It's us, Ally. Us against the world."

"Carved in scars."

He nods. "You know it."

"Can I see it?"

He turns, and I lift the hospital gown. I count the stitches running across the angry, bruised skin.

"How bad is it?" he asks.

"Not that bad," I tell him. "Devon? You know what's been bothering me?"

He turns toward me again and props his head up on his elbow.

"What's that?"

"I keep thinking about Darci—now that we kind of know what happened to her. I keep thinking about what I could have done differently and how that might have saved her. What if I told her about Mark and Grace? Or what if I had told her the truth about us and you two never had that fight? Would she still have left that night?"

"Ally, we could do that all day long—all day, every day even, until the day we die. There are maybe a million things we could have done differently, and maybe they would have changed the outcome, and maybe they wouldn't have. But you were a victim, too. You have to let go of that guilt. You didn't kill Darci—Mark did. He was a predator, and he groomed her."

"I know that. I can't help it, though."

Jeff walks back into the room with a tray of food and drinks and sets two coffees on the tray next to Devon's bed. "I didn't know if you wanted one, but I got you both some coffee just in case."

I pick up the cup and take a drink. "Thank you. I was never allowed to have coffee when I lived with them. I always loved it. The only place I ever had coffee was at your house."

"I have a really nice espresso machine back at the townhouse," he says. "I'll show you where the coffee pods are when we get home."

"Thanks for letting her stay, Dad," Devon says.

We talk for just a few minutes longer—until the nurse comes in and tells us visiting hours are over and we have to go. Jeff tells Devon that we'll come back and see him tomorrow, but it still physically hurts me to pull away from him.

"I love you, Ally," he says. "You better be here when I get out. No running."

I nod. "I'll be here."

33

"Ally, come here," Devon says. "You got another email from one of those properties you applied for."

Devon's hospital stay lasted an additional four days. He's been home for about a week now. I know his dad said I could stay for as long as I wanted, but I'm feeling a lot better now, and Devon will return to school next week.

Then what am I going to do? I can't stay. I can't get a job here when I can barely leave the house.

I've been trying to find a place to rent near Eugene, Oregon. There are a lot of decent, affordable options (if I can just get approved), and it's still a big enough city that I shouldn't have too much trouble finding a job waiting tables and an apprenticeship with a tattoo artist.

"Which one is it?" I ask.

"The one-bedroom duplex," he says. "The little blue one."

"Oh, god. I love that one. What does it say?"

"It says...you can have it. You have to wire them the first two months' rent when you sign, and you can move in as early as Monday."

"Monday? Really?" That's only two days from now. "That's so soon."

"It's what you wanted, right?"

I nod. "I can't stay here."

"I know. It doesn't change anything, though."

I blink back tears. As much as I want that to be true, how could it not? Long distance is hard enough as it is, and maybe once I'm gone, Devon will realize how much simpler everything is without me. Then, he'll just stop calling. He'll find a girl who laughs easily and doesn't have a tortured past spelled out in scars across her body. She'll wear a bathing suit and have a big family to share Thanksgiving with, and she'll make him happier than I ever did.

"Hey," he says. "Where'd you go?"

"Oh, um. Nowhere. I'm here. I'm okay. That house is going to work out really well. I'm really excited for it."

"Really? Because you look like you just got the worst news of your life."

I shrug, and he pulls me into his lap.

"I love you," I tell him.

"I love you, too. Nothing is going to change that."

"I guess I should sign the lease and start looking for bus routes."

"Ally, I'm going to drive you down there."

"Really? Are you sure you can even do that?"

"Yes, I'm sure. I'm fine, and I can't wait to see the place. I can't wait to meet your mom."

I've spoken to my mom several times since that night. I hoped I'd be able to keep what happened to me a secret, but unfortunately, with the publicity all of this got, it wasn't possible. It broke her heart, and that broke mine, too. Each time we talk, all she does is cry.

She feels guilty like I do. I bet it keeps her up at night, too.

Devon helps me sign the lease, and once we get confirmation that it was received, he wires the money over from the bank account he set up for me with our illicit funds.

Not that I ended up needing it in the end. Jeff set up a GoFundMe to help with my fresh start. I could have paid for the entire year in advance. Money probably won't be a problem for a while.

Monday rolls around far quicker than I'd hoped. Devon starts to load up the car, and I try my best to be excited, but the idea of leaving him again hurts too badly.

"Don't," he says.

"What?"

"Whatever you're thinking. I can see that it's something you shouldn't be thinking about. You're going to try to break up with me in the car and tell me it's for my own good or something and how it's okay for me to be happy without you and some other bullshit—I can feel it."

I laugh and shake my head, but I can't deny it. It is kind of along the lines of what I'm thinking.

"Find something to be excited about," he says. "We're going to see your mom, and you get to go furniture shopping. You'll get to make that place look however you want. I can't wait to see what you'll do with it."

He kisses me, and we get into the car and start the long drive to Eugene. When we're finally on the 5 freeway, I ask, "How long do you think you'll stay?"

"I don't know," he says. "I was thinking...forever."

"What do you mean?"

"I told you already, Ally. You're not getting rid of me. I'm going with you. My dad is going to ship the rest of my stuff. It's us against the world, remember?"

"But what about school?"

"I dropped out, too," he says.

"You what? Devon, you can't!"

He shrugs. "I know, but I did. I can't go back, Ally. You know how it feels just going grocery store there now."

"Do you think it will be any different in Eugene?"

"I think so," he says. "They might recognize us, but they won't know us. They won't know any of them, either. They won't have their own notions about who Mark or Darci were or who we are. I think that will make a difference."

"You didn't even ask me."

He smiles. "Can I be in your space, Ally?"

I shake my head and try to hide my own smile. "Yeah, Devon. You can be in my space. But...what about your parents? And your sister?" I ask. "You'll miss them."

"It's not that long of a drive. Besides, I'd miss things if I stayed, too. I'd miss waking up next to you and making you laugh. I'd miss your smile and the way you taste." He runs a finger down my cheek and then takes my hand in his. "And we *will* smile again, Ally. Someday, it'll just be easy—the other stuff, too, whenever you're ready."

"But what are you going to do there? What about college and being an architect?"

"I want to do tattoos," he answers.

"Really!?"

"And I'm going to take care of you every day," he says. "I'll fuck you every night. And once summer comes, I'm going to take you to the beach. You're going to wear a bathing suit, and we'll go swimming. We can even camp out in the car when we're done if that's what you want."

"That is what I want. I want all of that. I meant what I said before—I can't picture myself happy without you. I don't even want to try."

"Get ready to be happy then, Ally. We're going to have a lot of good days."

I sigh and rest my head on the center console while Devon runs his fingers through my hair. And I do feel happy.

I finally made it to the next part. The good part.

34

ally

Almost Four Years Later

I run across the hot sand and into the surf, letting the cool salt water wash over my bare feet.

"There's no way I'm getting in that," I tell Devon. "You're crazy. The water is fucking freezing."

We've had one of the hottest summers on record here; this is the third straight week of temperatures around ninety degrees. Still, even with the hot July sun bearing down on me, the water here is cold enough to take my breath away.

He still takes my breath away, too. I wonder how he does it. A lot has changed in the almost four years since we moved to Oregon, but that's one thing that remains a constant.

We both smile easily and often now. I breathe easier. I sleep deeply at night next to his warm body, surrounded by cedar and sandalwood and the scent of our own fabric softener, and don't wake up frightened by even the slightest of sounds. Our home is always peaceful and adorned with beautiful things we've created together—artwork and photographs, souvenirs and other things that matter to us.

We visit Devon's parents a few times a year, but we don't leave the house much when we're in Black Rock. It still doesn't feel quite right there—it brings back a lot of bad memories that, when I'm here, I'm able to put out of my head. It takes me back to the things I could have done differently, to the questions that were never answered, to the dark place and the scars it left on me.

But the scars made me who I am, whether I wanted them to or not. And I'm happy with who I am now.

I leave flowers on Darci's grave each time we visit. And every time, I tell her I'm sorry. I'm not angry anymore.

We both finished our apprenticeships last year. We took a chance on us and have been able to ride both our talent and notoriety to success. Admittedly, it made me a bit uncomfortable at first, but I learned to roll with it. With our books always full, our waiting lists long, and our ever-growing following on social media, we decided to open Killer Ink earlier this year. It has become somewhat of a tourist attraction in Eugene. People travel from all over the state and sometimes further to see us.

And we escape to the beach and the mountains as much as our schedules allow. It turns out I am a little outdoorsy.

"Swim with me, Ally," Devon says from where he wades in nearly waist-deep water.

"No way. I have fresh ink. Maybe next time."

"The skull is healing nicely," he says. "It looks amazing. Who's the artist? They must be really talented."

I shake my head. "You."

He smiles. "Oh, that's why, then."

Over the last few years, I've decorated my body the way that I always wanted to. I pierced my eyebrow and double-pierced my lip, and it does feel good when Devon pulls it through his teeth. My hips and thighs are completely covered in beautiful art, and the scars aren't noticeable unless you know exactly where to look. I can wear a bikini now and feel proud of my body, of who I am, and of what I've overcome.

The things that happened to me changed me, but they don't have to be the sum of who I am. I can be etched in ink instead of carved in scars. I can be happy; I'm worthy of love. I can tell my story. I can bring joy to others through my art and try to make a difference in small ways for someone else when it matters.

We walk back to our spot on the beach, hand in hand, and sink into our chairs, grateful to be under the shade of the umbrella. Devon reaches into the cooler and pulls out a couple of beers.

"You want one, Ally?"

"Yes, please," I tell him.

He removes the bottle cap and hands it to me, leaning in and kissing me when he does. I thread my fingers through his long-again hair and deepen it, sliding my tongue into his mouth before remembering we're not alone and breaking away.

"What about you, Kate?" he asks my mom. "Do you want a beer?"

"Mine is still full," she tells him. "Thanks, though, Devon."

She did end up getting out of jail in time to buy me a drink when I turned twenty-one. She's endlessly proud of me, and I gave her her first tattoo at age thirty-eight. She and Devon both have my name etched into their skin.

Which is fitting. Because they're never getting rid of me.

Hours pass just like this before we pack up and head home. The one-bedroom duplex was great for the first couple of years, but now we rent a three-bedroom house just outside town. A small sunroom off the back makes for a perfect art studio; it gets the best light in those early morning hours. There's a backyard with plenty of room for our dogs to run around. We have only two, not seventeen, and even that seems excessive with their energy at times. But the shelter said they were a bonded pair and couldn't be separated; they needed to be adopted together. I told Devon that's what we were, too—a bonded pair—and we brought them home.

On our way home, we drop my mom off in front of her building. She stayed in the guest room for about six months but recently moved to a small apartment near downtown. She got a job cleaning a nearby office building and helps us out around the studio whenever we need her.

It was nice having her around, but it's nice having the place to ourselves again, too. Someday, we'll fill it with small people. But for now, we'll take full advantage of this space we've made our own. When we get home, we fuck on the kitchen table while we wait for Uber Eats to deliver our food and then again against the shower wall before bed.

We don't bother dressing afterward. I climb under the covers, and he wraps his body around mine. He's etched in ink, too, from both shoulders down to his wrists, and I've started on a piece that will cover his back.

And in the morning, I know I'll wake up with his hands and mouth on me, and it will be okay because it's him—and it will always be him. There is no version of me happy that doesn't include Devon West.

Etched in ink or carved in scars. It's us. Against the world.

Known as the (mostly benevolent) Queen of Angst, Elle Mitchell writes new adult contemporary romance ranging from shades of grey to morally pitch black with a hint of taboo. A mix of plot and spice, her books follow flawed, relatable characters as they rage against the machine or struggle against the darker parts of humanity and themselves. They're messy—like real life—and emotional.

She can't promise that all her books will depict what a healthy relationship should look like at every turn. She rejects purity themes. The best she can do is promise an eventual HEA when it's all said and done.

When she isn't reading or writing, it's unlikely you'll find her anywhere. She's probably at home with her family, minding her own business.

Find her on IG and TT: @ellemitchellbooks

Join her Facebook group: Elle's Angsty Babes

The stars really have to align to make dreams come true, and I've been lucky enough to have that happen for me. And there are so many people who helped make this all happen—who made a difference in my life in small ways that maybe they didn't even notice, but I did, and it mattered to me.

See what I did there?

To my husband, I'm eternally grateful for your unwavering support. Thank you for being my very first fan.

Thank you to my dear friend, PA, and my emotional support influencer, Shelbie, for everything you do. From managing my street team to just being there to listen to me talk to myself about my characters, you've helped make this book happen more than you know.

To Genesis, Legacie, Harlee, Hannah, Sara, Sofi, and Kelli for taking the time to beta read Ally and Devon's story. Both your time and your input are so important to me, so thank you from the bottom of my heart.

To Ember, Emily, and Rose for being there to hold hands and scream with me through all of this.

To all the outcasts and the black sheep of the family—me too. It wasn't your fault, and it's *their* loss. It's time to heal. Do it for yourself, and find your people.

Runaways (Coming June 2025)
Pretty Poisoned (Gods of Tomorrow #1)
The Road to Ruined (Gods of Tomorrow #2)
The Pieces We Leave Behind (Lost Hollow #1)
The Pieces We Try to Forget (Lost Hollow #2)
A Little Unstable
Broken People (Broken #1)
Broken Apart (Broken 1.5)
Broken Reverie (Broken 2)

Made in the USA
Monee, IL
27 June 2025